THE UNCLE DUNCLE CHRONICLES

Escape *from* Treasure Island

The Uncle Duncle Chronicles, Escape from Treasure Island
Text © 2006 Darren Krill

Published by Lobster Press™
1620 Sherbrooke Street West, Suites C & D
Montréal, Québec   H3H 1C9
Tel. (514) 904-1100 • Fax (514) 904-1101 • www.lobsterpress.com

Publisher: Alison Fripp
Editors: Alison Fripp, Karen Li, & Meghan Nolan
Editorial Assistant: Morgan Dambergs
Cover Illustration: C.R.É.É. Alain Salesse
Graphic Design & Production: Tammy Desnoyers

We acknowledge the financial support of the Government of Canada through the Book Publishing Industry Development Program (BPIDP) for our publishing activities.

The Canada Council | Le Conseil des Arts
for the Arts | du Canada

We acknowledge the support of the Canada Council for the Arts for our publishing program.

Library and Archives Canada Cataloguing in Publication

Krill, Darren, 1967-
     The Uncle Duncle chronicles : escape from Treasure Island / Darren Krill.

ISBN-13: 978-1-897073-31-5
ISBN-10: 1-897073-31-3

     I. Title.

PS8621.R54C47 2006   jC813'.6   C2005-904990-1

Printed and bound in Canada.

To my parents, Ron and Ester,
For sparking my imagination,
And fanning the flames throughout my life.

And to my wife, Kelly,
For not letting the flame die.

– Darren Krill

THE UNCLE DUNCLE CHRONICLES

Escape *from* Treasure Island

Written by **Darren Krill**

Lobster Press ™

ACKNOWLEDGMENTS

Writing a book is a very personal journey, but one that very quickly becomes a team project. I'd like to thank everyone who helped make *The Uncle Duncle Chronicles* a reality.

To my wife, Kelly, for allowing me to pursue my dream, and for encouraging me to see it through to the end. You are my partner and traveling companion, and our future together will be our greatest adventure.

To my parents, Ron and Ester, for instilling in me a love of reading from a very early age, and then encouraging it throughout my life. You've both been true inspirations, and I appreciate everything you've done for me.

To my brother and sister, John and Sabrina, for a lifetime of stories to weed through. When writing a book, they say "write what you know," and thanks to you both I now have enough material for a career. Thanks for a lifetime of laughs.

To my many nieces and nephews — Matthew, Erin, Leanne, Brendan, Ethan, Estella, Aimee, Joel, Braedon, Brooklyn, and Ainsley, I wrote this book for you, and I hope it opens your eyes to the amazing world around you. You'd better love it!

To the many friends who have stood tall beside me for so many years, especially Matt, Carrie, Zac, Doug, Mike, and Peter.

To the incredible family support network I have from both the Krill and Gagliardi side, as well as my in-laws, the Hames.

To everyone at the Edmonton Oilers Hockey Club for their ongoing support and encouragement, and for teaching me how to be a true champion. Go, Oilers, Go!

To Robert Louis Stevenson for creating such wonderful characters in the original 'Treasure Island,' and for inspiring me to revisit the shores of your island.

Finally, to everyone at Lobster Press for putting their faith into my manuscript, and giving me the opportunity to achieve a dream. Especially my editors, Alison Fripp, Karen Li, and Meghan Nolan, whose hard work polished *The Uncle Duncle Chronicles* into a jewel. Also to Stephanie Hindley and Stephanie Normandin who work so hard to promote my work throughout North America, and around the world.

With wings of wind, I fly!

Darren Krill

CHAPTER 1

SAGE SMILEY WOKE to the clanging and clanking of pots and pans in the kitchen below. Straining to pry his left eye open, he peered over at the alarm clock on his bedside table. 7:14 a.m. As the irresistible weight of sleep pulled his eyelids shut once again, a smirk slowly seeped across his face. It was Saturday, but not a regular Saturday morning by any means.

Saturday. The word echoed in Sage's head as he glided in that dreamy space between being awake and falling deeper into sleep. *What was it about Saturday?*

On Friday, the day before, the Spruce Ridge Elementary School bell had rung at precisely 3:20 in the afternoon. Merely seconds later, the doors to every possible exit of the school had burst open as hundreds of kids surged out, screaming gleefully and tossing their notebooks and textbooks in the air. The final bell had officially announced the start of summer vacation, and the end of sixth grade for Sage.

And if that wasn't enough gut-busting excitement for any kid to absorb, the final day of school also marked the last unblemished square on Sage's *Hockey Heroes* calendar. More than a month ago, Sage had circled the date of Saturday, June 28, in thick red ink and had been counting down the days to the momentous occasion. On Saturday, June 28, Sage's mom and dad would take him on summer vacation—his first *real* summer vacation outside of Spruce Ridge. On Saturday, June 28, he would find out when and, more importantly, *where* they were heading. It was a double-barrel blast of excitement to cap off Sage's final year of elementary school, and now vacation day had finally arrived. V-day!

"It's Saturday!" The words burst out of Sage's mouth like lava from an erupting volcano. His eyes shot open, and Sage flung back the bed sheets and swung his legs out onto the floor. There was no time for lazing the day away, no time for even a shower. *It was Saturday!*

Sage raced to his dresser and yanked open the bottom drawer. He snatched a pair of white athletic socks and hopped clumsily on one foot and then the next as he pulled them on. Then he shimmied into a well-worn pair of blue jeans and slipped on a fresh white T-shirt. Once dressed, Sage grabbed a red felt pen off the dresser top and added the final X to his calendar. He had finally made it.

For weeks, visions of possible destinations

had been racing through his head—touring the many worlds of Disneyland, sauntering down the main street of Tombstone like Wyatt Earp and Doc Holliday, riding a burro down a treacherous trail in the Grand Canyon, or simply frolicking in the waves on the beach—*any beach*. One way or the other, the suspense was about to end.

Placing the red felt pen back on the dresser top, Sage quickly glanced over his impressive collection of brightly colored postcards from all corners of the earth—Africa, Russia, Peru, Egypt, China, Alaska, and many, many more. There were exactly fifty-seven postcards tacked to his bedroom wall, and every one of them had been sent by Dunkirk Smiley, the famed adventurer and explorer. He was also Sage's uncle. With an eager grin, Sage realized that this summer he would be adding a postcard of his own to the collection.

As if it were Christmas morning, Sage barreled down the stairs, roared through the living room, and blew into the kitchen where, judging by the unmistakable aroma of fresh coffee, he knew he'd find his parents. Sure enough, his mother, Irene, was standing by the stove, looking comfy-cozy in her usual Saturday sweat suit, frying up a load of French toast, while his father, Wyatt, was seated in his regular spot at the kitchen table, cradling a cup of coffee. Directly across from him sat a stranger.

Surprised by this unexpected intrusion on his morning agenda, Sage skidded across the freshly waxed linoleum in his socks, the words "good morning" firmly lodged in his throat as he gave the stranger a second look.

There was something familiar about the man. He had short black hair, swept up boldly in the front, with white streamlines across the sides, like racing stripe stickers pasted to a Revell model. Under his strong nose sat a meticulously trimmed black mustache, the ends of which came to a rigid point on either side of his mouth. His face was rugged, with well-worn wrinkles entrenched deeply into his skin, but his blue eyes reflected warmth as they sparkled mischievously from below two bushy black eyebrows. As he glanced over from the kitchen table, a smile crinkled across the stranger's face and a deep baritone voice rang out, "*Sa wat dee*, Sage."

Sa wat dee. Sage had heard those words before, but where? Then it came to him—he hadn't actually *heard* those words, he'd *read* them. *Sa wat dee* was a greeting from one of the fifty-seven postcards tacked to his bedroom wall. A postcard sent by Uncle Dunkirk Smiley, the adventurer. In every postcard Uncle Dunkirk had included a greeting in the country's native language. Over the years, Sage had memorized all of the greetings, and he quickly recognized *sa wat dee* as the Thai word for "hello."

Sage's jaw dropped in disbelief. "Uncle Dunkirk?"

"Don't you mean Uncle *Duncle?*" replied the man. When Sage was a toddler, pronouncing "Uncle Dunkirk" had been nearly impossible. One day while trying to articulate the name, "Uncle Duncle" simply rolled off Sage's tongue. And from that moment on, Uncle Dunkirk had been branded for life.

Uncle Dunkirk slid his chair out from the table and crossed the kitchen. "Look how you've grown!" he said, giving Sage a brief once-over. "I think the last time I saw you, you were just pint-size, like the Baka pygmies of Cameroon."

And it was true. The last time Sage had seen Uncle Dunkirk face-to-face was when he was five years old. But for someone he only remembered meeting once before, Uncle Dunkirk Smiley was a major influence on Sage's life. For as long as Sage could remember, brightly colored postcards from exotic ports and cities around the world had landed on the Smileys' doorstep in Spruce Ridge. Before he could read, Mom and Dad would tuck him into bed and read him mesmerizing tales of Uncle Duncle's latest adventures, painting a vivid picture of fantastic sights and remarkable people in his impressionable young head. For Sage, story time quickly became Uncle Duncle time, and Dr.

Seuss was relegated to the back of the bookshelf. After all, who needed imaginary plates of *Green Eggs and Ham* when you had a relative like Uncle Duncle, with real-life tales of drinking Nepali chicken wine and eating otter feet?

And at the age of five, when Sage met Uncle Dunkirk, the man proved to be everything Sage had imagined, and then some. He had shown up on the Smileys' doorstep unexpectedly, laden with gifts and trinkets from Africa. There was a rich-looking carved elephant for Mom, which Uncle Dunkirk claimed had been carved by a member of the Zulu tribe, and an ashtray made out of an ox hoof for Dad's pipe. For Sage, Uncle Dunkirk brought a small brass telescope that folded into itself. He told Sage it was an antique, once owned by a pirate named Captain Kidd, and that by looking through it you could see new worlds to be conquered. The telescope still sat in a place of honor on a shelf by Sage's bedroom window, ready at a moment's notice to peer across the rooftops of Spruce Ridge.

Then, as quickly as Uncle Dunkirk had sprung off a postcard and into Sage's life, he was gone—out of the country on another adventure. The only notice the Smileys received that he was alive and well came with the postman once a month in the form of a postcard, embellished with yet another exotic postmark, a brief synopsis of his adventures, and the latest foreign greeting for Sage to memorize.

"I thought you were in Thailand," said Sage, showing off his knowledge of Uncle Dunkirk's comings and goings. "That was the last postcard I got from you."

"I was," Uncle Dunkirk smiled. "I spent two months in Thailand searching for one of the fabled nine-masted treasure junks that Zhu Di, the third emperor of the Ming Dynasty, launched in 1421. I'd been following a trail of ancient bronze coins along the ocean floor in the Gulf of Thailand, and if my months of research and calculations proved correct, I was just hours away from proving that Zhu Di's treasure junks actually existed. That is until I was, how should I phrase it, politely asked to leave the country."

"Did you do something wrong?" Sage asked breathlessly.

"No, of course not. When you work in foreign locales, you learn quickly enough to follow the letter of the law." Then, with a wink to his brother, Wyatt, Uncle Dunkirk added, "Well, most of the time. My guess is that Zhu Di's treasure junk is either still resting somewhere on the ocean floor in the Gulf of Thailand, or its plunder now resides in King Rama's royal treasury. But what can you do? Sometimes you win, and sometimes you lose. That's the game of life. But enough about Thailand

and lost treasures. Uncle Duncle is here now, in Spruce Ridge! How's that for a surprise?"

"Well, it's a great one, Uncle Dunkirk," Sage replied warmly. Then he added with a frown, "But your timing isn't too good. We're taking a summer vacation. Right, Dad?"

Sage's father replied, "Well, sort of, Sage. Why don't you come sit down, have a few slices of French toast, and we'll fill you in."

Sort of? Sage suddenly felt ill, thanks to his father's vague answer, but reluctantly followed Uncle Dunkirk back to the table and slid into his usual seat.

The French toast had turned a light golden brown on the stove, and his mom forked two slices onto Sage's plate. She filled the remaining plates on the table and then joined everyone at the table.

"Sage, there's something your mom and I have been keeping from you about your summer vacation," began Wyatt. Sage held a bottle of maple syrup, drizzling a thin, golden stream onto his French toast, but as his father began to speak, the syrup was instantly forgotten.

"Just over a month ago, your Uncle Dunkirk phoned when he was in Thailand. He told us he was coming to visit for a few days, and that he wanted to spend some time with you."

As much as Sage tried, he couldn't keep the disappointment hidden from his face. His smile was now slowly sagging into a hangdog frown. Sure, he was excited to see Uncle Dunkirk. At any other time of the year, Uncle Dunkirk's visit would have been trumpeted like the arrival of a Roman emperor, and Sage would have counted the days down on his calendar just as enthusiastically. But today of all days was *V-Day*. The day that Sage had waited for all month, never mind the twelve years he had waited for a real summer vacation.

Wyatt continued, "So your mother and I have decided to let you go on a trip with your Uncle Dunkirk."

The cuckoo clock above the kitchen table ticked away. The fan behind the fridge whirred lightly. In the kitchen, the silence seemed to last an eternity, as if his dad's words hung suspended in the air, floating somewhere above the kitchen table, and just wouldn't sink in. Sage was going on a trip with Uncle Dunkirk. The same Uncle Dunkirk who had hopscotched the globe endlessly and whose every adventure had painted Sage's dreams for years.

Finally, the silence was broken by the squeak of Sage's voice. "Really?"

Uncle Dunkirk's eyes twinkled, and the pointy corners of his mustache seemed to curl inwards an inch as his smile reached full wattage. "Oh, it's true, Sage. It's very true. But first I think you had better put the syrup down."

Sage blinked once, as if waking from a dream, and noticed the pool of syrup drowning his French toast. "Oops. Sorry."

Irene Smiley shook her head, amused, and Sage's father continued, "We would have told you earlier, but we wanted you to concentrate on your schoolwork. It's been a big year for you, and this is a little graduation present from your mother and me."

"And Uncle Duncle," added Uncle Dunkirk.

"That's right," corrected Wyatt, "and Uncle Duncle...er...Dunkirk."

Four weeks of bottled anticipation finally burst free and carried Sage out of his seat. He danced around the kitchen, jumping ecstatically and waving his arms, before restoring enough self-control to embrace both of his parents in a hug. Then, giving his Uncle Dunkirk an enthusiastic high five, Sage breathlessly asked, "So where are we going, Uncle Dunkirk?"

"Sage," announced Uncle Dunkirk grandly, "that is the beauty of travel. We're simply going to follow the wind and see where she blows us."

CHAPTER 2

THE INFAMOUS SATURDAY was a whirlwind of packing and unpacking, checking and double-checking, and the first item to be jettisoned by Uncle Dunkirk was the powder blue suitcase Wyatt unearthed from under the stairs and laid open on top of Sage's bed.

"This will never do!" remarked Uncle Dunkirk. He borrowed the keys to the Smileys' blue minivan, raced out of the house, and returned thirty minutes later with a ball of green canvas tucked under his arm. Tossing it to Sage, he announced, "Now *this* is a pack worthy of travel."

Sage pulled the canvas ball out of the air and quickly unrolled it to discover the same stout canvas backpack sported by his favorite actors in war flicks at The Strand theater.

Sage chased Uncle Dunkirk back upstairs and watched in awe as his uncle attacked Sage's bedroom closet. As hangers screeched across the metal rod, Uncle Dunkirk selected five shirts, three pairs of pants, and two jackets. Then, satisfied, he shifted his assault to the dresser, adding socks, underwear, swim trunks, t-shirts, and a bulky wool sweater to the pile. Finally, he added Sage's running shoes, hiking boots, sleeping bag, toiletry bag, and what seemed like a million other little tidbits—nail clippers, a canteen, shoelaces, and even a fork and spoon from the kitchen. With a stack of items piled high on the bed, Uncle Dunkirk proceeded to position each item into Sage's new army surplus backpack.

"Don't forget the *Kids' Cough*," came a helpful suggestion from the doorway.

Uncle Dunkirk and Sage both looked up to see Irene stroll in, holding a box of *Kids' Cough Natural Cold Remedy*. Sage's mom had always trumpeted the value of natural remedies, and for the past week her trusty box of *Kids' Cough* had been a staple on Sage's bedside table—with its potent blend of echinacea, beta-carotene and vitamin C— as he battled a dreaded summer cold. "Sage has been getting over a head cold, Dunkirk, so I'd appreciate it if you'd keep him healthy. And naturally so."

"*Mom*," groaned Sage. "I'm feeling better now. The sniffles are gone, and I didn't even have to blow my nose this morning."

"You'd best listen to your mom," countered Uncle Dunkirk wisely. "You never know when a cold will spring up."

Irene gave Sage a smug nod as he took the box of *Kids' Cough* from her. He passed the box to

Uncle Dunkirk, who tucked it neatly into Sage's toiletry bag.

As his uncle continued to balance the load in Sage's backpack, Sage scoured his room for any overlooked items. He picked up the brass telescope Uncle Dunkirk had given him—after all, they were out to discover new worlds—and his lucky Jim Hawkins compass, an antique Disney movie tie-in Sage had bought for a dime at a garage sale, which had led many a Saturday bike excursion. The telescope slid tightly into the backpack, while Sage opted to tuck the compass into the front pocket of his jeans—ready at a moment's notice to point out the way. Once Uncle Dunkirk was satisfied that all the essentials were packed, he laced up the top of the bag and hefted it onto Sage's shoulders.

"Now stand with your legs far apart, Sage," instructed Uncle Dunkirk. "It helps distribute the weight."

Once Sage was in position, Uncle Dunkirk released the pack and let Sage absorb its full mass. The shoulder straps complained noisily as the backpack settled onto Sage's slender frame, but Sage was determined to act like a man and carry his own load. Standing still, Sage braced himself against the crushing onslaught of weight—*when did Uncle Dunkirk pack the pallet of bricks?*

"Good," noted Uncle Dunkirk as he stepped

back to admire his handiwork. Sage stood completely immobile before him, teetering slightly.

"It feels kind of heavy," commented Sage, his voice wavering a bit. "Especially on my shoulders. The straps are starting to dig in."

"Shrug your shoulders. It will shift your pack forward a bit."

Sage wiggled his shoulders and felt the backpack shift slightly. He tried it again, more forcefully this time, and the shoulder straps slid forward into a more comfortable position. Sage grinned. Then he cautiously brought his legs together until he was completely upright.

"Good, Sage, good," commended Uncle Dunkirk. "I think you've got it!"

"I do!" exclaimed Sage. "I've got it!" Then, with his body as straight and stiff as a ruler, Sage leaned back and promptly tipped over.

A contagious laugh rang throughout the room, and Sage opened his eyes to see the stark white ceiling and the grey undersides of the model airplanes that hung from fishing twine, in flight, over his room. Lowering his eyes, Sage spotted Uncle Dunkirk laughing uncontrollably at the sight of his nephew, stuck and kicking like a turtle on its back. Uncle Dunkirk's laugh was a long, hitching wheeze that ended in a low chuckle. Once silent, he would suck in a fresh breath of air and continue the cycle, cheerfully wheezing away.

"I think it might be a shade too heavy," sputtered Uncle Dunkirk, as he wiped a loose tear from his eye. He latched onto Sage's hand and pulled him off the floor. Then he lifted the pack off Sage's shoulders and placed it carefully on the bed. "We'll have to rethink your pack, Sage. I just might have to lug some of your gear."

Together, they transferred a quarter of Sage's supplies into Uncle Dunkirk's backpack, and then reloaded the green canvas monster onto Sage. This time, the weight of the pack seemed acceptable to Sage's shoulders and, more importantly, to gravity.

By the time Uncle Dunkirk and Sage finished their preparations, the smell of pot roast and gravy permeated the house. When the tantalizing aroma reached Sage's nose, his stomach rumbled noisily. With all the excitement of the day, he had forgotten to eat the lunch that his father had left for him in his room. When supper was finally dished onto his plate, Sage wolfed down three slices of pot roast, two potatoes, a tossed salad, and three spears of asparagus—to the delight of his mother.

After supper, the four Smileys retired to the living room, where Uncle Dunkirk held court over coffee and dessert. He regaled his family with breathtaking tales of his adventures around the world. He told them about the search for a missing 35-ton obelisk in the Nile River and the lost city of Catalhöyük in Turkey. He also described a ritual called the *Nagol*, performed by a remote tribe on Pentecost Island, in which boys and men would plunge headlong from a 75-foot tower, with vines tied to their ankles to stop their fall the instant before their heads touched the ground.

Although Sage could have listened to Uncle Dunkirk's tales all night long, the excitement of the day caught up to him. Sometime during Uncle Dunkirk's hunt for the mysterious Canadian sea serpent, the Ogopogo, exhaustion overtook Sage, and he slipped into sleep.

CHAPTER 3

"GOOD-BYE, MOM! GOOD-BYE, Dad! Thanks again for the surprise!" Sage called out of the rear window of the Checker Cab as it slipped away from the curb. The fresh morning air gusted through Sage's blond hair as the car accelerated. A whole new world was opening up today, and his face was positively beaming with anticipation. He watched until his mom and dad disappeared from sight, lost below the crest of a hill on Wellington Street. Then, with a grin, he faced forward—ready to tackle the road ahead on his first summer vacation.

Uncle Dunkirk was in fine form, leaning forward in his seat, his finger pointing directions over the cabby's shoulder, while he spouted instructions in the man's ear. As Sage watched, he wondered if Uncle Dunkirk felt the same tingling sensation under his skin at the start of a journey, or if the many years of living out of a backpack had diminished travel's magical appeal. But watching Uncle Dunkirk in action, Sage realized that this *was* his life. This was where Uncle Dunkirk felt most at home—*on the road*.

The Checker Cab cruised along Wellington Street to the corner of Delwood Road, and then it hung a right. Uncle Dunkirk had opted for the winding scenic route that passed through the outskirts of Spruce Ridge. Sage watched the familiar sights of Spruce Ridge roll past his window: Ducey Diamond, where he had twice cracked a baseball over the far chain-link fence; Bing's Grocery Store, with the best chocolate-vanilla-swirl soft ice cream in town; and then Hobbit's Book Emporium, the only used bookstore in town, where Sage would trade in two dog-eared comics for a single used one. As the cab coasted past Cheap Charlie's Used Car Lot, the unofficial city limits of Spruce Ridge, Uncle Dunkirk finally relaxed, sitting back in his seat, and gave Sage a reassuring pat on the knee. Sage grinned back, anxious to begin their adventure.

The cab continued rolling down the highway, leaving Spruce Ridge as a memory in Sage's mind. The I-18, which fed traffic to and from Spruce Ridge, was fairly quiet for a Sunday morning, and devoid of the usual eighteen-wheelers that delivered goods into town seven days a week. Other than a few random vehicles passing in the opposite lane, the road remained practically deserted.

A few minutes later, Uncle Dunkirk instructed the cab driver to take the next right. The cabby edged the vehicle onto the shoulder of the highway and then turned right onto a barren dirt road—two ruts for tire tracks covered completely with gravel and dust.

"Now just follow this road for two miles," added Uncle Dunkirk.

Looking out the window, Sage felt a twitter of hesitation in his chest. This was definitely not the route to the bus station, nor the road to the train station. And the closest airport was fifty miles away—in the other direction. They were completely out of the Spruce Ridge city limits and driving on a dirt road that looked as if it hadn't been traveled on in years. But Sage held his tongue and kept his faith in Uncle Dunkirk.

After a few more minutes of silence, in which the cab jostled over every pothole and dip in the road, Uncle Dunkirk spoke up. "Do you see that grove of trees up ahead on the left? You can drop us there."

The cabby's eyes flitted to the rearview mirror. "You do realize that you're in the middle of nowhere?"

"Actually, I am approximately 8.7 miles north of the town of Spruce Ridge," replied Uncle Dunkirk. "Trust me, young man, I have traveled the world extensively and this is nowhere near nowhere."

"Hey, it's your money," replied the cabby

nonchalantly, his eyes returning to the road. He braked slowly, pulled the cab off to the side of the road, and stepped out. Then he popped the trunk and helped Uncle Dunkirk unload both backpacks. "That'll be sixteen bucks for the ride."

Uncle Dunkirk slipped his hand into the pocket of his khaki pants and pulled out a messy wad of cash. Sage noticed that many of the bills weren't American. Instead, the assortment of notes seemed to mimic every color in the rainbow— blue, red, green, yellow, violet—and they were covered with enough foreign symbols to confuse even the most seasoned traveler. Finally, Uncle Dunkirk peeled off two ten dollar bills and passed them to the cabby. "Keep the change."

The driver gave Uncle Dunkirk a tip of the hat, and then returned to his car. Then, after pulling a sharp U-turn, he tooted the cab's horn twice and drove off in a cloud of dust.

Sage stood next to his backpack and puzzled over this deserted dirt road 8.7 miles from Spruce Ridge. A flurry of questions raced through his mind, each a little more panicked than the previous. *Does the bus come this way? Are we meeting someone else? Is our summer vacation going to be a lousy camping trip this close to Spruce Ridge? Has Uncle Dunkirk been out in the sun too long?*

"Uncle Dunkirk," Sage finally asked, "is there a reason why we're out—here?" Sage caught himself before saying "in the middle of nowhere."

Uncle Dunkirk turned to Sage. "Well, Sage, our adventure begins here."

Sage took a good look around. A large thicket of trees blanketed the left side of the road. To the right, fields of wheat rolled from hill to hill, and in the far distance, smaller squads of trees marked the countryside. The dirt road rolled like a discarded ribbon to the horizon in either direction. Other than that, there was nothing in the area— *absolutely nothing*—that Sage might have taken as the starting point for their summer vacation.

"Right here?" Sage asked glumly, pointing at the dirt road beneath his feet.

"Well, not right *here*," corrected Uncle Dunkirk. "But in the general vicinity."

"I don't see a bus stop," Sage ventured.

"Who said anything about a bus?" Uncle Dunkirk asked with a wink. Then, hoisting his backpack onto his shoulders, Uncle Dunkirk brushed aside his nephew's puzzlement. "Saddle up, Sage. Time's wasting."

Sage slung his backpack onto his shoulders and curiously followed his uncle down a steep embankment into the ditch bordering the dirt road, and then clambered up the far side. Wading through knee-high weeds, they followed the northern edge of the copse. Then they turned away from the road and tracked the trees along the western side.

After another ten minutes, the back side of the copse presented itself. But without any explanation, Uncle Dunkirk turned, stayed against the tree line, and hiked along the southern edge of the copse, heading back east. With a look of complete confusion on his reddening face, Sage reluctantly followed.

As they trudged along, Sage glanced about, expecting to find a car, a camp, a house—*anything*. But still all he could see was wheat, dirt, trees, and patches of scrub.

Finally, Uncle Dunkirk stopped, spun around, and began studying the trees and ground around them. Sage watched patiently, bending down to yank a stem of grass from the ground, which he deposited between his teeth. "Correct me if I'm wrong, Uncle, but we seem to be walking in a circle around these trees."

"No, you're absolutely right, Sage," Uncle Dunkirk answered, before turning his back on the boy to scan the face of a massive bush. Sage glanced at the bush, and noticed that it seemed rather odd. It easily dwarfed every other bush in the area, and it seemed to be tucked tightly between two huge trees, from stump to stump.

"So, let me get this straight," Sage said, pressing a finger down to emphasize each point. "We're not taking a bus. We're not going to the airport. We have no car. And Mom and Dad would probably ground me, *and you*, for life if we hitchhiked."

"And rightfully so," Uncle Dunkirk agreed over his shoulder.

Exasperated, Sage pressed on. "But how are we going to start our summer vacation by standing in the middle of a field?"

Uncle Dunkirk finally tore his eyes away from the bush and gave Sage an all-knowing smile. "I thought we'd take along a little friend," he said. "I hope you don't mind."

With that, Uncle Dunkirk grabbed hold of the curious bush and pulled. Like Superman ripping a brick wall off a building with his bare hands, a massive wall of branches and leaves broke free in Uncle Dunkirk's arms. Before Sage could blink, the propeller of an airplane appeared.

"Sage," announced Uncle Dunkirk, "meet my traveling companion, Willy C."

CHAPTER 4

SAGE'S JAW DROPPED in surprise. "An airplane!" he exclaimed.

"Not just an airplane," corrected Uncle Dunkirk, "but one of the greatest fighter aircraft of all time—a Supermarine Spitfire!"

Sage rose on wobbly legs and stepped toward the giant four-bladed propeller that loomed above him. He reached out, gently touched the black metal blade, and then ran his palm across its cool surface. Although the propeller had been shaded from the morning sun, Sage could almost feel a ghostly heat beneath his fingers, as if the Spitfire was communicating its war-torn history through his touch. With a tone of utmost respect, the word *"Coooooooooooool!"* oozed from his mouth.

There was something about airplanes that had always fascinated Sage. When he was younger, he had spent hours on end lying on the grass of his backyard, staring into the sky, and marveling over the jet aircraft that crisscrossed the heavens above Spruce Ridge. He'd trace out the long smudges of exhaust the planes trailed behind, and then watch fascinated as the smoke gradually dissipated into nothing—a forgotten remnant of a journey gone by.

Recently, Sage and his friends would imagine that they were pilots valiantly protecting the skies from enemy attack. They'd haul empty cardboard boxes into the backyard from the garage and carve out cockpits with scissors. Then their imaginations would fuel their battles—the grassy backyard becoming the wild blue yonder and their cardboard boxes airplanes—and they would dive and charge gallantly in aerial combat.

And one constant of all their make-believe battles was the Spitfire—the sleekest, fastest, deadliest flying machine of the Second World War. And now Sage Smiley was about to fly in one.

"I can't believe you own a Spitfire," gasped Sage in awe.

"Not just any Spitfire," replied Uncle Dunkirk, with a gleam in his eye. "What you are looking at is a Mark IX trainer. When this plane originally flew during the Second World War, it only had a single cockpit. But after the war, it was converted into a trainer. They shifted the front cockpit forward and added a second cockpit behind it. You even have a raised seat, so you can see over your uncle's big head."

Sage's jaw still hung limply, his mouth wide open. His uncle's description of the Supermarine Spitfire had not registered. "I can't believe you own a Spitfire," Sage repeated.

Uncle Dunkirk chuckled and ruffled Sage's hair. Then he clapped his hands, "All right, Sage, it's time to earn your keep. We need to clear out the remaining leaves and branches so we can get Willy C out."

"By the way," Sage asked as he grabbed an armful of branches, "why do you call it Willy C?"

Uncle Dunkirk was already ahead of him, laying down a large branch about twenty feet away from the plane. "Why don't we save that story for the ride, Sage? It's a long flight to where we're going, and a good tale will help pass the time."

With the promise of a story floating in his head, Sage worked quickly. He added his bundle to the top of his uncle's pile and returned for another load. Soon enough, Uncle Dunkirk was ready to guide the plane out into the clearing.

"Now stand by the wood pile," instructed Uncle Dunkirk. "I need to get Willy C out of the trees and into the clearing. I don't want you anywhere near the propeller or the wings while the engine's running." With that, Uncle Dunkirk climbed up onto the wing, and slid the canopy back. He vaulted into the cockpit and did a quick pre-flight check before sparking the ignition. Willy C sputtered and coughed, spitting out a few huffs of black exhaust, before the propeller bit the air and began to spin at full pitch. After releasing the hand brake, Uncle Dunkirk gently taxied Willy C out of its hiding place and into the clear. A long, flat field stretched out before the plane, and for the first time Sage realized the significance of their hike around the trees—it made a perfect hiding place and provided a nice, secluded runway for the Spitfire.

Uncle Dunkirk killed the engine and then climbed out of the Spitfire while calling Sage over. Together they managed to stow both backpacks securely inside a rear storage compartment located in the tail of the plane. Then Uncle Dunkirk walked Sage around Willy C, pointing out the various features on the plane—the strengthened airframe, the V-12 supercharged Merlin engine, the four-bladed airscrew, the rear fuselage, and the eight 0.303 Browning machine guns imbedded in the wings, which Uncle Dunkirk stressed had been completely neutralized. Sage listened in fascination to every description of the Spitfire, still not fully believing that he was about to fly off in one.

Finally, the moment arrived, and it was time to go. Uncle Dunkirk gave Sage a few brief tips on how to best climb up onto the wing, but Sage was a natural. Like a monkey scaling a tree, Sage swiftly clambered onto the wing. Then he scrambled into the rear cockpit, dropping into the navigator's seat. A battered leather flying cap was tucked beside the seat, and Sage shook it out and jauntily positioned it on his head. Now that he looked the role of a pilot, Sage took in the variety of official-looking instruments presented before him—from dials to knobs to monitors, and Sage's eyes darted from one to the next, desperate to soak up the interior of the airplane. *My friends will never believe me.*

Moments later, Willy C's supercharged Merlin engine sputtered to life once again, and this time Sage felt the power of the aircraft beneath him. Willy C vibrated wildly, shaking Sage until he felt like a jumping bean. He wrenched on the strap of his seatbelt, and felt his body press deeper into the navigator's seat. "Hold on, Sage," called Uncle Dunkirk over the din of the engine. "We're about to take off."

Sage eagerly peered out the cockpit window as Willy C began to roll forward. The plane's thick rubber wheels bounced roughly over every bump, rut, and dip in the field. Then, as it gradually picked up speed, Sage watched the trees on either side of the plane lose their rigidity and fade into a blur of green, yellow, and brown. Finally, he felt a tremor of anxiety as the tail of the plane lifted off the ground and Willy C took flight. The jarring sprint across the field turned into a silky smooth glide as Uncle Dunkirk eased back on the stick and guided them into the air.

Out the cockpit window, the countryside fell away, and Sage marveled at his stunning new vantage point, floating high with the birds over the treetops. Willy C soared over emerald forests. Turquoise lakes spotted the countryside, the water glittering white light in the morning sun. They followed ribbons of highway far below, and watched the ant-sized cars bustle from lane to lane. As they climbed higher and higher, they began to slip into pockets of white fluffy clouds, and hazy strands swished by the cockpit window to reform into odd shapes behind the plane. The sun beamed through the canopy glass. It was truly a glorious day.

Finally, Uncle Dunkirk broke the silence, "I promised to tell you about Willy C, didn't I?"

"Yes," Sage replied eagerly.

"Well, Sage, picking a name for a plane is a tricky business. There's a lot of superstition involved in selecting the right name. Some pilots, especially those who flew during times of war, picked the names of their wives or girlfriends in hopes that it would keep them safe. When it came to naming my Spitfire, I had to look elsewhere for inspiration. Since I've never been married, and have never been much of a boyfriend, I decided to name my Spitfire after a very brave pilot—Willy Omer François Jean Coppens de Houthulst."

"Willy *who*?" exclaimed Sage.

"Willy Omer François Jean Coppens de Houthulst. He was better known as Willy

Coppens, but you've probably never heard of him. He was way before your time—actually, he was before my time, too," Uncle Dunkirk added.

"Willy was an ace during the First World War with the famous *Compagnie des Aviateurs*. He flew a single-seat Hanriot and was considered an expert at shooting down enemy observation balloons. He'd soar into battle with the sun at his back, dodging enemy artillery and shrapnel, and he'd take out the observation balloon with a single burst of his guns. Once the balloon dropped from the sky, he'd execute aerial acrobatics over the enemy."

"Kind of like celebrating a touchdown?" Sage offered.

"Exactly! Just like spiking the ball. He was a great pilot and one of the original aces. I remember reading about him and the other aces when I was young. There was Edward Rickenbacker, the American ace, and Brumowski from Austria. There was René Fonck from France, the Brit's Ed Mannock and Canada's Billy Bishop. And, of course, there was the infamous Red Baron—a German ace named Manfred von Richthofen. They were all amazing pilots, but there was one story about Willy Coppens that really sparked my imagination.

"It took place during a fierce air battle in the First World War when Willy was attacking one of the enemy's balloons. Now you would think that it wouldn't be much of a challenge for a biplane to shoot down a hot air balloon, but when you consider how often the wind shifts and changes, and that the balloon is more or less riding on the wind, it wasn't a walk in the park by any means. On this particular day, Willy learned that himself. He was diving down on an enemy balloon, ready to tear it open with a burst from his guns, when a freak gust of wind suddenly shot the balloon straight up at Willy's plane. Poor Willy had nowhere to go. He had already committed his Hanriot into a dive, he had no time to turn, and he couldn't get out of the way quick enough."

"So what did he do?" asked Sage.

"Most pilots would have simply given up at that moment, realizing that they were about to meet their maker. After all, if the Hanriot crashed into the balloon, both plane and balloon would have gone up in a ball of flame, and Willy Coppens's eulogy would have been written there. But our friend Willy, being the ace that he was, attempted the only maneuver that would have given him a chance to survive."

"What was that?" Sage asked breathlessly.

"He landed his plane on top of the balloon," answered Uncle Dunkirk, with a deep-seated tone of respect.

"*No way!*" The words burst forth from Sage's mouth like a shotgun blast.

"It's true," replied Uncle Dunkirk. "Willy

landed his Hanriot smack dab on top of the enemy balloon. Then he killed his engine to save the propeller. When the plane finally slipped off the top of the balloon, he started it up again and flew away."

"Wow!" Sage exclaimed. "It sounds like a scene from an Indiana Jones movie."

"Exactly, except this was real life, not the movies. This was piloting at its highest level of skill—when a man had to make life or death decisions in a split second and live with the consequences."

"Did Willy Coppens die in the war?" Sage asked, hoping that this war story had a happy ending.

"As a matter of fact, he survived. He was shot down and had a leg amputated, but good old Willy Coppens led a long and productive life. He was a military attaché in Europe, but passed away in 1986. To me, he'll always be an Ace. Quite a pilot, that Willy C."

"I'll say," Sage agreed, storing away Willy Coppens's adventure to one day relive it in a cardboard Hanriot in his backyard. Content, Sage turned his attention back out the cockpit window. He was startled to see that the once patchy fields of green, brown, and yellow had grown distant. Sage hadn't noticed how high they'd flown in such a short time, but he could now see that the Spitfire was still clawing at the air, climbing higher and higher above the clouds.

"But there's something else I should tell you about Willy C," continued Uncle Dunkirk. "This is a very special plane, Sage. It's been with me for twenty years and has taken me all over the world. It has been my friend and traveling companion, but, most of all, it has been the portal to all of my adventures."

Then, Uncle Dunkirk twisted round in his seat, glanced at Sage, and asked, "How do you feel about magic?"

CHAPTER 5

"MAGIC?" ASKED SAGE. "Why?"

The Spitfire continued to climb through the air, the earth now nothing more than a hazy collage of colors splashed about on a massive canvas. Willy C's engine roared powerfully, but every now and then, Sage would hear an unmistakable stutter in the plane's voice— nothing much, just a slight hiccup in the plane's smooth purr that made the hair on the back of Sage's neck stand.

Uncle Dunkirk was impervious to the slight skips in Willy C's engine. He continued speaking, "Years ago, back when I was just a young lad out of University, I set out to make a name for myself by finding the mythical kingdom of *Shambhala* that had served as the inspiration for Shangri-La in James Hilton's book *Lost Horizon*. I trekked deep into the Himalayan backcountry, spending weeks crossing mountain ridge after mountain ridge, until I reached an area so remote that the sherpas carrying my gear refused to follow."

"What's a sherpa?" asked Sage curiously.

"Sherpas have to be the toughest people in the

world. They live in the high mountain regions of Nepal, working as traders and farmers, but they're probably best known for their skills as guides and porters. They lug massive baskets on their backs, sometimes just as heavy as they are, and carry them up steep mountain passes and along treacherous trails. Practically everyone who treks into the Himalaya is guided by a sherpa, especially in areas as forbidding as those that I was trekking in. You see, I was off the map, which is usually where a *real* journey begins.

"I bid adieu to my sherpas and proceeded alone, taking only what I could carry on my back. One morning, as I plodded along, I heard a terrible roar that drowned out all sound, and shook the ground like an earthquake. I realized that I had come within minutes of stumbling into the path of an avalanche, but luckily enough, the trail I was following had taken me behind an outcrop of rock, and I had a front row view of the landscape in front of me being completely obliterated under an onslaught of snow. It was an amazing sight to witness—Mother Nature in all her angry glory.

"When the snow finally stopped, I strapped on my snowshoes and began picking my way across the snow-covered valley. I was halfway to the opposite side when I saw something strange out of the corner of my eye. A *flash*. I glanced up the hillside and once again saw a bright flash of light a couple hundred feet up, almost as if someone were trying to signal for help.

"I raced up the valley, as fast as my legs would carry me, following the flashes that kept glimmering before me. Halfway up, I realized that whoever was signaling had either seen me, or was growing weak, because the flashing finally stopped. I marked the spot and closed the distance, and as I climbed up, I saw the oddest thing—a man's bald head sticking out of the snow. From the features of his face, I could see that he was obviously a Nepali or Tibetan. Stranger still, he had no glasses to reflect light from, and both his hands, not to mention every other part of his body, were buried up to the neck in snow. How he managed to make those flashes, I had no idea.

"I scrambled up beside him and let him know I was there to help. A small smile lit up his face, and he whispered in heavily accented English, "Bless you," before his eyes rolled back and he passed out. I tore at the snow around him, digging for all I was worth. And as I unearthed him, I noticed that both his legs were broken. I wouldn't have been surprised to find that he had some internal bleeding also. After all, it looked like he had been tossed around quite severely in the avalanche. I also noticed the robes that he wore— those of a *bhikkhu*, a Buddhist monk.

"When I finally managed to free him from the

snow, I could tell he was living on borrowed time. I wrapped him in my sleeping bag, tenderly massaging his frozen limbs to get his circulation flowing, and then dug a snow cave for shelter. Any wood for a fire had been carried away in the avalanche, so I knew that his chances of survival were slim. This deep into the Himalaya, there was no hospital, no doctor, nothing. Just a person's will to survive.

"Later that night, he regained consciousness for a moment. I had made some tea using my portable camp stove, and I held his head up while he drank. When he finished, he smiled again, and then reached into his robes and pulled a necklace from around his neck. At first, I thought it was just a cheap relic. A bauble of no real value. But as I looked closer, I could see that this necklace was unique. There was an amber stone of some sort attached to a thin leather band. To this day, I've never seen anything like it. It was a light yellowish-brown in color, but you could see through it, almost as if it were translucent. And in the middle of the stone, there was a burst of light—like a captured star that pulsed with a life all its own. He pressed the stone into my hand and said in halting English, 'Seek truth and enlightenment on your path in life.' In layman's terms, he was telling me to search for *nirvana*."

"*Nirvana*?" asked Sage, his curiosity peaked. "I take it you're not talking about Kurt Cobain, are you?"

"Not even close," chuckled Uncle Dunkirk. "You see, Buddhist monks seek *nirvana* through the course of their lives. Nirvana is not a place, but more of a culmination of a lifelong journey, or the realization of an absolute truth. Life is just a cycle to Buddhists, and when a person who has achieved nirvana dies, their death is known as *parinirvana*— they have *fully* passed away. Their life was the last link in the circle of death and rebirth, and they will not be reborn. I don't know if the monk had found nirvana during the course of his life's journey, but I know that he had accepted his fate, and was at peace with it. He simply meditated while I investigated the stone. Seconds later, his body was writhing in pain. I tried to help, but he seized my hand, stared into my eyes and said, 'With wings of wind, I fly.' And then he died."

"With wings of wind, I fly?" asked Sage. "What does that mean?"

"I hadn't a clue," replied Uncle Dunkirk. "But I wondered if it had anything to do with those mysterious flashes."

Uncle Dunkirk paused. In the interim, Sage glanced out the cockpit window to watch the earth pass by far, far below. Willy C's engine was still stammering away, but the sputters were becoming farther apart. Suddenly, the plane's propeller ground to a halt, and then burst into action again.

Sage tore his eyes from the vista and watched as the propeller continued to stop and start, again and again. The color quickly drained from his face, and his heartbeat quickened.

"For days I played with the amber stone," continued Uncle Dunkirk, lost in another time and seemingly oblivious to the deathly lurches of the propeller. "I'd lie awake in my sleeping bag at night, squeezing it tightly in my hand, and chanting 'With wings of wind, I fly' over and over, but nothing happened. After a while, I simply slung the thing around my neck and forgot about it.

"Then, one day, your Uncle Dunkirk was hiking along, staring up at a tough climb that I would soon have to ascend. The ridge was two hundred meters up, and my legs were jelly, feeling as if they'd be hard-pressed to take one more step, let alone climb another few hundred steps. I was daydreaming, wishing I could just fly to the top, when the monk's words simply crossed my lips: 'With wings of wind, I fly.'

"The next thing I knew, there was a blinding flash that enveloped my whole body. When I opened my eyes, I found myself standing at the top of the ridge, looking down on the trail I had just been hiking."

"That's weird," commented Sage.

"Tell me about it," replied Uncle Dunkirk.

With a piercing screech, Willy C's propeller

came to a complete stop, and with it, all sound from the engine. Sage leaned forward, straining against his seatbelt, and peered over Uncle Dunkirk's shoulder to watch his reaction. However, Uncle Dunkirk simply flicked the ignition switch off and took a firmer grip on the stick as Willy C began to pitch down toward the ground.

"Which brings us to our present situation," Uncle Dunkirk noted offhandedly. "Which has come around a bit faster than I had anticipated." Leaning on the stick, he pitched Willy C into a dive, pointing the plane's propeller straight down at the earth far below. Then he continued his story, hardly missing a beat.

"The amber stone, I discovered, is some sort of ancient teleportation device. The incantation makes reference to the wind, which is *motion,* when you think about it. After experimenting a bit, I surmised that once you had achieved a certain degree of motion, you could teleport yourself anywhere in the world. All you had to do was picture a destination, say the chant and, like magic, there you would be. It also explained those mysterious flashes I saw from the mountainside. The monk was trying to flash himself to safety, but he was trapped in the snow, and unable to move with two broken legs, so he went nowhere."

The soothing whistle of the wind that had been lightly drafting outside the cockpit window increased to a shrill howl as gravity's fingers encircled Willy C and pulled with all her might. With his heart in his throat, Sage peeked out the cockpit window and watched as Willy C rocketed toward a massive blanket of clouds that seemed to grow in size by the second. A low groan seeped out of Sage's mouth as terror threatened to overwhelm him, but Uncle Dunkirk calmly carried on.

"I continued to experiment with the stone while in the Himalayas. I next tried the incantation on an icy slope. I had been traversing a razor sharp ridge when I slipped. My feet shot out from under me, and I landed hard on my back. Unfortunately, before I could twist around and sink my ice axe, I found myself hurtling down a sheer mountain face.

"With nowhere to go but down, I muttered the chant again and was once more enveloped in a flash of energy. This time, when I came through, I found myself standing at the top of the Mother of the Universe herself—*Chomolungma*, which you probably know as Mount Everest."

"Get out!" sputtered Sage, as he fought back the urge to scream. His fingers were clamped to the sidewalls of the cockpit, pressing him firmly into his seat, but Uncle Dunkirk's intriguing story served as a distraction from their blistering trajectory. However, as the peculiar reality of his uncle's magical amber stone began to fully register inside of Sage's mind, a torrent of goose bumps swept over his arms. "You ended up on *top* of the *highest* mountain *in the world*? What did you do?"

"Why, I planted a flag that I'd brought for just such an occasion, took a quick picture, and then flashed back to the trail. But as breathtaking as the view was on top of the world, the discovery that went along with it was even more amazing—the faster I went, the farther I could travel."

Willy C tore through the sky, shearing through the wind and carrying them closer to what Sage figured was their certain death. Suddenly, the clouds were upon them. Willy C rocketed through, and wisps of snowy white ether whizzed past the cockpit window—there one second, gone the next. Then, just as suddenly, they broke through the clouds and the patchwork quilt of earth was once again in sight.

"I continued experimenting with the amber stone over the next few years, learning more about its powers with each successive flash. Finally, one day when I was back in the United States, I tried the stone in Willy C, which was new to me at the time," continued Uncle Dunkirk, calling out over the roar of the wind. "I'd found the plane forgotten and gathering dust in a farmer's barn, and it was love at first sight. Some enterprising farmer had bought it after the war as a crop duster, and gladly parted with it after a long year of drought. I gave him every penny I had, then taught myself to fly a stick before taking it for a spin."

Sage's curiosity in Uncle Dunkirk's tale barely restrained his fear of crashing. But with a little courage, he clenched his sweaty palms and managed to concentrate on Uncle Dunkirk's words. "Where did you end up that time?"

"That time, I ended up in Montana," Uncle Dunkirk replied nonchalantly as he cranked the ignition. With a belch of black smoke, Willy C's engine turned over and the propeller burst back into life. The shrill *whoosh* of air hurtling past the cockpit was replaced by the powerful thrum of Willy C's supercharged engine, and Sage felt the plane lurch forward.

"Montana?" Sage sputtered.

"Yes, Montana. Along the Little Bighorn River to be exact."

"But that's not so far away," said Sage, tugging on his seatbelt tensely. "It's not like magically appearing on top of Mount Everest."

"That's true," replied Uncle Dunkirk. "However, what's shocking was not that I transported myself to Little Bighorn, Montana, but that I unknowingly stumbled onto a way to break every known law of time and space, and somehow managed to skip through time to arrive moments before Lieutenant Colonel George Armstrong Custer made his final stand. I arrived on June 25, 1876, and witnessed one of the greatest defeats in

American military history—Custer's Last Stand."

"No way!" Sage exclaimed in surprise and shock. "You can travel through time?"

"With enough speed, yes. Both of us can," replied Uncle Dunkirk. "By putting Willy C into a dive from over thirty thousand feet, we can achieve enough forward momentum and speed to teleport our combined body weights, plus Willy C, anywhere we want to go. And by anywhere, I do mean *anywhere*.

"So, I'll leave our destination to you, Sage. Wherever you want to go for your summer vacation is fine with me. Just pick a destination." With that, Uncle Dunkirk twisted round and reached his hand out. The amber stone dangled from its leather band, glittering brightly.

Sage quickly grasped the amber stone and held tight. The altimeter embedded in the control panel in front of Sage spun wildly. Sage took one last look out the cockpit window, and was certain that he could now make out specific vehicles driving on a highway below and farmhouses spotting the countryside.

"Sage?" pressed Uncle Dunkirk. "We don't have much time. Slip the amber stone around your neck. Then, concentrate on a place that you've always wanted to see, close your eyes, and chant 'With wings of wind, I fly.' Got it?"

Sage clutched the amber stone in his damp

palm and thought for a second that he could almost feel a mystical heat permeating from it. He slid the leather band over his neck and felt the stone's weight press against his chest. A flurry of destinations raced through Sage's head—places he had always wanted to see, places he had seen in movies and on TV, places he had only dreamed of. How was he supposed to concentrate on selecting just one when he could now clearly see the yellow lines on the highway?

Sage felt a scream curdling inside of his stomach like sour milk, and sensed it creeping up his throat to his lips. The ground was rapidly rising, and he had a horrifying premonition of Willy C slamming into the earth, and shattering into a million unidentifiable pieces. Desperate for something familiar and comforting, Sage dug his hand deep into the pocket of his pants and clutched his lucky Jim Hawkins compass. The good luck charm had served him well in the past, and Sage prayed that it would continue to do so. Then, right before he could let loose a bloodcurdling scream, Uncle Dunkirk called out, "Now, Sage! Now!"

"With wings of wind, I fly!" Sage chanted loudly, clenching his eyes shut to escape the sight of the rapidly-rising ground, and clutching the compass with equal vigor. "With wings of wind, I fly! With wings of wind, I fly!"

CHAPTER 6

SAGE FELT A sudden heat infuse his body, and a blinding flash enveloped the cockpit. He clamped his eyes shut, but a brilliant orange light still shone through his eyelids.

And then all was normal, yet strangely so. The regular, soothing purr of Willy C's engine suddenly reappeared without the chilling sounds of a strained propeller or an overworked engine. And the incessant howl of the wind that had ridden with them all the way to the ground had vanished. From somewhere near, Sage recognized a voice, his *own* voice, chanting, "With wings of wind, I fly! With wings of wind, I fly!" until Uncle Dunkirk finally spoke.

"You can open your eyes now, Sage."

Sage pried his eyes open a fraction, and was relieved to find that he was no longer plummeting toward Earth. Willy C was flying on an even keel, its engine humming as if nothing unusual had happened. However, out the cockpit window, the landscape had changed dramatically. Where there had once been gently rolling hills and random pockets of forests, there was now water—

and lots of it.

To the left of Willy C, an ocean of water, dark blue with foamy whitecaps, stretched into the distance. Sage scanned the horizon, trying to pick out an identifiable mark—a boat, a sail. But there was only water stretching to the very edge of the earth.

Sage turned to look out the right side, and was startled to discover that Willy C was skirting a landmass in the middle of an expanse of water. The island was maybe five miles long and half that wide. Three large hills, blanketed with emerald green scrub, rose to the sky, giving the island the look of a camel with three humps. Thick forests of palm trees circled the base of each hill, sheltering the ground beneath from the air. Farther down the coast, the island was speckled with pristine white sand beaches, and the outline of a magnificent coral reef could be seen through the waters.

"Where are we, Sage?" asked Uncle Dunkirk, his voice full of wonder.

"In all honesty," replied Sage nervously, staring at the island below, "I don't know. The ground was coming up so fast that I couldn't concentrate on one place. I was too scared."

"Well, we're nowhere near Spruce Ridge, so something must have crossed your mind," said Uncle Dunkirk. Then, with a grin, he added, "We might as well make the best of it. Why don't we explore this little island?"

With that, Uncle Dunkirk banked Willy C to the right. The Spitfire immediately responded, soaring down through the skies to follow the contours of the island. As they skirted the northern tip, a small inlet appeared, shorn from high cliffs on either side. Sage peered between the two massive cliff faces and guessed that the inlet snaked far into the island's interior, dragging a trail of water with it. Otherwise, the north side of the island seemed completely impregnable.

The eastern side of the island also seemed secure. Tall cliffs rose high above the water, and massive boulders jutted up from the surf to protect the eastern shore from the endless onslaught of ocean rollers that crashed upon them and sent blasts of spray skyward. As Sage gaped at the huge plumes of water exploding every which way, Uncle Dunkirk noted, "No sign of life so far."

And he was right. So far, they hadn't seen a single sign that man resided on the island below. No village or shelter passed by the canopy window. There were no lavish mansions, or even lookouts built atop the three hills. There were no tourists sunning themselves on the beach, or children splashing in the surf. And, stranger still, the waters surrounding the island were devoid of any speedboats, Jet Skis, or cruise ships— something unheard of in this day and age. From their vantage point, soaring high above the island in Willy C, it appeared as if the island below was totally deserted.

"That might be a good landing spot over there," Uncle Dunkirk said, as he motioned to a long valley near the center of the island. A natural clearing seemed to be sheared out of the forest, tucked between two of the hills. "We'll have to take a closer look once we've finished our reconnaissance."

By now, Willy C was nearing the southern tip of the island, flying past the last of the island's three hills, when Uncle Dunkirk called out excitedly, "Sage! Down there!"

Following Uncle Dunkirk's lead, Sage spotted what looked like a small wooden fort built on a slight ridge. The building was square, and a small perimeter had been cleared out of the forest surrounding it. The walls of the fort had been hewn from trees, lashed tightly together, with the tips carved to points and aimed at the sky. Inside the small compound stood a single blockhouse, but again, no one raced out to investigate Willy C's noisy intrusion.

"If there's anyone on this island, we'll know soon enough," remarked Uncle Dunkirk, before veering from course and banking Willy C sharply toward the fort. Uncle Dunkirk dropped the plane's altitude to only fifty feet above the treetops, and then charged over the compound with a deafening roar.

Sage twisted around in his seat to watch for any reaction to their flyby. To his dismay, there wasn't one. No one dashed out of the shelter or raced for cover. Either the fort was long deserted or nobody was home.

"We'll take a closer look after we land," said Uncle Dunkirk, with a trace of disappointment in his voice.

Leaning on the stick, Uncle Dunkirk returned Willy C to the southern coast of the island, to continue their aerial tour. As they skirted the final hill, a large lagoon appeared, nestled safely on the island's opposite shore and sheltered from the breakers that ravaged the island. Crystal blue water sparkled like a brilliant diamond, promising a refreshing swim. But as Willy C soared nearer, something menacing came into focus—black silhouettes slinked across the lagoon floor, their tails lashing to and fro.

"Sharks," explained Uncle Dunkirk. "You can tell by their..."

Ka-Boom!

A loud report echoed over the island, sending a panicked flock of birds skyward. Sage twisted in his seat to look behind them when a large, black object whistled past Willy C.

"What was that?" Sage yelled, twisting from

side to side in the rear cockpit, trying to improve his view.

Uncle Dunkirk reacted quickly, throwing Willy C into a hard right turn. "I think we might be under attack." He, too, craned his neck, peering out the cockpit window, trying to find where the mysterious report had come from.

Ka-Boom!

Once again the thunderous roar shook the serenity of the island paradise. Out of the corner of his eye, Sage spotted a puff of white smoke coming from an area of the lagoon that was masked by a wall of palm trees. But before he could say anything, his world turned upside down.

The second black shot caught the tip of Willy C's right wing, sending a gut-wrenching tremor throughout the plane, and throwing Sage and Uncle Dunkirk hard to the left. Sage quickly regained his wits, and peered out the cockpit window. He was horrified to see a hole ripped through the right wing.

Ka-Boom!

In the front cockpit, Uncle Dunkirk fought for control, gripping the stick between two clenched fists and bucking the tremors that rippled through the plane. Taking action in order to evade the attack, he increased the pitch of Willy C's engine and pushed the plane higher, climbing rapidly out of range of enemy fire. Willy C passed over the lagoon and rocketed away from the island, farther out to sea.

"We've been hit, Sage, and we have to land," announced Uncle Dunkirk. His eyes darted from instrument to instrument, and out the cockpit window to watch the right wing. "I'm going to try to reach that clearing in the center of the island. We don't have any other options."

Uncle Dunkirk cautiously banked Willy C back toward the island, careful not to exert too much pressure on the damaged wing. At this point, Uncle Dunkirk seemed to have Willy C under a semblance of control. But, all the same, Sage knew he'd feel much safer with his feet back on the ground.

Willy C powered over the ocean and skirted the shore, veering away from the lagoon. Soon enough, the island's first large hill sat directly outside their left window, and Sage could feel Willy C begin to decelerate.

"We don't have time to take a closer look at the clearing, so this could be a rough landing, Sage. Make sure you're buckled in tight, and hold on!"

Sage yanked at his seatbelt, but it was already uncomfortably tight. Sitting back, he watched as Willy C coasted along, barely feet above the trees. The foliage flashed below the plane in a blur of green and brown. Finally, the forest below the plane vanished, and the ground rushed up to meet them. Willy C glided over the clearing and skimmed the floor of the valley.

"Here we go, Sage. Hang on tight."

Uncle Dunkirk dipped Willy C the remaining feet to the ground, risking a rough landing over a shortage of runway. Willy C seemed to hover for a moment before its wheels touched down and bounced off the hard-packed earth. With a jolt, they landed again, and this time the wheels found land, carrying them speedily along the valley floor toward an embankment of trees on the far side of the clearing.

Sage felt like a can of paint in a mixing machine. His body shook violently in the rear cockpit as it absorbed the shock of the rough landing and the uneven ground beneath their wheels. In the front cockpit, Uncle Dunkirk seemed to rise out of his seat. Using every bit of strength in his body, he was pressing on the brake, trying to curb Willy C's headlong momentum. As the edge of the forest loomed ahead, Sage thought of how sad it would be to survive a death-defying plunge from thirty thousand feet, not to mention a vicious attack from a mysterious enemy, only to die in a plane crash when the plane was already on the ground.

The trees on the far side of the clearing closed in fast, their thick trunks rising high over the clearing and threatening to snap off Willy C's wings. Uncle Dunkirk continued to strain against the brake, pressing harder and harder, finally slowing Willy C to a crawl. The long, dangling fronds of the palm tree directly in front of the plane came under the propeller and flew every which way. Then, with a welcome jerk, Willy C stopped.

They had survived yet again. They were on the ground and safe. Or so they thought.

CHAPTER 7

"NOT MY BEST landing," observed Uncle Dunkirk dryly. "But given the circumstances, definitely not my worst."

After unbuckling his seat belt, Uncle Dunkirk slid open the canopy and climbed out onto the wing. Sage managed to hoist himself up and climb out as well. He still clutched his Jim Hawkins compass. And after checking to see if it was still working—*north, south, east, west*—Sage slipped the instrument back into the pocket of his jeans for safekeeping, and wiped his sweaty palms on the seat of his pants. After the numerous close scrapes they'd had today, there was no doubting the luck that the compass provided.

"We'd better move quick, Sage," instructed Uncle Dunkirk, glancing around the clearing, which, for the time being, was deserted. "Whoever shot at us could be on their way to find us."

Uncle Dunkirk jumped off the wing, and Sage followed, stepping down for the first time onto the ground of this mysterious island. "Grab the backpacks out of the rear storage while I take a few measurements. We'll have to worry about fixing the wing later."

Following his uncle's instructions, Sage opened the rear storage compartment and managed to pull the backpacks free. Then, grabbing them by the shoulder straps, he lugged them fifty yards away and stored them behind the coiling roots of a large banyan tree, where he was certain they would be out of the way.

In the meantime, Uncle Dunkirk was busy counting off the yards between the trees immediately in front of Willy C. With a clap of his hands, he reported, "This spot is perfect. And Willy C was kind enough to trim a few palm fronds for us. Sage, I need you to gather as many palm fronds and branches as you can find and bring them here as quickly as possible. I'm going to park Willy C." As he climbed back onto the wing, Uncle Dunkirk cautioned, "Oh, and don't go too far into the woods. We don't know what's out there yet."

Wiping the sweat from his forehead with the back of his arm, Sage ran into the forest and started collecting bundles of palm fronds. The ground throughout the forest was littered with an array of suitable branches, which had probably been cast aside by a previous tropical storm or hurricane. Once his arms were weighted down completely, Sage retraced his steps back to the clearing and dumped his bundle near the plane.

Sage was on his third trip into the woods

when he heard Willy C's engine turn over once more. The wash from the propeller sent a wall of dirt and leaves billowing throughout the forest, and Sage was forced to cover his eyes and dash deeper into the woods to outrun it. As he raced forward, Sage spied a beam of sunlight streaming through the treetops maybe a hundred yards in front of him. Staring ahead, Sage wondered why the overhead canopy thinned in that particular spot, allowing such a brilliant band of sunlight to peek through. *Is there another clearing? Maybe a homestead, built in the middle of the forest?*

Sage decided to do a quick investigation. After all, one extra minute wasn't going to make much of a difference in the scheme of things, and he might have just stumbled onto a significant discovery.

He jogged toward the light, dodging back and forth between the trees. As he moved closer, a shower of brilliant sunlight rained down from the canopy to blind him. Raising his arm to shield his eyes, Sage stumbled forward. He tried to stop, but found that his feet didn't obey. The hard-packed forest floor had given way to loose shale, and, carried along on a dusty wave of pebbles and dirt, Sage's sneakers seemed to move by themselves. As Sage slipped down an embankment, he quickly realized that there was only one direction to go—*down*. And he wasn't about to gamble on how far down.

Frantically, Sage spun around and looked for something to grab hold of. To his left stood a gnarled tree rotting with arthritic branches. As Sage fell to his knees, his right arm snaked out and clutched a branch. A fiery needle of pain announced itself in his left shin, but Sage ignored it for the moment. Pain could wait. Right now, stopping was more important.

Although the branch crackled noisily under his weight, it held firmly to the tree, allowing Sage to stop his descent. With a sigh of relief, Sage began to carefully churn his feet against the loose shale, sending a jet of rocks and dirt tumbling over the ledge behind him. Eventually, he was finally able to scramble up to the top of the embankment, where he collapsed, exhausted.

With his heart thundering in his ears, Sage took a quick look at his left shin. There was a ragged tear in his jeans that revealed an ugly wound swathed in red dust. Sage spit onto his fingers and gently cleansed the nasty, red abrasion, careful not to brush the area too hard. "Great," he muttered. "What next?"

Using the tree beside him for support, Sage pulled himself up to his feet. Once he found his balance, he carefully leaned forward, clutching the branch tightly, and glanced over the embankment. What he saw dried out the saliva in his mouth—

the shale embankment slid down for only ten feet before plummeting hundreds of feet into a gorge far below. A rock-strewn creek trickled at the bottom, which Sage surmised was fed by the inlet they had seen from the air. If it hadn't been for the tree, Sage and his sneakers would have slid right off the edge and down to his death.

Sage gave his Jim Hawkins compass a pat for luck. Then, as he turned back toward the clearing, he noticed for the first time that the woods had gone silent once more. The roar of Willy C's engine was gone. *Uncle Dunkirk must be done.*

Sage scooped a handful of branches from the ground, and trudged back to the clearing. Uncle Dunkirk had parked the plane tightly between two trees, just as he had in the field outside of Spruce Ridge. A few palm fronds had already been laid against the fuselage, partially camouflaging the plane, but Uncle Dunkirk was nowhere to be seen.

"Uncle Dunkirk," Sage called out, careful not to be too loud. He walked toward the plane, expecting Uncle Dunkirk to appear, but there was no reply. Even the chatter of birds in the trees had seemingly fallen silent. A trickle of worry seeped into Sage's mind. "Uncle Dunkirk, where are you?"

Once again, an eerie silence was the only reply.

Sage peered into the woods surrounding the plane, but Uncle Dunkirk was nowhere to be seen. *He must be gathering wood*, Sage thought as he dropped his bundle of branches near Willy C. Three quarters of the plane was still uncovered, and sunlight shimmered off the plane's sleek exterior. Knowing they were nowhere near complete, Sage decided to set out for another bundle. This time he would try the woods directly behind Willy C.

As Sage circled the tail of the plane, his heart leapt into his throat, and a gasp burst from his lips. An unkempt giant of a man lay on the ground. He must have been nearly seven feet tall, with long black hair and bulging muscles. He had a jutting square jaw and a flat nose that looked as if it had been broken a time or two. He wore a red vest, unbuttoned, with fancy gold stitching throughout, and a pair of baggy, black trousers, which were tucked into a pair of black, shin-high boots.

A spatter of blood glistened in the sunlight on the giant's forehead, and next to him lay a broken tree branch. *He must have been hit on the head with the branch*, Sage thought. But one question remained: *where was Uncle Dunkirk?*

Sage could see from the giant's rising and falling stomach that the man was still breathing. Not wanting to wake the leviathan from his slumber, Sage crept back, never taking his eyes off the giant. As he slipped past the tail of Willy C, his ears perked up. There was something there. An unnatural sound floating on the wind. Something distant, yet not so far. It sounded almost like...*whistling?*

Sage stopped and turned his head from side to side, trying to determine where this mysterious noise was coming from. As the sound became louder, Sage realized that he was right. Someone *was* whistling a tune, and it was getting closer. *It must be Uncle Dunkirk.*

However, because of the strange circumstances laid out before him, Sage thought it wise to exert a little caution. He ran as fast as his scraped shin would carry him, and dodged behind a large tree, dropping to his stomach and extending his legs behind him. Then, peering through the underbrush, Sage watched, hoping to see Uncle Dunkirk come swaggering out of the trees, whistling a happy tune.

Moments later, across the clearing, Sage spotted a dark silhouette slip from the foliage and stride toward Willy C. Sage squinted his eyes against the sunlight and wished that he had his trusty telescope so that he could take a closer look. But there was no need. As the figure neared, the shadow fell away and the man's features became clear. With a nervous gulp, Sage saw that the man was not Uncle Dunkirk, not in the least.

And then he managed to pick out the tune the stranger was whistling:

Fifteen men on the dead man's chest
Yo-ho-ho and a bottle of rum.

CHAPTER 8

THE MAN WHO strode into the clearing was a wiry fellow, and not nearly as large as the giant. He stood maybe five feet seven and had shoulder-length brown hair, which was clasped back into a tidy ponytail. His face was a burnt shade of crimson, and covered in patches of bristly scruff. A hawk-like nose led the way from the middle of his face, and it perched boldly above a pair of thin lips that were puckered for whistling.

The man wore a loose-fitting white shirt, with large, puffy sleeves, and black, baggy trousers. As he moved forward, Sage took particular note of his belt, or rather the long, deadly looking sword that hung from it. He also appeared to be carrying a wineskin of some sort over his shoulder, which swung back and forth as he continued to whistle gaily.

The stranger walked up to Willy C, and paused for a moment in front of the black, four-bladed propeller. He stared longingly at the airplane and then tentatively reached out to touch the propeller. When his fingers glanced off the metal, he jerked his hand back suddenly, as if the simple touch had scorched his hand. Then, timidly, the stranger sniffed at his fingers.

Sage watched this curious display from his hiding place behind the tree. The man's apprehension was clear, but Sage detected something else behind the nervous demeanor—*greed*. Whoever this man was, he was completely enraptured by Willy C.

The stranger's peculiar behavior stopped the moment a pained groan broke from the lips of the downed giant. The wiry fellow darted away from the propeller without a second glance, and circled the wing. Then, standing over the fallen giant, he loosened the cap off the wineskin and poured a steady stream of water over the man's face.

"What the..." sputtered the giant. His massive hands burst into action, flinging water from his face, and with the agility of a cat—a *very* large cat—he scrambled to his knees and then to his feet, his fists raised, ready to fight.

"Easy, Red, easy," soothed the wiry man, stopping the flow of water. "'Tis I, Mr. Hands."

Although the giant continued to sputter, reality seemed to thin the fog in his head. His colossal fists—hoisted and ready to pummel the nearest threat—slowly dropped to his side. Then, with a voice as deep as the ocean's dark depths, Red asked, "What happened?"

"You took a mighty blow to the noggin," explained Hands, amiably offering the wineskin.

Red grabbed the wineskin and swallowed a few mouthfuls of water before looking about, as if trying to put together the scrambled puzzle pieces in his head. Finally, his eyes settled on Willy C. He traced the outline of the plane from front to back before stating, "It was that bird from the sky."

"Cap'n fired upon the bird from the lagoon and clipped one of its wings," explained Hands. "We were searching for Flint's treasure near the base of Spy-glass Hill and saw the bird land in the clearing."

"I remember now," replied Red, though his voice still seemed uncertain. "We snuck through the woods and came out into the clearing...." A look of bewilderment crossed Red's face. He brushed a hand through his damp hair and winced as his fingers grazed the bloody wound on his head. "And that's all I remember."

"I tell you, Red, the devil must have had eyes in the back of his head, because he saw us coming," said Hands. "He was hiding behind a tree like a lily-livered coward. When you stepped past him, he clobbered you on the head with a branch—broke it clean in two over that thick noggin of yours."

At the mention of being ambushed, a vein as wide as a shoelace suddenly emerged on the giant's forehead, twisting and curling above his brow before vanishing alongside his left eye. His voice deepened to a growl of frightening proportions. "Where's the coward now?"

"After he clobbered you, the lads surrounded him. The devil didn't seem to have much fight left in him when he was faced with the tip of my cutlass. I cracked him over the skull with the hilt of my blade, and the lads took him back to the *Hispaniola* for the Cap'n to decide his fate."

"I'll string him to the mainmast," snarled Red angrily, his voice seething with menace. "And tear the skin off his back with the lash."

"Or," offered Hands, "a walk on the plank with the sharks below might make for a good evening's entertainment. We know the devil can fly, but can he swim?"

While Sage listened in horror to the two men exchange vile ways to torture Uncle Dunkirk, a feeling of dread washed over him. He and his uncle were in dire straits. These weren't the type of men who listened to reason. They were bloodthirsty bullies. Uncle Dunkirk's only hope for survival would be a swift rescue.

Or the amber stone, thought Sage. With Uncle Dunkirk's magical amber stone, he could easily flash back to Willy C and get them off this perilous island. But Sage didn't want to count on the magical stone. Uncle Dunkirk was a prisoner, and there were too many what-if's floating about in his mind—*what if Uncle Dunkirk's possessions were seized? What if he has nowhere to run—like the monk stuck in the snow? What if they are trapped on this island for all eternity?*

With a determined nod, Sage realized that he just might be Uncle Dunkirk's only fighting chance for survival. He would simply have to follow these bullies, and hope that fate might provide him with an opportunity to free Uncle Dunkirk from their clutches. There was no other sure alternative.

As Sage shifted his weight, preparing to follow the two men, a twig snapped beneath him. Red and Hands immediately spun toward him, drawn by the sound, and peered suspiciously into the woods. With the lithe moves of experienced fighters, Hands silently unsheathed his cutlass, while Red crouched down to pick up the broken branch that had earlier knocked him cold. With a powerful turn of his mighty fists, he completed the break so that he clutched a separate club in each hand.

"What do you reckon?" asked Red quietly, his eyes carefully scanning the trees and the underbrush.

"Maybe the devil slipped his noose and is returning to his nest," replied Hands, his eyes also darting from tree to tree.

An evil smirk slithered over Red's face. "I hope you're right, Hands. I would like nothing more than to return the favor of a knock to his skull."

With his heart in his throat, Sage risked a

quick glance around the base of the tree. Red and Hands were twenty-five feet away and advancing slowly, carefully checking behind each tree and within each bush. Hands's sword was slashing at the underbrush, throwing volleys of leaves skyward. He flourished each unsettling slash with a deep plunge into the denser foliage.

Red, in the meantime, had silently waded through the brush across from Hands, and was advancing from tree to tree toward Sage. He, too, was carefully eliminating each tree and bush by prodding the underbrush with a meaty stab from his club. Sage knew that in seconds he would be completely trapped.

With only moments to spare, he searched desperately for an answer. If he ran, he had no doubt that Red and Hands would see him. The forest was thick with trees, but the two thugs were near enough to spot him. *Can I outrun them?* Sage glanced across the clearing, judging the distance to the far side, and thought that in a dead sprint he might be able to make it. Then he could lose them on the other side of the forest. Speed wasn't much of a concern for Sage. During the past school year, he had won the second place ribbon in the Spruce Ridge Elementary School Track Meet.

He knew that beating Red wouldn't be too much of a problem. The giant was too big for speed, and he had the additional handicap of a throbbing head wound—not an ideal running condition. Hands was another story, though. The man was wiry, and didn't seem to be carrying much extra baggage around the waist. How he would hold up in a race, Sage didn't know, but the man could probably give him a run for his money.

Time was wasting, and Red and Hands were edging closer and closer. One way or another, it was time to act, and sprinting across the clearing appeared to be Sage's only option. As he steeled himself for the starter's pistol, ready to sprint across the clearing, a rough hand slid over his mouth and clamped down tightly. Sage felt the chilling weight of a knife blade press against his throat, and then heard an unnerving whisper in his ear: "Move one muscle and I'll slit your throat."

CHAPTER 9

SAGE FROZE ON the spot. Not a blink, not a breath. He could feel the rough calluses of the stranger's palm brush like sandpaper against his lips. He tasted the bitter tang of dirt on his tongue. Yet nothing felt as disturbing as the icy steel blade pressed against his throat.

The callused hand slowly guided Sage's head to the side. With wide, fear-filled eyes, Sage dared to look at the man, fully expecting to see another muscle-bound ruffian. But, to his surprise, he found that his assailant was an old man.

The old man whispered, "Shhhhh," before removing the knife from Sage's throat. Then, putting a dirt-encrusted finger to his lips, the old man removed his hand from Sage's mouth.

By now, Red and Hands were only fifteen feet away, beating the bushes frantically and closing in fast. The old man glanced briefly in their direction, and then turned his attention to the ground below him. Quickly sifting through the dirt, he uncovered a small rock and held it up to show Sage. Then, with another quick glance toward Red and Hands, the stranger lobbed the stone in a high overhead arc toward the woods on the far side of Willy C.

Ker-chak!

Red and Hands both spun around at the sound of the rock ricocheting off a tree. "The devil!" cried Hands, his cutlass pointing the way. "He's over there!"

Red and Hands charged out of the woods like angry bulls, and roared past Willy C and across the clearing in a frantic assault. As soon as they had entered the far bush, the old man whispered in Sage's ear, "This way." Then, in a crouch, he dashed deeper into the woods.

At this point of his summer vacation, Sage was in a definite predicament. There was no doubt in his mind that he had to get as far away from Red and Hands as possible. But on the other hand, the old man had threatened to cut his throat—going so far as to place the blade of a knife against Sage's neck. However, in doing so, he'd also saved Sage from what would surely have been a most violent fate with Red and Hands. With a head jumbled full of more questions than answers, Sage quickly realized that his options were few. And if the amber stone had been seized, and Sage had to rescue Uncle Dunkirk, the old man might prove helpful. Looking back once more at Willy C, he crouched down and followed the old man deeper into the forest.

The going was tough, and Sage was constantly slowing to dodge trees, hop over fallen logs, and glance over his shoulder for his pursuers. It was a good five minutes before the old man finally slowed to a stop in the middle of a creek. With his bare feet soaking in the water, the stranger stood stock still and listened intently to the sounds of the forest. Sage followed his lead, trying to identify any noise that seemed out of place. Finally, when the old man seemed satisfied that they were safe, he crouched down and cupped a mouthful of water into his lips before finally glancing up at Sage.

Sage suddenly realized that the old man wasn't so aged after all. He now saw that the stranger was probably closer in age to Sage's father, maybe thirty-five or forty. What had fooled Sage was the man's appearance. He was wearing a suit of rags—a shirt as frayed as it was filthy and a pair of pants so tattered that they would have been discarded from a homeless shelter. His feet were bare and equally grimy, but his soles must have been as tough as shoe leather to survive the dash through the woods without as much as a whimper. The most startling part of him, though, was his hair. His hair was as white as a snowy mountain pass, and it hung halfway down his back. On his face, he sported a matching beard that draped a good foot from his chin.

"I guess I should thank you," Sage panted. His

chest was heaving from their headlong run, but he was desperate to break the ice with his savior. He also wanted to know all he could about this strange island, and the men who had abducted his uncle. "Thank you for saving me from those men."

"You should stay clear of those men," the man replied brusquely between drafts. Water streamed messily through his beard and down his shirt, but he didn't seem to mind.

"Yeah, I figured that out," Sage agreed. "I didn't mean to bump into them. I was collecting wood in the forest—"

"Yes, I know," the man interrupted. "I saw the whole thing."

"You saw the whole thing?" Sage asked, with a shimmer of hope in his voice. "Then you know what happened to my uncle?"

The man stepped out of the creek and walked toward Sage, trailing a stream of water behind him. "You are with the one that fell from the sky?"

Fell from the sky? "Yes," Sage replied cautiously. Choosing his words carefully, he explained, "My uncle and I were shot at while we were flying over the island. We had to land or we would have crashed."

"Are you a sorcerer?" asked the man with distrust.

"A sorcerer?" Sage sputtered. "No, I just graduated from elementary school."

"Then how is it that you can fly?" the man asked, his pale blue eyes boring into Sage. Sage could tell that he still had some answering to do.

"Why in a plane, of course," Sage answered, dumb-struck. Then, with a surge of pride, he added, "A Spitfire, as a matter of fact."

The old man suddenly sprang back, horrified, his arms shielding his face for protection. Sage spun around, his tiny fists raised to fight, expecting to find Red or Hands charging at him with cutlasses brandished. But there was nothing.

Sage was confused, and turned back to the cowering man. "What is it? Why'd you do that?"

"You can spit fire!" the man cried, frightened. He pointed a finger at Sage. "You *are* a sorcerer!"

Sage suddenly understood. He tried to calm the man down. "No no no," he soothed. "You don't understand. A Spitfire is a type of airplane. It's a fighter from the Second World War."

The man slowly dropped his hands. "Second World War?" he asked. "You mean between Spain and England?"

Once again, Sage was at a loss. *This guy definitely flunked history.* "No, the Second World War between America, England, and Germany. Oh, and Japan too." Then, after a moment, Mrs. Minckler's history lessons came back to him. "And Canada," added Sage. "And Russia. And Italy. And France. Well, and a lot more countries. It was a *World* War, after all."

A look of sheer bewilderment crossed the man's face, and Sage realized that the stranger had probably been on this island for a long, long time. He was *really* out of touch with the world around him—kind of like Robinson Crusoe.

"Maybe we should start from the beginning," Sage offered. "My name is Sage. Pleased to meet you." He held out his hand, and, after a moment, the man took it in a handshake.

"My name is Ben," he replied timidly. Then, slightly more comfortable with the formality, he added, "I, too, am pleased to make your acquaintance."

"Good." Sage smiled. "We're making progress. I'm from the U.S."

Once again, a puzzled look slipped over the man's face.

"You know," Sage embellished, "The United States of America."

"*Ahhhh,*" replied Ben, nodding. "You are from the colonies. I knew there was something different about your accent." He gestured at Sage. "And your clothing."

"Well, I guess we once were the colonies," Sage replied, slightly perplexed. "Now, I live in a town called Spruce Ridge. Where are you from, Ben?"

"I am from Cardiff," answered Ben, becoming more and more comfortable with the conversation.

"But I've been on this island for three years now. In fact, you are only the second person I've spoken to in three years."

"Really?" Sage exclaimed. "I thought you might have known those other two men somehow."

"Oh, I know *of* them," replied Ben bitterly. "But they're no mates of mine. They're scurvy cutthroats, one and all."

Scurvy cutthroats. That sounds about right. "Were you shipwrecked?" Sage asked.

"No, I was marooned. Left alone on these shores three long years ago—and all because of greed. You see, years ago, I sailed with Captain Flint. You might have heard of him in the colonies."

"No," Sage replied. "I've never heard of him."

"You've *never* heard of Flint the pirate?" remarked Ben, surprised. "That's odd. I'd thought everyone had heard of Captain Flint. Oh, he was an evil man with a heart black as coal. Just mention the name Flint at any tavern or inn from Cardiff to Madagascar, and the room would go silent as a church. He had that kind of effect on people, Flint did. And I saw it personally, with mine own eyes. Grown men would drop to their knees in terror, whimpering like children, when they came under his blade."

Sage listened, enraptured, as Ben told his tale. "Years ago, I was young and strong, and an able seaman. Flint's legend was known far and wide, and although he was feared by the upper classes, he was a hero of sorts to the poor. You see, Flint came from poor roots. He was born on the streets of London and managed to make something of his life—though it came with a heavy price.

"One day, my skills as a sailor came to the attention of Flint's First Mate, Hannibal Blight, and before I knew it, I was offered a berth on Flint's ship, the *Walrus*. Like any dim lad out of Cardiff with dreams of escaping his lot in life, I jumped at the chance. I saw an opportunity to escape the poverty and hard work on the docks of Cardiff. And you have to admit, it seemed a glamorous way of life, sailing with the infamous Captain Flint across the seven seas.

"My glamorous vision of a pirate's life quickly changed, though. A few days out of Cardiff, we came across an English schooner riding low in the water. She was heavily laden with goods, sailing in English waters, and only a day away from port, but that didn't stop Flint. As a new conscript, I was given the duty of watching for English Man O' Wars from the topmast. As I scanned the horizon, I also had a bird's-eye view of Flint's crew storming the rails of the schooner. What had seemed like a lark quickly turned terrifying. Flint's crew slaughtered the schooner's sailors. Anyone without a blade to defend himself was forced into the sea to drown or feed the sharks. I watched, horrified, as man after man fell under Flint's blade that day, and I realized that a human life wasn't worth a single doubloon to that madman. After the crew had finished plundering the ship, they scuttled it and sent its remains to Davy Jones's locker.

"And that was only the first of many such attacks. Flint was a bloodthirsty pirate. The glimmer of a gold coin was enough to drain any compassion from his black heart. And I watched, time and time again, as Flint and his men plundered and murdered innocent men, women, and children. It was quite an eye-opener for a poor lad from Cardiff—and not at all what I had expected.

"A few months later, once the *Walrus*'s hold was bursting with plunder, Flint anchored us in the lagoon of a deserted island. He chose six strong seamen and rowed ashore with his treasure piled high in the skiff. Then, once the treasure had been buried, Flint murdered all six men...his *own* men...in cold blood to keep his secret safe.

"Tired of his murderous ways, I left Captain Flint and the *Walrus* far behind when we sailed into the next port. I simply vanished amongst all the sailors in port and kept well hidden in the hills above town until the *Walrus* had sailed on the tide a week later. Later that year, I heard word that the *Walrus* had been sunk off the Cape of Africa by a British Man O' War, and that Flint had gone down with the ship. With Flint and his crew gone, I realized that I was probably the only survivor who knew where Flint had stashed his gold. And it was now mine for the taking.

"I convinced the owner of a ship to bring me here for half of Flint's treasure. For twelve days we scoured the island, but Flint had shrewdly hidden his loot. The men became discouraged, and some even started to spread shipboard rumors that I had seawater on the brain. After a while, they simply decided to go. Out of spite for their lost wages and time, they left me here alone to search for Flint's treasure. And here is where I have been these three long years."

"Wow," Sage replied in a daze, not knowing what else to say. Ben's tale had shaken him to the core—Captain Flint, pirates, English Man O' Wars, hidden treasure—but the pieces were all starting to fall into place. *No wonder Ben thought I was a sorcerer and dressed funny*. As Sage struggled to make sense of the big picture, a simple question came to mind. "By the way, Ben, do you know exactly where we are? You know, the name of the island?"

"Of course," replied Ben. "This is Treasure Island."

CHAPTER 10

UNCLE DUNKIRK CAME to as the salty ocean water closed in over his head. He sputtered and panicked, and as he struggled to make sense of the situation, a hand grabbed him roughly by the hair and yanked his head out of the water.

"That's it, Gov," a Cockney accented voice chided in his ear. "Wakey, wakey!"

Salt water streamed off Uncle Dunkirk's face, leaving the tips of his proud, black mustache drooping like limp spaghetti. He wiped his face and blinked salt water off his eyelashes. Then, shaking his head from side to side, he tried to clear the cobwebs from his head. When the fog started to dissipate, two thoughts immediately came to mind—his head hurt *immensely*, and there was something in the water.

"You might want to get your arm out of the water, Gov," suggested a voice that seemed to drift from the ether around Uncle Dunkirk's mind.

As he slowly lifted his throbbing head, Uncle Dunkirk struggled to figure out what was happening. He found himself lying on his stomach at the front of a large longboat, his left arm dragging in the warm water. Four men sat behind him, oars clenched firmly in hand, and pulled with all their might against the tide, while another sat guard beside him. Uncle Dunkirk studied the rowers and noticed that each man looked as if he were on loan from a police lineup. They were hardened men, muscle-bound, with peculiar tattoos crisscrossing their backs. With the next forward thrust of the oars, Uncle Dunkirk realized that the odd tattoos *weren't* tattoos at all. They were whip marks. Some were fresh, some old, but each was a heinous sign of a brush with cruelty.

The sailor with the Cockney accent was sitting next to Uncle Dunkirk and offered a crooked smile. The stubs of three decaying teeth jutted out from between his cracked lips. "The water, Gov," he repeated, this time a little more forcefully. "Get your arm out."

When the Cockney's words finally slipped through the fog, Uncle Dunkirk turned his wobbly head away from the longboat and looked below. No fewer than ten feet away, a large fin knifed through the water, leaving a bubbling wake. And below that fin, under the waterline, a shark was bearing down on Uncle Dunkirk's dangling arm, its mouth gaping in anticipation.

Suddenly alert, Uncle Dunkirk yanked his arm from the water just as the shark's head broke the surface and bumped roughly down the side of the longboat. The mouth on the beast was enormous, like a massive bear trap, with glistening rows of razor-sharp teeth on full display. As the shark brushed past, Uncle Dunkirk heard the unsettling *snap* of its powerful jaws.

"Twelve footer," commented the Cockney. "With teeth as sharp as me blade."

A feeling of nausea bubbled up inside Uncle Dunkirk, and he found himself suddenly coughing and gagging. Using what little strength he had left, he managed to prop himself up and plunk himself down on the front bench, clear of the shark-infested waters.

Sage! The thought exploded in Uncle Dunkirk's mind and, in a moment of clarity, he realized exactly what had happened. He had landed Willy C in the clearing and sent Sage out into the woods to gather camouflage. Once he had parked the plane between two trees, he had begun laying palm fronds and branches against Willy C to hide it from sight. When he'd slipped into the woods behind Willy C to secure a second bundle of fronds, he had spotted a welcoming committee creeping through the woods up to the plane. However, judging by the weapons clenched menacingly in the men's hands, this committee wasn't welcoming him to the island.

Uncle Dunkirk had looked for an escape route, but discovered that he was trapped. The strangers had already fanned out in the trees, and they were obviously planning on surrounding Willy C before making themselves known. That was when Uncle Dunkirk had decided on a different tack. With Sage expected back at any second, Uncle Dunkirk decided to buy as much time as possible for his nephew. He slipped behind a large palm tree and waited for the first marauder to cross his path.

After jumping out behind a giant of a man and swinging with the might of Babe Ruth, the last thing Uncle Dunkirk remembered seeing was the tip of a cutlass pointed at his face. Then all went black.

For a split second, Uncle Dunkirk considered swimming for shore. He had to get back to Sage. But the incident with the shark quickly dashed those thoughts. It was one thing to encounter a shark when properly outfitted for a dive, which Uncle Dunkirk had done on numerous occasions. It was another to make a frantic dash across a lagoon, splashing wildly like an injured seal. That was suicidal.

Realizing that he was trapped for the time being, Uncle Dunkirk dropped his head into his hands and groaned. A throbbing pain pulsed inside his skull, and a quick self-examination with his fingers uncovered a lump on the back of his head the size of a silver dollar. Other than that, he seemed as fit as he usually was. Just a little foggy.

It was then that he spotted the most magnificent tall ship that he'd seen in his lifetime. The vessel was a breathtaking sight, lying at anchor in the turquoise waters of the lagoon. She had two tall masts, which soared majestically above the deck, draped with swags of pristine white sails. A tall quarterdeck commanded the rear of the ship, while a slightly shorter forecastle deck guarded the front. The main deck was long, and populated by a large number of seamen, who were hanging over the rails and shouting encouragement— whether they shouted to the rowers or the shark, Uncle Dunkirk didn't know.

After a moment, Uncle Dunkirk managed to tear his eyes away from the view to focus on his new reality. He examined the scenery around him, and noted that he was in the middle of a lagoon, obviously somewhere tropical. He was a prisoner, but, now that his mind was clearing, Uncle Dunkirk realized that escape was just six words away. After all, he still had the amber stone.

Inconspicuously glancing down the length of the longboat, Uncle Dunkirk performed a few quick calculations in his head. The boat was maybe fifteen feet long, but the short distance should be ample to flash him back to the shore, at least. Once there, he could extend his running space by racing down the beach, and then he could flash back to Willy C, and, he hoped, Sage. Then the two of them could take off before the marauders returned, and flash to somewhere safer—like Disneyland.

Careful not to attract attention, Uncle Dunkirk turned his back to the marauders, acting as if he were simply taking in the scenery. Then, when he was sure no one was watching, he slipped his hand into his shirt. The only thing he found was the stringy patch of hair on his chest. Uncle Dunkirk slid his fingers to his neck, frantically feeling for the leather band. His heart skipped a beat. The necklace was missing—and with it the amber stone.

Uncle Dunkirk spun in his seat and peered anxiously at the seamen, who were busy rowing. They had all taken their shirts off for the row back to the tall ship, but no one wore the leather band around his neck. A feeling of dread engulfed Uncle Dunkirk—Sage was on his own in a strange land, and the amber stone was missing. *What do I do?*

Then, suddenly, Uncle Dunkirk's desperation was thinned by a bright, new emotion—determination. With a dogged look in his eye, Uncle Dunkirk knew that he had to escape his captors, locate Sage, and then find the whereabouts of the amber stone. All told, there was no other option. If he failed, they would be trapped here forever, wherever this may be. Or worse, they would be killed. Not exactly the summer vacation he had hoped to give Sage.

"Ahoy, mateys!"

Uncle Dunkirk glanced up to see that the

longboat had now closed within yards of the tall ship. A number of coarse- looking sailors hung over the rail, calling down uncouth greetings and mocking the prisoner. As the longboat slipped up against the ship, the rowers stowed their oars, and then secured the boat against a web of netting that hung off the ship's side.

Jumping to his feet, the Cockney sailor unsheathed his sword and gave Uncle Dunkirk a rude prompt with the tip. "Climb on up, Gov. The captain's expecting you."

Uncle Dunkirk took hold of the rope netting and managed to pull himself out of the boat. He climbed up the side of the ship, rung by rung, and as he neared the top, a collection of hands grasped him by the shirt and hauled him over the rail, dropping him carelessly to the deck. Wincing, Uncle Dunkirk rolled over onto his back, and then sat up, glaring at the callous crew of sailors before him.

They were a hardened bunch of men, and each shared the same appearance as the oarsmen— criminal. More than two dozen men circled Uncle Dunkirk, and each had stopped his shipboard duties to watch the spectacle unfold on deck. Oddly enough, no one spoke or took action.

After an uncomfortable minute, a murmur rippled through the crew, and the circle parted to allow one man through. He was an imposing figure, and Uncle Dunkirk noticed most of the sailors drop their eyes and slink to the side to give the man ample room to pass.

The man wore a tri-point hat that shielded his long, ebony hair from the hot sun. He was dressed in a suit of obvious finery, with gold stitching and glittering brass buttons. His eyes were black like coal and held no warmth. His nose was long and pointed, and flanked by sunken cheeks. And a cruel, thin-lipped smirk was painted on his face. Uncle Dunkirk felt a chill settle upon him with the man's first glance.

As the man took another step, Uncle Dunkirk heard a slight *knock* on deck, and he noticed for the first time that the man was missing most of his right leg. It had been cut off above the knee, and his right pant leg was tucked up and tied with a small band of string beneath the stump. A hand-hewn wooden peg stretched down to the ground from the stump, and a Y-shaped crutch was propped under his right arm to help support his weight.

Tramping forward, the man stopped at Uncle Dunkirk's feet and gazed down at him grimly. Uncle Dunkirk met his eyes and felt another shiver roll down his spine—it was as if he had looked the devil in the face.

Finally, the man spoke, and his voice cut like shards of broken glass, "Welcome to the *Hispaniola*. I am the Captain of the ship, John Silver. We have much to discuss."

CHAPTER 11

"TREASURE ISLAND!" SAGE exclaimed, his mind reeling in shock. "This can't be Treasure Island!"

Ben stood before him with a look of complete confusion. "Of course this is Treasure Island. I sailed the coordinates myself! And those were the exact same coordinates that Captain Flint sailed years ago too."

"No, you don't understand," Sage countered, trying to make sense out of the situation. "Treasure Island isn't a real place. It's fiction. A story."

"Of course it's a real place," retorted Ben angrily. "We're here, aren't we?" He scooped a handful of rocks from the creek bed. "And these rocks are real, aren't they? And this dirt? And the water in this creek?"

"No, Ben, you're the one who doesn't understand," Sage struggled to explain. "*Treasure Island* is a book written by Robert Louis Stevenson. It's make-believe."

"Well, I don't know much about reading, or about the books of Mr. Stevenson, but I do know that Treasure Island is a real place. Just as I am a real person. I don't know what they teach you in the colonies, Sage, but books hurt brains. Don't you know that?"

"I'm serious, Ben," Sage sputtered on, digging himself a little deeper, but helpless to stop. "I don't remember much about the book, but I saw the movie on TV a while back. There was this pirate who pulled the wool over everyone's eyes while trying to steal a hidden treasure. He was a mean one. Oh, and there was even a guy like you, Ben. A man who had been deserted on the island. What was his name? Gunn! That's it, Ben Gunn!"

Sage stopped cold. The name had passed over his lips before it had even registered in his head. *Ben Gunn. A marooned sailor. Pirates.*

Ben stood before Sage, his mouth open wide and his eyes as round as wagon wheels. Then he raised his arm shakily, a finger pointed directly at Sage, his voice quivering, "You *are* a sorcerer!"

Ben turned, and in an instant was gone. He sprang effortlessly over the creek, and broke through the underbrush on the far side. Three years of solitary confinement on Treasure Island seemed to have left Ben full of fear and uncertainty.

Sage took chase, running for all he was worth and trying to keep up with the frantic marooned sailor. As he ran, he tried to placate the man, calling, "Ben! Stop! You have to believe me! Stop, Ben!"

It was no use, though. Ben was in full flight,

running at an all-out sprint, and this was unfamiliar terrain to Sage. Sooner or later, Sage would lose sight of Ben in the endless maze of trees and bush, and then any hope of rescuing Uncle Dunkirk would be shattered. He would be lost and alone on this perilous island.

He searched his head for something, anything, to calm Ben down. Some little nugget of knowledge that would prove to Ben that he wasn't a sorcerer, and that he hadn't fallen from the sky out of nowhere. And then it came to him in a burst of lucidity—how the whole situation had happened. Sage knew without a doubt how he and Uncle Duncle had ended up on Treasure Island.

It was a few seconds before impact, and Willy C was screaming out of the sky. Sage's mind was racing as the ground rushed up at them. Uncle Dunkirk was calling out, "Now, Sage, now!" And Sage did something natural to him—he clutched his lucky compass, and chanted "With wings of wind, I fly." His lucky compass. His lucky *Jim Hawkins* compass that had probably been excavated from the bottom of a cereal box when the *Treasure Island* movie first played in theaters.

"There was also a boy," Sage called out to Ben's back, which was already disappearing into the distance. "Jim Hawkins was his name!"

With that, Ben stopped cold.

CHAPTER 12

IN ALL HIS years of flashing from place to place and from time to time, Uncle Dunkirk had seen many wondrous and even historic sights, but never had he come face-to-face with a literary creation. And Long John Silver was a vicious and dangerous one.

Hiding his astonishment, Uncle Dunkirk looked up into Silver's black eyes and agreed, "Yes, we do, Captain. We have much to talk about."

With a slight nod of Silver's head, two men broke from the pack and grabbed Uncle Dunkirk beneath the arms. They hoisted him up, and then twisted one of his arms behind his back.

"Mr. McGregor," called Silver, and one of the oarsmen from the longboat pushed his way through the crowd. Uncle Dunkirk recognized him as the three-toothed man with the Cockney accent.

"Aye, Captain," McGregor called out officiously as he strode up to Silver.

"What seems to have become of Red and Mr. Hands?" inquired Silver in an icy voice.

"We had a wee spot of trouble with the

prisoner, Captain," stammered McGregor. "He clobbered Red over the head with a club. Knocked him clean out, he did."

"And Mr. Hands?" demanded Silver. The news of their predicament obviously did not sit well with him.

"Hands stayed behind to fetch a dram of water to wake Red from the dead," sputtered McGregor. "I reckon they should be along mighty quick."

"And what about your task on shore?" continued Silver, his voice chilling by a few more degrees.

"Begging your pardon, Captain, but Spy-glass Hill looked as bare as Lippert's head," replied McGregor, tossing a light-hearted barb at the *Hispaniola's* bald cook.

Any hope that McGregor had about lightening the captain's foul mood quickly vanished. Silver simply turned his back on the oarsman to gaze across the lagoon. "Send the longboat back to shore with a party of two. Wait an hour for Red and Mr. Hands to return. That should be plenty of time to recover from a simple knock to the head. If they're not back by then, return to the *Hispaniola*, and tie down for the night."

"Yes, sir, Captain," McGregor replied smartly, turning quickly.

"Oh, and McGregor," added Silver. "Keep the

men on the beach. I don't want anyone leaving your sight, or the sight of the *Hispaniola*. You are responsible, McGregor, and the lash will fall to your back if you fail."

Once McGregor had departed, Silver strode up to Uncle Dunkirk and stopped inches before him. Then, leaning so close that a pungent stream of Silver's foul breath curled the hair in Uncle Dunkirk's nostrils, he snarled, "You had better pray that my man returns with his wits, or mark my words, you will find not only your arm but your whole body dragged behind my ship for the sharks."

With that, Captain Long John Silver spun on his heel and stormed off to his cabin.

CHAPTER 13

"**WHAT DO YOU** know of young Jim Hawkins?" called Ben Gunn from fifty yards ahead of Sage.

Sage slowed to a stop, grateful that Ben had finally stopped running. Panting heavily, he managed to call back between breaths, "I know all about Jim Hawkins, Ben. I know that he came to the island with the pirate Long John Silver. He was tricked, along with everyone else on board the ship, into believing Silver was a good man. But I know the truth about Silver. I know that he is a deceitful man—and a murderer."

Ben shifted his balance from one foot to the other, and Sage knew that one wrong word, one small misstep on his end, would send Ben charging through the forest again. And then all would surely be lost.

"Look, Ben," Sage implored, "the pirates took my uncle. You know as well as I do that he's in trouble. Deep trouble. And if Silver is as cruel as I remember, I don't have much time." A wave of emotion was welling up inside Sage, threatening to overtake him, but he pressed on. "My uncle brought me here, Ben, and he's my only chance of getting home. Without him, I'll be no better than you—marooned on Treasure Island."

Ben shuffled a bit more, weighing his options, as Sage patiently stood by. Sage wished he could tell Ben about Uncle Dunkirk's magical amber stone, and how easy it would be to flash him back to Cardiff, but there was only so much that Ben would believe. For the time being, Sage thought it best to simply keep the secret, and hope that Uncle Dunkirk would soon be flashing them back to safety.

"Please, Ben," Sage pleaded, his voice cracking with emotion. "I need you."

With those three simple words—*I need you*—Ben gave in. With an inviting wave of his hand, he said, "Come on, then. The sun will be down soon."

A bright smile lit up Sage's face, and he walked the remaining fifty yards to catch up to Ben. "Thank you, Ben. You have no idea how much this means to me."

"Oh, yes I do," replied Ben. "I wouldn't want anyone to suffer as I have over the years. Especially one as young as yourself."

"So, where do we go from here?" Sage asked, looking around. They were engulfed by the forest, and his sense of direction had been skewed during their mad dash through the woods.

"We go to my home," announced Ben. "We

need food and water. Then we'll decide on the best course of action to rescue your uncle."

With that, Ben and Sage set off together. Now that they shared an equal purpose, a sense of camaraderie had come over them. The trek to Ben's home was fairly hard, so talk was sparse, but they trudged on in comfortable silence—Ben leading, and Sage following.

After Sage and Ben hiked for a while, the trees around them began to thin out. Golden shafts of sunlight streamed through the thick canopy. Raising his head to feel the sun, Sage saw a large ridge looming above them through the treetops.

"That's Mizzen-mast Hill," said Ben. "It's the southern-most hill on the island, closest to the lagoon. It's followed by Spy-glass Hill and Fore-mast Hill, farther to the north."

"Yes, we saw them from the air," Sage replied, offering up his limited knowledge of the island's terrain. "We also saw a small fort. Is that where we're heading?"

"No, unfortunately not," replied Ben forlornly. "That was my home. I built it with my bare hands the first year I was marooned on the island. But when the *Hispaniola* anchored in the lagoon, I knew that I was either saved or in a heap of trouble. Until I knew exactly who I was dealing with, I moved into a cave on the west side of Mizzen-mast Hill that I stumbled onto a few years ago while exploring the high ground. I've been watching them ever since. From my vantage point, I can see every move they make on their ship."

"And they don't know that you're here?"

"As far as I can tell, no," answered Ben. "But you're right about one thing. Silver is a cruel man—and not one to be trusted. He treats his sailors like mangy dogs, working them to the bone and lording over them through fear. Why, in just the past few days, I've seen him put the lash to three of his men for nothing more than—"

Ben stopped in mid sentence, suddenly aware of the impression his words could have on Sage, and he mumbled a heartfelt apology. "I'm sorry, Sage. I didn't think."

"That's all right, Ben," Sage replied forlornly. "We'll get Uncle Dunkirk back."

Trudging on, Ben led the way out of the thinning forest and along the rocky base of Mizzen-mast Hill. The ridge towered majestically over them, covered in a lush, though brambly, scrub. Ben side-stepped the boulders that littered the ground surrounding the base of the hill, before veering up a well-hidden wildlife trail that was invisible to the untrained eye.

They crisscrossed the face of Mizzen-mast Hill to ease the climb. Soon enough, they were high above the treetops, and Sage could see the vast ocean stretching off to the horizon. After another hundred feet, the lagoon came into full view below them.

Ben paused for a moment and pointed toward its shores. A large two-masted schooner lay anchored in the lagoon, and from it, a small longboat rowed toward shore. Sage squinted his eyes to try and distinguish the men in the longboat, but the distance was too far.

"It looks like a landing party," said Ben, his hand shielding the sun from his face. "Three men. Probably just coming ashore to pick up the two they left behind." Then, turning inland, Ben pointed toward a bare patch of land in the middle of the island. "And that's where we came from—the clearing between Mizzen-mast and Spy-glass Hill."

For the second time that day, Sage peered across the island toward the clearing. He could plainly see the ring of trees that circled the clearing, and the mass of wide-open space that had served as the plane's makeshift runway. But Willy C, which was only partially camouflaged between two trees, was not visible from this angle.

After a moment's rest, Ben turned and continued climbing Mizzen-mast Hill. Sage took one last look at the tall ship before following. He could see a mob of indistinguishable figures gathered together on the deck, and wondered if Uncle Dunkirk was one of them. One man seemed to stand alone, separate from the pack. He had caught Sage's eye for the simple reason that he was the only man on deck who didn't seem to be moving. While others jostled about busily, he seemed to be pointing and gesturing, maybe even issuing orders. A sliver of ice crept down Sage's spine as he realized, with an unnerving shudder, that he was probably looking at Long John Silver. "Don't worry, Uncle Duncle," Sage muttered quietly to himself. "I'm coming for you."

Moments later, Ben scrambled over a slight embankment, and turned to wait for Sage. Once the boy had joined him, Ben pointed to the far edge of the embankment, and said, "Be careful. That edge is a shortcut to the bottom, but with a deadly first step."

Sage cautiously crept up to the edge, and peered over the embankment. Sure enough, the face of Mizzen-mast Hill dropped a sickening five hundred feet down, but the drop wasn't sheer. A person could, perhaps, descend with the benefit of climbing gear, but after climbing down, a bare-handed ascent would have been next to impossible.

Sage stepped back from the edge and joined Ben, ready for their next stage of climbing. But Ben only turned and walked directly into a curtain of vines draped over a rock wall. To Sage's amazement, the vines parted, and Ben disappeared through to the other side.

Following Ben's lead, Sage carefully inched

his way through the dangling foliage, feeling its cold, creepy stems brush against his body, until he slipped through to the other side and into the mouth of a tunnel. Darkness swept over him, and his eyes struggled to find light. As he stood perfectly still, deathly afraid to step into a chasm or walk into a wall, Sage heard the clacking of two rocks coming together, and dazzling blue and orange sparks sputtered like mini fireworks in the back of the cave. A moment later, a small flicker of light appeared in Ben's hand and illuminated the mischievous smile on his face.

"Welcome home," said Ben, as he touched the burning wad of coconut husk to a homemade candle. The light expanded throughout the cave, bouncing off wall after wall, and nearly blinding Sage with its glare. It was then that Sage noticed why the walls of the cave glittered as brilliantly as they did—Ben's cave was full of treasure.

CHAPTER 14

"I GIVE UP, already," moaned Israel Hands. He and Red had been searching the bushes for the last ten minutes, and they had seen absolutely nothing. Not a single hide or hair of the demon that fell from the sky. "The devil's probably back at the ship under lock and key."

Red wandered back through the forest until he was standing next to Hands. His arms hung resigned against his sides, the two halves of the branch still clutched within his beefy hands. He was tired, and his head was throbbing with a dull, pulsing pain that rose and fell, rose and fell. "I hope you're right. I've a score to settle with him before the night is out."

"Easy, Red," cautioned Hands. "Did the devil knock the sense out of you? This devil that fell from the sky is our ticket to fame and fortune! Just think about it, Red—a flying machine! You saw how fast it swooped through the sky. Like a bird, it was. Why it was sheer luck that Cap'n clipped its wing with a cannon. With that contraption, we could rule the high seas. We could spot ships miles off and lead the *Hispaniola* to riches we've only dreamed about. We need the devil alive. We need him to teach us how the flying machine works. And then, Red, *we* take control. *We* captain the *Hispaniola*. And *we* get rich."

Red pondered Hands's suggestion warily. Just a rumor of mutiny was enough to send Silver into a murderous rage, and Red knew that Hands would be nothing more than an appetizer for the sharks if Red saw fit to inform the captain about this conversation. But knowing the way Silver's twisted mind worked, Red could also picture himself following Hands off the plank—simply for having being present when mutiny was discussed. After all, why should the captain trust him?

But Israel Hands was the *Hispaniola*'s coxswain. He had been sailing the high seas for most of his life and was considered by the crew to be wise in the matters of ship politics—especially when it came to handling the enraged tirades of the captain. Hands was also considered to be fair with the crew, and there was no doubt in anyone's mind that Hands knew the workings of the ship as well as the captain, if not better. As such, his offer was not taken lightly.

"And what if we can get the prisoner to explain his flying machine? What then?" asked Red, hoping for a token gesture that would cement their partnership.

"Why, you'll get your revenge then, Red,"

replied Hands generously. "You can do anything you like with the devil once we know how to fly."

Red nodded in agreement, then he reached out his hand and grasped Hands's sword. Drawing it forward, Red slid his palm over the blade until a smear of scarlet blood appeared. "A pirate's agreement it is," said Red, holding out his bloody hand.

Hands grinned and followed Red's lead. Drawing a bead of blood on his own palm, he clasped the giant's hand and shook heartily. "Partners until the end."

The two men strode out of the forest, and back into the clearing. Willy C remained parked in its hiding place.

"What should we do with the flying machine until then?" asked Red.

"We'd best leave it be," replied Hands. The sun was high over their heads, but it was dropping fast. "I don't want to be stuck in this godforsaken jungle after sunset."

The two men circled Willy C, again admiring its sleek lines. They had watched from the base of Spy-glass Hill as the plane had soared through the air with the agility of a hawk. Soon it would be theirs, and they would soar through the skies as captains of both air and sea.

Leaving Red to admire the four-bladed propeller, Hands continued around the right wing. He wanted desperately to climb onto the flying machine, but he still felt a superstitious dread about getting too close. After all, this was a toy of the devil, and who knew what evil spell or sorcery was contained within its enticing walls.

As he looped around the plane, studying its streamlined dimensions, Hands's foot came down on a particularly unyielding lump. Glancing down, Hands spied a stone of some sort sparkling in the dirt, with a band of leather swirled about it. Curious, he reached down and grasped the object.

The amber stone shone brilliantly in Hands's palm, even with the fine coating of red dust soiling its surface. Hands wiped the stone clean with his thumb, and then admired the peculiar gem. It was fairly large for a gemstone—much too large for a ring, but perfect as a bauble to hang around a woman's neck. Running his fingers along the smooth edge, Hands noted that the lines of the stone were very well cut, and must have passed through the hands of a master craftsman at one point or another. But the most spectacular feature of the stone appeared *inside* the gem. As he turned it to best catch the receding sunlight, Hands noticed that a fire of sorts, only brighter, and without any flickering movement, seemed to be encased within the stone—the gem was a treasure. And, best of all, it was all his. No one would need to know about his find—not Red, and especially not Captain Silver.

This is turning out to be a very good day, thought Hands. Then, with a satisfied grin, he pocketed the amber stone and called out, "Come on, Red. We'd best get back to the ship."

CHAPTER 15

"**DOWN YOU GO**, matey," came the brusque order, and the sharp end of a cutlass pressed the point home with a persuasive jab to the small of Uncle Dunkirk's back. Followed by two guards, Uncle Dunkirk ducked through the low doorway, and then treaded down the six wooden stairs that led into the interior of the forecastle.

The corridor inside the forecastle was gloomy, and Uncle Dunkirk squinted his eyes, straining to peer through the darkness. Four doors lined each side of the passage, providing ample quarters for the crew. Two oil lanterns swung lazily from nails imbedded in the ceiling beams, waiting to be lit when the sun set.

"Move along," prodded the uncouth pirate, with another nudge from his blade. Uncle Dunkirk shuffled deeper into the gloom, passing closed doors on either side, until he came to the end of the hall.

"Hold up," ordered the gruff voice behind him, and Uncle Dunkirk was relieved that the guard's cutlass wasn't used as an exclamation point this time. As Uncle Dunkirk waited, the second guard stepped around him and up to the last door in the hall. A humungous metal lock hung from a metal clasp attached to the doorframe. The guard unlocked the catch, and then stepped aside quickly, after swinging the door open.

"Get in there," barked the guard with the cutlass. This time his obligatory jab returned, digging painfully into Uncle Dunkirk's back. *I guess he owed me one*, thought Uncle Dunkirk as he stepped into the dark room. The door slammed promptly behind him, and the metallic *clank* of the lock immediately followed, sealing Uncle Dunkirk's fate.

"Good day, sir," came a clipped English accent from somewhere deep within the gloom. Uncle Dunkirk jumped at this unexpected greeting, but then, as his eyes began to adjust to the murkiness, he saw the outline of a man sitting across the room. And the man wasn't alone. There were others in the room. Four others, at best count.

"Hello," replied Uncle Dunkirk warily. "Who's there?"

One of the shadows rose from behind a table and slowly walked over. As he neared, the darkness fell off him like a discarded cloak, and Uncle Dunkirk was able to make out the finery of his uniform—that of an eighteenth century British sailor, complete with shiny brass buttons, gold epaulets on the shoulders, and the requisite white, powdered wig.

"I am Captain Smollett," the man said, holding his hand out, "the *true* captain of the *Hispaniola*."

Uncle Dunkirk shook the offered hand and replied, "Dunkirk Smiley, at your service."

"I take it that you are a prisoner of John Silver?" asked another voice from across the room. This voice, also English, sounded less authoritative.

"Yes," replied Uncle Dunkirk. "I am a prisoner. And you?"

"We are all prisoners of Silver," answered the same man. He had now risen from his seat, and walked toward Uncle Dunkirk and Captain Smollett. The man wore a trim suit of dark blue, a white, ruffled shirt, and matching white knee-high socks. His brown, shoulder-length hair was pulled back neatly in a ponytail, and he had a kindly face, with warm hazel eyes and a smile. "Allow me to introduce our menagerie to you," the stranger offered. "I am Doctor Livesey, a simple passenger on this ill-fated voyage. You've already met Captain Smollett, who is indeed the *true* captain of the *Hispaniola*." Dr. Livesey then gestured to two other wraiths who appeared out of the gloom. "This is Squire Trelawney, a businessman with goods on board, and the young lad is Jim Hawkins, who is traveling in my company."

Uncle Dunkirk shook all the offered hands,

and then followed the men deeper into the quarters. His eyes grew quite accustomed to the gloom, and thin strands of light shone through slight cracks between the ceiling beams, adding faint outlines to the remainder of the cabin. The rectangular room looked fairly simple in design. Four sets of bunk beds leaned against the walls. A small table, flanked by two pairs of chairs, stood in the middle of the space.

As the men took their places around the table, Captain Smollett asked conversationally, "Mr. Smiley, might I implore you to tell us how you came under Silver's blade?"

"Certainly," replied Uncle Dunkirk warmly. If he were going to work with these men to escape, he might as well gain their trust immediately. Unfortunately, that would require a few innocent fibs. Uncle Dunkirk had already figured out that he and Sage were trapped on Treasure Island. And meeting the four other prisoners—who he had already been introduced to in Robert Louis Stevenson's classic novel, long ago—helped to reawaken his spotty recollection of *Treasure Island*. If memory served him correctly, he had read Stevenson's classic on an expedition down the Nile in 1973. Or maybe it was trekking through Peru in 1974.

Uncle Dunkirk knew there were limits as to what men would believe, especially men who had yet to experience the many wonders of modern science and technology. For these men, it was the age of ocean travel and carriages, and the thought that a man could fly would be seen as simply preposterous. An act of witchcraft, even. And explaining the time-traveling powers of the amber stone would have been akin to informing them that the British Empire no longer spanned the globe. It would have been sheer sacrilege. With that in mind, Uncle Dunkirk put his imagination to work, and wove a tale that incorporated a few fibs, some improvisation, and an element or two of truth.

He began with a white lie to place himself and Sage in the area—a shipwrecked schooner—and then expanded on it, explaining dramatically how he and his nephew had managed to save themselves. "As we splashed about in the water, I spied a cask bobbing on the waves, and managed to grab hold. My nephew and I clasped hands over the cask, holding each other out of the water, and there we floated throughout the night, riding on the tide. Whatever happened to the rest of the passengers and crew, I can only guess. But it's my belief that they went down with the ship, as we heard no cries for help in the dark."

Another slight fib delivered Uncle Dunkirk and Sage to Treasure Island. "When the sun rose the next morning, we spied land on the horizon.

Kicking our feet, we managed to steer our way to shore. After what seemed like days in the water, we finally felt sand beneath our feet, and we thanked God for delivering us from certain death."

From there, Uncle Dunkirk found it easy to begin inserting elements of truth into his tale. He explained how he had sent Sage into the woods to collect firewood—a slight fib, and not really worth counting—and that while he had been busily preparing camp, he had spotted the pirates of the *Hispaniola* advancing through the trees. From there, the story completed itself.

"Of course, once they had me down on the ground, there was little I could do. They were armed to the teeth with swords and cutlasses, and I had nothing but my bare hands and my broken branch. One of the ruffians clobbered me over the head, and the next thing I knew, I was being rowed out to this ship."

"And what of your nephew?" asked Jim Hawkins breathlessly.

"That's the part that fills me with dread. I don't know what became of Sage. The last I saw of him, he was heading into the woods to gather firewood. I just hope that he's all right."

There was silence throughout the cabin as Uncle Dunkirk's tale came to a close. Finally, Captain Smollett, a true gentleman of the sea, offered his heartfelt condolences. "I'm sure your nephew is fine, Mr. Smiley. If he were a prisoner of Silver's, he'd be locked in the brig with all of us. So I'm sure he's still safe on shore. I'm also sorry to hear about your ship. It's a shame that so many perished when she went down. I will be sure to document its loss in my logbook for posterity's sake, and I will report it to my commander if we ever get out of this predicament. What was her name again?"

The first ship name that sailed across Uncle Dunkirk's mind tumbled out of his lips: "The *Titanic*." Then he added, "She was part of the White Star Line out of Liverpool."

"Odd," replied Captain Smollett curiously. "I've sailed into Liverpool on numerous occasions, and have never heard of her. Was she a two-master?"

"Yes," replied Uncle Dunkirk quickly. "She seemed very similar to the *Hispaniola*."

"Who captained her?"

"Oh," muttered Uncle Dunkirk, his mind searching for an answer. *A name. A Liverpudlian name.* "McCartney was his name. Captain Paul McCartney."

"No, sorry, I've never heard of him," responded Smollett. However, the speed of Uncle Dunkirk's answers seemed to pacify the captain. "I will make note of it, though. At least that way, if we ever get free of Silver's grasp, Captain

McCartney's family, and those of his passengers and crew, might be notified."

"I'm sure they would greatly appreciate that," offered Uncle Dunkirk, struggling to keep his composure.

"I would have loved to have seen you break that branch over that pirate's head," grinned Jim Hawkins. For the duration of Uncle Dunkirk's fabricated tale, Jim had sat cross-legged on the wooden floor, enraptured by the action-packed story. "I wonder who it was?"

"Judging by your description," weighed in Captain Smollett, "I'd guess that it was Red. He hired on in London and is definitely a giant, as you say. Plus, he does wear a fancy red vest."

"If that's the case, then I'd suggest that you step lively around him," offered Dr. Livesey. "From what I've seen of Red, he seems to have the strength of an ox. He's not someone you want to cross."

"Thanks for the warning," replied Uncle Dunkirk. "I'll keep it in mind. Now, if you don't mind, I'd like to hear your story—how you were all taken captive."

Each prisoner immediately looked to Captain Smollett. The captain nodded, and began their sorry tale.

According to Captain Smollett, they had all been aboard the *Hispaniola*, sailing from London to Havana, Cuba, when a vicious mutiny broke out.

The mutiny had come swiftly, as the evening meal was coming to a close, catching Captain Smollett and his guests unaware. When the smoke had cleared, the prisoners discovered that John Silver, a simple crewman who had hired on in London, had incited the crew to revolt. The *Hispaniola's* crew, given the option of joining Silver or leaving the ship via the plank, quickly pledged their undying allegiance to the new Captain, while Smollett and the passengers were imprisoned below decks.

As Smollett spoke, Uncle Dunkirk noted that he wasn't the only one holding his cards close to his chest. Captain Smollett didn't say a word about the treasure for which Treasure Island was named, a detail too important for him to simply have forgotten.

"Any idea why Silver wanted to come to this island specifically?" asked Uncle Dunkirk innocently, playing along with Captain Smollett's ruse.

"No idea whatsoever," interjected Squire Trelawney rather abruptly, launching a spatter of spittle off his thick, stout lips. "For all we know, Silver might simply be laying low for the time being, staying downwind of trouble. Don't you think, Dr. Livesey?"

Dr. Livesey jumped at the mention of his name, and stammered a hasty reply. "Oh, yes, quite right." But Uncle Dunkirk could see that the respectable doctor wasn't an accomplished liar.

"How long have you been captive?" asked Uncle Dunkirk, carrying on the charade.

"Eight days now," replied Dr. Livesey wearily. "And we're only allowed on deck for a few brief minutes each day, for a spot of fresh air."

"What do you think Silver's intentions are?" continued Uncle Dunkirk.

The prisoners once again turned to Captain Smollett for the answer. After a moment's hesitation, Captain Smollett spoke grimly. "I don't think our chances are good. Unfortunately, gentlemen, we are in the terrible position of being witnesses to a shipboard mutiny, which, I don't have to remind you all, is a hanging offense according to English law. I think Silver is smart enough not to leave any loose ends, especially because, if he did so, he would tighten the noose around his own neck."

A morbid silence descended upon the room. Although every one of the prisoners understood the ramifications of their imprisonment, no one had voiced it aloud as of yet.

Finally, as thoughts of Sage alone on a foreign island once again clouded Uncle Dunkirk's thoughts, he broke the silence and asked, "Can we escape?"

"And go where?" retorted Captain Smollett. "We're locked in this putrid cabin from morning to night, and Silver won't even give us a match for the lantern, lest we burn down the ship. We're escorted onto deck only once a day, while the crew is up and about. And even if we could simply dive overboard and hope to outswim Silver's guns, the waters are shark infested. I'd venture that even the strongest swimmer wouldn't make it halfway to shore."

"Yes, I think it's best to eliminate swimming from any escape plans," agreed Squire Trelawney wholeheartedly. Then, as a blush of red glazed over his pudgy cheeks, he added bashfully, "I'm afraid that my swimming skills are akin to skipping a stone across the water. I splash about a few times, and then simply drop to the bottom. I'm actually quite afraid of the water."

Uncle Dunkirk ignored the squire's pathetic confession, and forged on, tossing out random ideas. "What if we stole the longboat in the middle of the night and rowed to shore?"

"We've already thought of that," replied a disheartened Captain Smollett. "In order for that plan to succeed, we would need to take control of the upper deck. But even in the darkest hours of the night, Silver has men on watch. We've all heard boots tromping overhead as we lie awake in our bunks. I'd guess that there are two, maybe three men on watch all night."

"But there are four of us," pressed Uncle Dunkirk.

"Five," corrected Jim Hawkins assuredly.

With a wink to the young lad, Uncle Dunkirk reiterated, "*Five* of us. We shouldn't have too much trouble overpowering them. We have the element of surprise."

"I'm sorry, but I don't think it will be that easy," disagreed Captain Smollett. "Mark my words, Mr. Smiley, the night watchmen will all be armed. If they give even one cry for help, we'll be awash in Silver's men."

"Once again, I must say that I agree whole-heartedly with Captain Smollett," piped in Squire Trelawney. "As it stands, we have bided our time like honest, respectable gentleman, and I think Silver might reciprocate when the time comes."

"Oh, come now, squire. You're closing your eyes to a great injustice," groaned Dr. Livesey. "We all know how Silver treats his own crew. Why just two days ago, we heard the screams of a man taking ten lashes on deck for sneaking an extra ration of salt pork. *Ten* lashes across a *man's* back, and all because the sailor was hungry. I think the sand has almost emptied from the hourglass. Whatever your plans may be, Mr. Smiley, you can count me in."

Uncle Dunkirk nodded. Dr. Livesey's courageous words added an additional layer of rouge to Squire Trelawney's cheeks, and he turned his head away in a shameful huff, but they also cemented his relationship with Uncle Dunkirk.

"We have to get off this ship!" stated Uncle Dunkirk, striking his fist into his open palm. "All we have to do is get to the island. Once on shore, there are a million places we can hide. The island is covered in thick forest. Silver couldn't hope to contain us amongst all those trees. Plus, there are three large hills, any one of which would provide us with unlimited sight lines over the island. We could take the high ground, and watch Silver's men coming from miles away."

"What about Ben Gunn's fort?" offered Jim Hawkins enthusiastically, caught up in the excitement of planning their escape. Then, as the startled eyes of his cell mates turned toward him, the boy realized that he had blundered, and he diverted his eyes to the floor.

However, Jim's mistake had not slipped past Uncle Dunkirk, who immediately recalled the deserted fort that he and Sage had seen while surveying the island. With a sprinkle of surprise coating his voice, Uncle Dunkirk asked, "Did you say *Ben Gunn's* fort?"

An uncomfortable silence filled the room. In shame, Jim Hawkins had gone completely mute, and was doing everything in his power not to meet the accusing glares of his friends.

Finally, Dr. Livesey broke the silence with a difficult admission. "I'm afraid we haven't been completely honest with you, Mr. Smiley."

"Please, call me Dunkirk."

"Thank you, Dunkirk. You see, we are aware of another man on the island—a man by the name of Ben Gunn, who has been marooned on these shores for quite some time. For some reason, Silver allowed Jim to accompany him during his first excursion ashore. That was when Jim discovered Ben. We don't think that Silver knows of Ben's presence, and, in all honesty, we don't know much about this Ben Gunn at all. We just know that he is marooned, and, obviously, looking for an opportunity to get off the island." Then, with his tail between his legs, Dr. Livesey added, "I hope you understand, Dunkirk. We would have told you at the right time. It's just that your sudden appearance seemed rather suspicious. You could have even been a spy for Silver, for all we knew. I hope you don't take offense, for none was intended."

"I appreciate your candor," replied Uncle Dunkirk sincerely. "And, rest assured, you have not offended me. You were simply doing what was best for your interests. In your shoes, I would have done the same."

However, deep inside, Uncle Dunkirk was kicking himself. He had completely forgotten about the character of Ben Gunn. But after Jim's abrupt reminder, Uncle Dunkirk recalled that Ben Gunn was one of the good guys, and he hoped that

Sage might somehow cross his path.

"Let me reassure you, gentlemen," stated Uncle Dunkirk, "that my only intention is to escape from this ship, find my nephew, and leave this island far, far behind. You have my word. Whether you choose to join me or not is your decision completely, and one that I will respect. However, if you decide to put your trust in me, I think we'll all find the task at hand easier."

A chorus of agreement rang out from the men in the room as Captain Smollett and Dr. Livesey jumped to their feet to shake Uncle Dunkirk's hand and seal their alliance. Uncle Dunkirk's words managed to perk up the red-faced Jim Hawkins and the bashful Squire Trelawney, who also added their votes of confidence. The prisoners were all in this game plan together, and escaping was their main goal.

"Now," continued a determined Uncle Dunkirk, getting down to business, "how do we get out of this room and onto the longboat?"

CHAPTER 16

"IS THAT WHAT I think it is?" Sage gawked from the mouth of the cave. His eyes bugged out as he stared unblinkingly at the brimming casks of treasure. Four large oak chests lay snuggled up against the back cave wall, their lids flipped open to flaunt a glittering array of gold, diamonds, silver, and other priceless relics.

"Aye, it is," replied Ben indifferently, the sparkle of the treasure having lost much of its luster for him over the years. "Flint's treasure."

Sage staggered farther into the cave. It almost felt as if he were Luke Skywalker caught in the Death Star's tractor beam as he was drawn toward the treasure.

Never in Sage's life had he seen wealth firsthand like this. For him, a Wayne Gretzky hockey card, won fair and square in the schoolyard during recess, was a treasure.

However, after seeing the four glittering chests, Sage finally understood the draw treasure had on others. He'd seen that glazed, wild-eyed stare in too many Saturday afternoon matinees at the local theater to mention, and if a mirror were hanging on the cave wall before him, he was sure he'd see the same look on his own face. After all, how could he not be impressed by the magnificence of it? The candlelight flickered off the treasure, reflecting a thousand beams of golden light across the cave, and transforming the chest into the most dazzling campfire Sage had ever seen.

Without realizing it, Sage had wandered the entire length of the cave, and found himself standing at the foot of the first chest. He glanced timidly at Ben for approval, and after Ben's slight nod, Sage dropped to his knees and dug his hands into the chest. His fingers burrowed deep into a heap of gold doubloons, wiggling back and forth. Then he clenched his hands, and pulled them out to watch the gold doubloons filter through his fingers like rainwater and jingle pleasantly back into the chest.

"When did you find Flint's treasure?" Sage asked over his shoulder, as he crawled over to the second chest and repeated the dip-and-drop process. This chest, though smaller in size, was full of brilliant diamonds, rubies, sapphires, opals, and other valuable gemstones. Scooping up a fistful, Sage held the stones at eye level, and peered through them at the shimmering candlelight on Ben's makeshift table. The colors tossed and turned before his eyes, as if he were looking through the peephole of a giant kaleidoscope, before Sage released them and let them rattle back into the chest.

"Shortly after I was marooned, a thought came to me," replied Ben. He had slipped into a handmade chair fashioned out of wood and palm bark, and watched Sage's progress with amusement. "And then finding the treasure wasn't that hard at all. You see, sailing with Flint had given me a bit of insight into the man's thoughts and actions. I already knew that Flint was a devious man, and that he trusted no one—which is why he murdered his own men after burying the treasure. But I also knew that Flint was a lazy man—not apt to lend a hand when there was work to be done. So, knowing this, I simply began scouring the island, looking for the remains of the six men, for I knew that Flint wouldn't have raised a sweat burying them. He would have simply left the bodies to rot in the hot sun, as fodder for the island's creatures.

"Once I'd stumbled over the remains, I simply began digging in the area. After a few hours, my hunch proved right. My spade came down on something hard, and when I unearthed it, I found the first chest. I kept digging, and soon I'd exhumed all four."

By now, Sage had already scrutinized the third chest, which was teeming with more gold doubloons, and was immersed in the fourth. This final chest was by far the ultimate toy box—a dream come true. It was a make-believe wonderland, complete with diamond-encrusted necklaces, glimmering gold rings, stately scepters, ceremonial daggers, and other equally exquisite ornaments.

Sage selected a majestic gold crown, and pulled it from the pile. The crown glittered in the candlelight as Sage propped it ceremoniously on his head. When he let go, the crown slid down over his forehead and eyes, and it would have kept going to encircle his skinny neck if his nose had not abruptly stopped its descent.

"I think that one might be a little big for you," observed Ben with a chuckle.

Bashfully, Sage slipped the crown back over his head, and returned it to the top of the pile. "How did you manage to get all this treasure up here?"

"I'd kept the treasure in the fort for some time," explained Ben, "waiting for a ship to come along and rescue me. Soon enough, a month became a year, and a year became three. But as I waited for rescue, I soon realized that I was in the same spot of trouble that Flint had been in. I was sitting on top of a heap of treasure—more money than a man could ever spend in a hundred lifetimes, but I couldn't trust a soul. After all, anyone who stumbled upon this island could easily steal the treasure from me and leave me here marooned. Or, even worse, *dead.*

"So I decided that it would be best to move the treasure to the cave. With all the vines hiding the entrance, I thought it would make a safe hiding place until I could discover the intentions of anyone who dropped anchor at Treasure Island.

"Then, about a week ago, I woke to find the *Hispaniola* in the lagoon. At first, I couldn't believe my eyes. I must have rubbed them raw trying to clear the mirage from my sight. But every time I opened my eyes, the ship was still there. I was ecstatic. I thought my prayers were answered. I could barely hold myself back from racing down to the beach to greet my rescuers, but something in the back of my mind made me pause. A nagging question just seemed to raise my hackles—why had the *Hispaniola* dropped anchor *here*? Treasure Island is quite a ways off the regular shipping lanes, and it isn't renowned for its spices or produce. It's simply a deserted island in the middle of nowhere. Not exactly the sort of desti-nation that gets a lot of law-abiding traffic, if you know what I mean. I decided that it would be in my best interest to watch from a distance until I could find out more about the ship.

"Later that day, I watched as the crew prepared their longboat for an excursion to shore. While they were readying the boat, I raced down to the lagoon so that I could keep an eye on the landing party. I hid in the bushes and watched as four men came ashore and set off into the forest, heading inland.

"The man I took for the Captain seemed to have a map of some sort, and as they counted off their steps from location to location, I realized where they were heading—to the exact spot where I had unearthed Flint's treasure. Right then, I knew that these men were not to be trusted. They've been searching the island ever since, trying to find the treasure."

"Is that when you met Jim Hawkins?"

"Yes, he came ashore with that first landing party, but never again. I could see that he was a prisoner. His hands were tied to a rope that the Captain led him about with, but I wasn't about to get my gizzard run by saving the lad. But young Jim, he's a clever one. He managed to slip away when the others had their backs turned, and he hid out in the woods—just like you did. I came across him, and he told me that there had been a mutiny onboard the ship, and that a pirate named Long John Silver had taken him and his friends captive."

"What happened to him?" Sage asked, although he knew the answer.

"The brave lad gave himself up. He went back on board to let the other prisoners know of my presence, and our plan to escape."

"You had an escape plan?" Sage sputtered excitedly, thinking that maybe Ben had an answer for saving Uncle Dunkirk. "What were you going to do?"

"It was fairly simple," offered Ben. "I was going to paddle out to the *Hispaniola* in the dark of the night, sneak on board, and overpower the guard. Then I'd free Jim and his friends, and we'd take control of the ship."

"It sounds easy enough," Sage added, a glimmer of hope sparking within him.

"Yes, it does. But Silver has been acting rather peculiar lately. He's doubled the guard on deck at night, and now with you and your Uncle showing up in that flying contraption of yours, I'm sure he'll tighten security once again. I might have been able to handle one guard, but two or more is too much."

"But there are two of us now," Sage replied bravely.

"Yes, but I don't think you'd be much of a match for a grown man, Sage," countered Ben honestly. "These men are brutes. They'd run you through without blinking an eye. And one peep out of their mouths, and we'd have all of Silver's men upon us. No, I'm sorry, Sage, but I don't think we can take them in a fight."

Sage dropped his head. He knew that Ben was right. Sage was an inexperienced 88-pound weakling, and there was no way he could topple a murderous pirate who slaughtered and maimed grown men for a living.

The cold claws of depression tightened their grip around Sage, pulling him into despair. Sage sniffled—it was a fading remnant of his summer cold—and wiped his nose with the back of his sleeve. He was lost in a strange land, and helpless to save Uncle Dunkirk. *Why didn't I wish for an African safari, or a trip to the Egyptian pyramids?*

And then inspiration struck like a bolt of lightning. It was an idea so simple that Sage thought it just might work. And if all went well, it would enable the two of them to get on board the *Hispaniola* and rescue Uncle Dunkirk, Jim Hawkins, and the other prisoners.

"I've got it!" Sage announced. "I know how we can get on board!"

CHAPTER 17

THE UNMISTAKABLE THUNDER of boots rolled down the stairs, and stormed across the hall of the forecastle before abating outside the makeshift brig. Seconds later, the door burst open. The menacing silhouettes of two pirates appeared in the open doorway. Both brandished swords.

"You!" barked one of the pirates, motioning to Uncle Dunkirk. "Out! Captain Silver wants to see you."

Uncle Dunkirk obeyed the command, ducking through the squat doorway and falling in line behind his captors.

The guards led Uncle Dunkirk across the length of the deck, down another set of stairs, and into the quarterdeck toward the Captain's cabin. Following a single rap to announce their presence, one of the men swung open a door, and reported officiously, "The prisoner, as you requested, Captain."

Uncle Dunkirk stepped tentatively into the room, and then glanced about as the thick wooden door slammed forcefully shut behind him. A pair of brass lanterns burned in the center of the room, throwing a wash of light and shadow throughout the spacious cabin. In the far corner, a four-poster bed with wrinkled white sheets sat upon a slight dais. A pair of solid oak chests resided in front of the bed, and, to the right, an intricately carved dinner table, stacked with plates, cups, and cutlery, was pushed up against the wall. Captain Silver sat at an imposing oak desk in the center of the room, scrawling in his logbook, with a feather quill in hand. A curl of blue smoke rose from the end of a black cheroot clenched tightly between his teeth, adding a slight, smoky haze to the already gloomy atmosphere. After a long moment, Silver glanced up, and ordered brusquely, "Sit."

Uncle Dunkirk strode across the room, and slipped into one of the two wooden chairs in front of the desk. Silver hospitably placed a chalice of wine in front of Uncle Dunkirk, and then refilled his own glass. "It's Spanish," commented Silver, removing the cheroot from his mouth. "I will say one good thing about the Spanish, they make a fine wine."

Silver slurped a mouthful of wine from his chalice, and then put down his cup. Satisfied, he replaced the smoldering cheroot between his lips, and turned his full attention to Uncle Dunkirk. "I'm a busy man, and I've not much time for idle chatter. Just a few questions that need answering. First off, your name?"

"Dunkirk Smiley," replied Uncle Dunkirk

stiffly, his military training coming to mind — *name, rank, and serial number.*

"You're obviously not English?" stated Silver.

"No, I'm an American."

"Ah, yes, an *American*," purred Silver, with a healthy dollop of distaste buttering his words. "You're a long way from the colonies, Mr. Smiley."

"I suppose I am," replied Uncle Dunkirk honestly, although he really had no clue where Treasure Island was exactly. Then, lifting his chalice of wine, he asked conversationally, "Do you mind if I ask a question of my own?"

Silver reclined in his chair, and, with a slight nod of his head, invited Uncle Dunkirk to continue.

"I was just wondering why I am being held captive?" asked Uncle Dunkirk. "I have nothing to do with your business on this island, Captain Silver, and I pose no threat to you whatsoever. However, you chose to shoot at me for no apparent reason. Would you mind explaining your motives?"

Silver stared at Uncle Dunkirk for a moment, as if determining how to best answer the question. Then he leaned forward, and calmly replied, "You are right, Mr. Smiley. You have nothing to do with my business here on the island. And the reason why you were shot at is quite simple. You see, I am what is commonly known as a pirate. Filthy word, if you ask me, but a better trade I've never found. Being a pirate affords me the opportunity to live life upon the high seas, and to do *whatever* I wish, *whenever* I wish. If I want something, I take it, and no one stands in my way."

"I guarantee, Captain Silver, that I won't stand in your way," assured Uncle Dunkirk firmly. "In my eyes, your business is just that—*your* business. All I want is to leave this island, and get back to *my* business."

"I appreciate that, Mr. Smiley. I truly do. But unfortunately, you just happen to be in possession of something that would be of great value to me in *my* business—a flying machine."

Uncle Dunkirk dropped his mouth open, skillfully feigning surprise. Of course, he'd already guessed that Long John Silver wanted Willy C. After all, in the eighteenth century nothing remotely resembled an airplane, and Silver was a greedy, thieving pirate. However, Uncle Dunkirk needed to pull the wool firmly over Silver's eyes, so he decided to play along. He sputtered a shocked reply. "My flying machine! You can't be serious!"

"Oh, I am serious, Mr. Smiley," answered Silver bluntly. "*Dead* serious."

Uncle Dunkirk dropped his head forlornly, and wrung his hands together. Then he pleaded his case. "Captain Silver, a flying machine is a very precise piece of engineering. It's made up of thousands of miniscule bits and pieces, and each piece needs to work hand-in-hand with the others in order for the machine to fly. When you fired on me earlier today, your cannonball ripped right through the wing. And, as you know, a bird can't fly with a broken wing. Neither can my flying machine."

Long John Silver remained emotionless throughout the plea. He stared coldly at Uncle Dunkirk. "So fix it."

"With what?" sputtered Uncle Dunkirk. "You don't have the proper tools. It needs much more than just a wooden mallet and a bucket of glue."

An angry crease suddenly gouged deeply across Silver's forehead, and the color seemed to drain from his face. The pirate's eyes were black and unflinching, and his teeth clenched around the cheroot, which glowed red like a volcano, ready to erupt with each breath. "Let me remind you, Mr. Smiley, that this is not a discussion. If you can't fix the flying machine, then your only use to me is as entertainment for my crew." Then, with a smirk polluting his face, Silver asked, "Have you, by chance, ever heard of 'the nick of time?'"

"'The nick of time?'" asked Uncle Dunkirk.

"Yes, it's quite entertaining, actually," continued Silver casually. A menacing edge crept into his voice. "You see, we take a prisoner and, using a sharp dagger, cover him from head to toe in tiny nicks. Nothing too deep. Just enough to draw a few drops of blood on *every* single part of his body—arms, legs, front, back, neck. I'm sure you get the picture."

Uncle Dunkirk swallowed and tried to maintain his composure, but he could see where Silver was going.

"We bind the prisoner's hands with a length of sturdy rope. The other end of the rope ties on to the longboat. Then my strongest rowers put their backs to work, and circle the lagoon, round and round, dragging the prisoner behind them in their wake."

Silver's cold eyes locked on Uncle Dunkirk's as he continued his chilling description of the dreaded pirate torture. "It's only a matter of time until the sharks catch scent of the blood in the water. They usually start slowly—circling their prey. They might nudge you at first, a glancing blow from their snouts. And then, bit by bit, they begin to feed. Maybe a nibble at first—a foot, or an arm. Then they become more confident, more aggressive. They'll go into a frenzy. They'll attack the legs, severing your knees, and then your waist, and your chest. And they'll continue, chewing and attacking, until there's nothing left tied to the rope, except maybe your hands.

"That, Mr. Smiley," completed Silver, with a ghoulish grin, "Is 'the nick of time.'"

A feeling of terror swept over Uncle Dunkirk. It was official: Long John Silver was a madman, a psychotic pirate with an unquenchable lust for blood. Uncle Dunkirk knew that he had to get off this ship, and he had to do it soon.

Thankfully, Silver's interest in Willy C could be the opportunity the prisoners were looking for. Silver wanted Willy C fixed, and no matter what, the wing needed to be repaired to leave Treasure Island. However, in order to fix Willy C, Silver would have to allow Uncle Dunkirk to go ashore.

"While your description of 'the nick of time' is interesting, to say the least," commented Uncle Dunkirk, slipping his game face back on, "I think I'd rather attempt to fix the flying machine for you."

With an arrogant guffaw, Silver retorted, "I had no doubt."

"Obviously, I'll need to go ashore to work on it," added Uncle Dunkirk, playing his cards as quickly and efficiently as possible.

"You'll be escorted to the flying machine first thing in the morning by my coxswain and a landing party. The coxswain will also see that you get whatever supplies and tools you need to make the necessary repairs." Then Silver added, as if he could sense Uncle Dunkirk's motives floating on the wind, "Of course, the men will be armed, and they will have direct orders to run you through with a cutlass if you so much as blink."

"May I ask one small favor?" asked Uncle Dunkirk, pressing on. "May I take the other prisoners to help? The more help I have, the quicker I'll be able to fix the flying machine."

A burst of sinister laughter belched forth from Silver. "Your opinion of me is unflattering," Silver chuckled, without humor. "I am not a stupid man, Mr. Smiley. Far from it."

"Then you might as well forget the flying machine," Uncle Dunkirk shoved back. "Realize this, Captain Silver—I *can't* fix the flying machine by myself. It's impossible. It would be like trying to sail the *Hispaniola* with an oar. You just can't do it. I need a few pairs of strong hands to help. If you want a flying machine that *works*, you are going to have to help me."

The room fell uncomfortably silent. For a moment, Uncle Dunkirk wondered if he had gone too far. From his initial examination of Willy C on the ground, Uncle Dunkirk already knew that repairing the plane wouldn't be too difficult. He figured that he could probably fashion a rough repair on the wing in a few hours. The patch probably wouldn't stand up on a long journey, but it would hold long enough for Willy C to flash back to safety—given that Uncle Dunkirk could find the amber stone before then.

But time was running out, and with it fell the ground beneath the prisoners' feet. Uncle Dunkirk had taken his shot, knowing that Silver would probably prefer having his own men scrounge the island for lost treasure, rather than waste a day toiling in the sun, working on the flying machine.

And if his plan worked, it would be worth goading Silver's wrath.

A sign of life finally passed over Silver's face, as the tip of his cheroot glowed red. Silver leaned back in his chair. "Smollett goes nowhere. I want him here, where I can see him, and not out on the island where he can poison the heads of my crew with threats of a mutineer's noose. The same goes for Trelawney. He is a spoiled upper-class twit who hasn't worked a day in his life. I doubt that he'd be of much assistance to you at all."

"What about Dr. Livesey?" asked Uncle Dunkirk. "The hands of a doctor are highly skilled. He could be of great assistance to me."

"You may take the doctor with you," agreed Silver, through a pungent cloud of cigar smoke.

"And Jim Hawkins?" pressed Uncle Dunkirk. "A pair of small hands might prove helpful for places that are hard to reach."

"Fine, fine," agreed Silver, with a dismissive wave of his hand. "I see no reason to keep young master Hawkins on board." Then, in a stern tone, Silver added, "But heed my words, Mr. Smiley—if any one of the prisoners fails to return to the ship by sundown, there will be repercussions. On that, you have my word."

"I assure you, Captain Silver, that we will be back on board before the sun sets."

With that, the meeting came to an abrupt end.

Long John Silver bellowed loudly for the guard, and the door swung open immediately. Without a backward glance, Uncle Dunkirk slipped out of the chair, and crossed the cabin toward the exit. As the guards stepped aside to let the prisoner pass, Silver called out once more from behind his desk, "Oh, and one other thing, Mr. Smiley. You have one day."

CHAPTER 18

THE LONGBOAT BUMPED up against the side of the *Hispaniola*, and McGregor quickly lashed a line to the netting for mooring. Israel Hands was first out of the boat, grabbing hold of one of the rope rungs and efficiently clawing his way to the deck. A moment later, Red swung a broad leg over the deck rail and pulled himself onto solid footing.

"Would you look at that?" called a grizzled old pirate, sitting on his haunches on deck, repairing a net. "It looks like Red's grown a raspberry patch on his head."

The malicious sound of the crew's laughter washed across the deck, and Red felt the throbbing return—*badump, badump, badump*—to his aching head, where a crusty patch of dried blood shone bright red. Word had quickly spread over the *Hispaniola* that Red had been bested, felled by a blow to the head by the new prisoner. The fact that it had, in all honesty, been a sucker punch made little difference to the crew. After all, the men of the *Hispaniola* were pirates and cutthroats, and cheating was as familiar as the water upon which they sailed.

"Easy, Red," cooed Hands softly from Red's side, as he watched the giant's hands flex open, and then closed. The man was obviously nearing his breaking point.

Jokes and rude comments from the crew of the *Hispaniola* were nothing new to Red. His shipmates had never truly accepted him as one of the men. For starters, Red stood out as the largest man onboard—weighing in at just under 300 pounds, and standing tall at nearly seven feet. But because they couldn't beat him with their size or strength, the crew turned to crueler forms of attack. They started by calling him names such as *Mammoth* and *Cyclops*—always behind his back, of course. But rather than confront the impertinent crew, Red simply shied away.

The persecution continued unabated, and the crew began pulling practical jokes on the giant. One time, Red woke to find his pants fluttering wildly in the wind from atop the flagpole of the ship. On another occasion, someone stitched his red vest closed, so that it was next to impossible for Red to pull it over his head. He had spent the entire morning that day sitting quietly on deck and undoing each stitch, one by one, to the callous chortles of the crew around him.

The only man who had shown Red any outward sign of respect at all was Israel Hands, the coxswain. Hands made good use of Red's Herculean strength, often taking him on excursions to the island, or including him in shipboard chores. And if it weren't for Hands's presence beside him now, Red surely would have snapped and taken weeks of bitter frustration out on this grizzled old pirate.

"Now's not the time to anger the cap'n," continued Hands, his voice still low and guarded.

Realizing Hands was right, Red suppressed the ferocious urge to pummel each and every one of the laughing hyenas onboard the ship.

Suddenly, the door to the quarterdeck swung open, and Uncle Dunkirk appeared on deck with his two-man guard. The simmering rage that Red had barely managed to get under control instantly boiled over as Red's eyes locked on those of the prisoner. Once again, Red's fists clenched angrily, squeezing every mighty inch of muscle from his tree trunk arms, until his nails dug painfully into his palms.

Uncle Dunkirk had also noticed the sudden appearance of the two new pirates on deck as he was led back to the prisoners' quarters. And now that he was once again face-to-face with the massive hulk of a man he'd clobbered over the head, a distressing twinge of regret for his earlier actions grew inside of him.

"You!" seethed Red, marching angrily forward until he stood toe-to-toe with Uncle Dunkirk. An angry blush of color had raced to the giant's face. "I was hoping we'd meet again."

Uncle Dunkirk's two guards stepped back warily. Obeying orders was one thing, but doing so at the risk of life or limb—well, that was a different situation.

The bulging mass of Red's beefy chest was now at Uncle Dunkirk's eye level. It expanded like a sail catching wind as Red inhaled. Slowly, Uncle Dunkirk raised his head and met the giant's eyes, looking deep into a bottomless well of fury and fire.

"I've been thinking about you all day," snarled Red.

"And I've been thinking about you," retorted Uncle Dunkirk casually.

A look of surprise flashed across the giant's face. "You have?"

"Yes, I have," replied Uncle Dunkirk calmly. "I've been wondering if you've ever seen a fourth down punt?"

Red's eyebrows arched in bewilderment. "A fourth down *what*?"

"A fourth down *punt*. It's all the rage in America."

With that, Uncle Dunkirk bent forward into a

three-point stance—right arm down, legs spread, head up. Then, he called a quick quarterback cadence, "Zero four. Zero four. Set, hutt, hutt!" Uncle Dunkirk pantomimed the snap of the ball and then held the imaginary pigskin at arm's length before him. Then, pulling his leg back, he swung with all his might, slipping his foot between Red's legs and into the giant's groin.

Red's eyes, once brimming with anger, blinked twice in confusion, and then registered a blinding surge of agony. His eyelids clamped into a pained squint as a stream of tears rolled down his face. Then the strength in the man's legs gave out, and he began to keel over on the deck.

All around Uncle Dunkirk came the chilling sound of a dozen *zings* as swords were unsheathed all along the deck, but Uncle Dunkirk stood firm.

The tip of a blade suddenly materialized under Uncle Dunkirk's neck, and he found himself staring down its length into the livid eyes of Mr. Hands. Hands pressed the blade against Uncle Dunkirk's skin, drawing a slight trickle of blood, and warned through gritted teeth, "Oh, that was a mistake! A terrible, terrible mistake!"

Suddenly, the door to the quarterdeck burst open, and a sharp voice rang out. "Hands! What the devil do you think you're doing?"

As quickly as it had appeared, Hands's sword dropped from Uncle Dunkirk's neck. Long John

Silver hobbled across the deck. A flintlock was clenched in his left hand, while his right hand held tight to his crutch.

"Cap'n," sputtered Hands. "The prisoner just assaulted Red."

Silver stopped above Red and glanced down. The giant was buckled forward in the fetal position, with both hands clenched between his legs. Shaking his head in disgust, Silver turned and faced Uncle Dunkirk. "I'd like to say that you are a brave man, Mr. Smiley, but I find it hard to commend an act as dim-witted as this."

Then, turning back to Hands, Silver cocked the pistol, and swept the barrel back and forth across Hands's chest. "Mr. Hands," asked Silver sarcastically, "when did you become Captain of this ship?"

Hands swallowed, choking back his anger. "Cap'n, I didn't mean any offense. I was just defending the honor of the crew."

"Why don't you leave the ship's honor to me," growled Silver loudly, his voice carrying over the deck. "This man is *my* prisoner. He is not to be harmed in any way unless I give a direct order to do so. Is that understood?"

Hands dropped his eyes to the deck. "Yes, sir, Cap'n, sir."

Then Silver turned his attention back to Red. "As for you, you oaf, I have put up with you for too long. This is your last warning, Red. You may have slipped the noose once before, but mark my words, the next time you litter my deck, I'll have you swept overboard." Silver pressed the heel of his pegged leg down onto Red's chest, pinning him to the deck.

As his watery eyes brimmed with pain, Red spoke through gritted teeth, "Yes, Captain. I'm sorry, sir."

"Now get off my deck, and stand like a man," ordered Silver, stepping back.

Red slowly rolled over onto his stomach, and then hesitantly lifted himself to his knees. With a slight groan, he clambered up off his knees, and managed to straighten his body tenderly.

"Now then," continued Silver, "Mr. Hands, at the crack of dawn tomorrow you will escort the prisoner, along with Dr. Livesey and Jim Hawkins, back to the flying machine. Mr. Smiley has graciously offered to fix the damage to the flying machine, and your job is to make sure that it gets done—and that it gets done right. You will provide Mr. Smiley with any tools or materials that he might need."

"What about guards?" asked Hands, thankful that he was back in Silver's confidence.

"Take four men with you, and make sure that each of them is armed. I want you all back on ship no later than sundown."

"Yes, sir, Cap'n," replied Hands smartly.

Then, addressing the crew, Silver barked, "Tonight's entertainment is over. You've all got work to do, so get to it!"

Instantly, the crew of the *Hispaniola* scattered, racing across the deck and scurrying up the riggings.

Then, to Uncle Dunkirk's guards, Silver bellowed a final order. "Take the prisoner back to his cabin."

The two guards immediately responded, and gave Uncle Dunkirk an unruly shove from behind. With a glance over his shoulder at the seething giant, Uncle Dunkirk treaded back to his prison.

CHAPTER 19

BEN AND SAGE were off just as a red-tinged sun began to peek over the distant horizon, ready to put their escape plan into motion. For now, the plan was simply to reach the clearing where Willy C had landed before Long John Silver had the chance to isolate "the mysterious flying machine."

Slipping back through the curtain of hanging vines, Ben and Sage stepped out onto the embankment. The morning air was crisp and cool, and it felt rather refreshing, but one could almost feel the temperature rising in accordance with the sun on the horizon.

In the distance, Sage spotted the *Hispaniola*, which appeared to be slowly stirring to life. A faint smudge of smoke drifted lazily over the lagoon, coming from somewhere on board, and the dark outlines of a pair of buccaneers, probably the night watch, were visible on the deck. Other than that, the ship appeared to be asleep.

"The longboat is still moored to the side," noted Ben from Sage's side.

"Perfect timing," remarked Sage, with a pleased grin. It looked as if they had a firm head start on Silver and his crew.

Scrambling over the embankment, Ben and Sage carefully snaked their way down the side of Mizzen-mast Hill. It was a difficult descent in the dim light, and both were careful about where they planted their feet, as a clumsy tumble down the steep face wouldn't have helped their cause.

Soon enough, Ben and Sage safely reached the forest perimeter at the base of Mizzen-mast Hill, and slipped into its protective shelter. Twenty minutes later, they crossed the small creek where they had stopped the previous day, and took a few brief moments to refresh themselves.

As they finally neared the edge of the clearing, the shadows of the forest began to fall away, and random streams of early morning sunlight streamed through the tops of the trees.

Holding his finger to his lips, Ben gestured to Sage to be silent. Then they crept to the edge of the clearing, and scanned the glade from side to side. Apart from Willy C, the clearing appeared deserted.

Ben and Sage stepped around the perimeter of Willy C. They purposely hugged the forest edge so that, at a moment's notice, they could easily disappear into the trees if Silver's men suddenly materialized. For now, though, the clearing was theirs alone.

"Well, we made it," whispered Ben. "Now what?"

"I don't think there's much that we can use in the flying machine," Sage replied. "But, if our luck holds, I think we'll find what we're looking for behind that banyan tree over there."

Sage skirted around Willy C and jogged the short distance to the banyan tree. All his hopes for rescuing Uncle Dunkirk were riding on this moment. It was sink or swim, and Sage was hoping that the life preserver he so desperately needed was still concealed in the forest.

Slowly circling the tree, Sage carefully stepped over its numerous roots that poked out of the ground. The banyan tree was ancient, and it must have grown to its present daunting size over the course of hundreds of years. Its haphazard array of roots looped and twisted, dipped into the ground, and then jutted out a few feet away, completely circling the massive trunk.

As Sage clambered over a final hurdle, his eyes settled on the prize. There, hidden behind the banyan tree, were the two army surplus backpacks that he had dragged from the belly of Willy C.

A sigh of relief whooshed out of Sage's mouth. He was thankful that Red and Hands hadn't uncovered the backpacks when they'd scoured the woods the day before. Quickly crossing the remaining distance, Sage hefted his backpack up and leaned it against the tree trunk. Then, unclasping the top, he untied the knotted rope and pulled the drawstring open. Everything was as he had left it, packed to the rafters in Spruce Ridge.

"Bingo!" exclaimed Sage, and a smile as bright as the Caribbean sun beamed from his face.

Chapter 20

UNCLE DUNKIRK WOKE to the sound of the prison door bursting open, followed by a pirate's rude order. "Get your lazy bones out of bed! The longboat sails within the hour!"

Before they could wipe the sleep from their eyes, Uncle Dunkirk, Dr. Livesey, and Jim Hawkins were dragged from their bunks and led topsides. As they gathered near the deck rail, Uncle Dunkirk noted that the longboat brimmed with supplies, and most of the landing crew appeared ready to depart.

Red, the final crew member to arrive, stormed across deck with what looked like a homicidal fire burning in his eyes. The giant had waited until the last possible moment to make his entrance on deck, and understandably so. Although he had wiped the blood from his forehead, and combed his hair neatly over the unsightly lump that remained from yesterday's blow, he strode a little bowlegged today, almost as if he had just climbed off a horse.

Uncle Dunkirk and Dr. Livesey climbed down the netting that hung over the side of the *Hispaniola*. They were given oars at the front of the vessel and instructed to row the longboat to shore. Red and another pirate took up the back oars, while the remaining crew sat fore and aft.

With each sturdy heave, the longboat pulled farther away from the *Hispaniola*, skimming across the lagoon.

Glancing up after a few minutes, Uncle Dunkirk couldn't help but notice that Red had slipped off his vest in the hot morning sun, and a large number of tattoos covered his broad back. Each tattoo was approximately the size of a matchstick, and maybe twice as thick, but they decorated Red's entire back. In places, the tattoos covered the healing scars of past whippings. Throughout his travels, Uncle Dunkirk had seen numerous tribal decorations—from the Iban tribesmen of Borneo, who decorated their bodies to ward off harm and disease, to the Pazyryks of Siberia, who some say inked proud badges upon their bodies to flaunt their noble birthright. However, Red's tattoos were different, peculiar even. Whether they were decorative tribal marks, or homemade shipboard tattoos, signifying an action of some sort—*a killing, maybe*, Uncle Dunkirk didn't know. Whatever they were, they added to Red's menacing appearance.

When the longboat finally slid onto the sandy beach of Treasure Island, the men slipped into the warm, thigh-high waters, and pulled the vessel to safety on shore.

Then, with arms piled high with tools and provisions, the landing party began the trek across Treasure Island to the clearing. Slipping into the forest at the shore's edge, they marched along in single file, keeping pace with the man in front.

Throughout the arduous trek, Uncle Dunkirk furtively glanced around, searching for any sign of Sage, and he also kept his eyes peeled for the amber stone, which had somehow been lost. Thoughts of his nephew all alone on the island had been troubling Uncle Dunkirk since his capture, but he had faith in the boy, and he felt that Sage had the gumption to stay safe through the night. He only hoped that his nephew had enough common sense to stay concealed if he heard the landing party trudging down the path. As for the amber stone, Uncle Dunkirk felt queasy every time he thought of the missing relic. For without the stone, Sage and he would be stuck on Treasure Island for all eternity. Or, at least, for as long as Long John Silver deemed fit. And that definitely wasn't acceptable to Uncle Dunkirk.

Sage busied himself placing the contents of both backpacks on the ground beside the banyan tree. The bags were propped on their sides, and from each Sage pulled a seemingly endless stream of items, which he organized and stacked as he went. Shirts went with shirts, pants with pants, and miscellaneous items were stacked separately. Through it all, Ben sat watching in amazement, his eyes sparkling, as he stared in awe at the riches that Sage pulled from each bag.

"Here," Sage offered hospitably, lobbing Ben a few pieces of Uncle Dunkirk's clothing. "A new outfit for you. Now you can get out of those filthy rags."

Ben snatched the garments from the air, and scrutinized them, piece by piece. It had been years since he had changed clothes, and the rags that adorned his skeletal frame were hanging by threads. Laying the shirt across his lap, Ben stroked the soft cotton tenderly, then held the shirt up, smiling at the vibrant floral print—red, yellow, and blue flowers shone brightly, as if the shirt had sprouted in a Technicolor garden.

"It's called a 'Hawaiian shirt,'" explained Sage, watching with amusement. "No visit to the islands is complete without one."

Ben grinned, clambered to his feet, and then pulled his tattered shirt over his head before discarding it on the ground. His equally brittle pants soon followed, dropping in a disheveled heap before being kicked aside. Then Ben slipped his arms into the short sleeves of the crisp, new shirt and carefully buttoned it up. Once he was done, Ben stepped into Uncle Dunkirk's khaki pants and pulled them up over his scrawny legs.

As Ben dressed, Sage couldn't help but notice the change in Ben's posture and attitude. Now that Ben was clad in a new outfit, he seemed to stand straighter. He also seemed to glow, almost as if the clothes had re-energized him. "Aren't you going to show off your new duds?" teased Sage.

With a grin, Ben spun around and flung his arms out to the sides. But being marooned on Treasure Island for three years had done quite a bit to reduce Ben's waistline, and when Ben let go of his pants, they dropped promptly to the ground.

Sage burst out laughing as the man scrambled to salvage both his pants and his pride. Ben's cheeks blushed brightly, but after a few seconds, the hilarity of the moment dawned on him, and he too began to chuckle. Soon enough, the two were laughing hysterically, with their arms clutched round their bellies, and salty tears streaming down their cheeks.

Finally, Sage managed to dig into Uncle Dunkirk's pack and pull out a belt. He tossed it to Ben. "Try that on for size."

Ben looped the belt around his waist and cinched it tight. The material at the front of his pants bunched up, but Ben didn't seem to mind. Holding his arms out, he posed once again for

Sage. If not for his snowy white hair and matching foot-long beard, Ben could have easily passed for a Californian beach bum.

"Now that we have you dressed, how about a pair of shoes?"

"Shoes?" sputtered Ben. *"Really?"*

Ben's incredulity hit Sage with a wave of sadness. The boy suddenly realized the crushing weight of loneliness the man must have felt while marooned on Treasure Island for three long years, and he was glad to be able to shine a little light into his new friend's life.

Sage pulled a rugged pair of leather hiking boots out of Uncle Dunkirk's backpack, and held them high for Ben to see. "I hope they fit," he said, as he lobbed them toward Ben's feet.

Without a moment's hesitation, Ben dropped to the ground and slipped his calloused feet into the boots. He pulled back on the laces, looped a quick knot, and then stood uncertainly.

"Give them a test drive," suggested Sage. But when a blank look stared back at him, Sage toned down his rhetoric. "Walk around a bit."

Like a toddler, Ben took a tentative step forward. The boots clunked heavily, and Ben took on a slightly comical appearance as his scrawny legs heaved the cumbersome boots off the ground and stomped them back down.

"They're too big," commented Sage. "But I

think we can fix that." As Ben removed the boots, Sage extracted a pair of thick woolen socks from Uncle Dunkirk's pack. Ben pulled the socks over his feet, and then slipped on the hiking boots once again. This time, the fit was definitely better. Ben tromped around the clearing, stepping spryly from side to side, with a grin.

"Thank you, Sage," muttered Ben from behind his beard. Sage knew that the words were heartfelt, but the look of pride on Ben's scraggly face was compensation enough.

"You're welcome, Ben," replied Sage. "But there's more." Sage had saved one of the most vital items for last. His fingers closed around the cool metal object inside the backpack, and he pulled it out, announcing with a flourish, "We now have a telescope."

Sliding the brass instrument to its full length, Sage carefully passed it to Ben.

Ben's face lit up at the sight of the telescope. "We'll have a fine view of the *Hispaniola* from the mouth of the cave."

"Yes, it should come in handy for keeping an eye on Long John Silver and his men," agreed Sage.

Suddenly, the smile on Ben's face vanished as his head snapped to the side. His eyes gazed into the far woods, flitting from tree to tree. "What is it?" asked Sage, following Ben's stare across the clearing.

"I think I hear someone coming down the trail.

We'd best take cover."

Sage rapidly grabbed the neat stacks of clothing and gear spread before him, and jammed them messily back into the backpack. Ben dashed about, gathering his tattered clothes and tossing them to Sage, while keeping his eyes locked on the trailhead. Finally, realizing that he held a telescope in his hand, Ben slipped behind the safety of the banyan tree, extended the lens, and peered through the viewfinder.

Moments later, he spied movement in the trees. A band of men was snaking through the jungle, and headed directly for them.

To Uncle Dunkirk's delight, Hands had taken no precautions to hide the crew's presence on the island. The prisoners talked freely throughout the hike, and Uncle Dunkirk used the time to prepare Dr. Livesey and Jim Hawkins for what they were about to see. After all, Uncle Dunkirk had told the prisoners that he had been stranded on the island after a shipwreck, and carried to its shores on the back of a floating cask. Within moments they would see the truth—that Uncle Dunkirk had actually landed on the island in what he would have to call a "futuristic flying machine."

"A flying machine?" asked Dr. Livesey, with a

skeptical smirk on his face. "Come on, Dunkirk, how daft do you think I am?"

"Dr. Livesey, please, I have nothing but the utmost respect for you. Put yourself in my shoes. As a doctor, how would you explain to someone without any medical knowledge that you've discovered an amazing machine—let's call it an X ray—that can look inside a man's body and take a picture of everything there? *Without* having to cut him open."

"I probably wouldn't be able to. Anyway, there's no such thing as an...X ray, and I won't be fooled into thinking that you can actually fly through the sky. That's just absurd."

"Then how would you explain that?" asked Uncle Dunkirk, as they slipped out of the woods and into the clearing. Willy C sat undisturbed on the far side of the clearing, glittering in the morning sun.

"They're here!" Ben whispered urgently, closing the telescope and slinging one of the backpacks over his shoulder. "We have to hide. Follow me!"

Together, Sage and Ben scampered from the safety of the banyan tree, and dashed into the nearest edge of woods. Once they had slipped into the safety of the forest, they hid behind the massive trunk of a tree, and peered around the edge.

"The telescope, Ben," said Sage, holding out his hand. Ben passed the telescope back, and Sage quickly raised it to his eye.

A moment later, Sage whispered excitedly, "I see him!" Uncle Dunkirk had just broken free from the trees, and was striding purposely across the clearing toward Willy C. "That's Uncle Dunkirk."

Ben watched the man named Uncle Dunkirk pass by in front of them, and then scanned the remainder of faces. "Jim Hawkins is here, too. And it looks like they're not alone."

Sage watched as a young boy, who was undoubtedly Jim Hawkins, walked into the clearing, holding a bucket. Another man, who was dressed much more fashionably than the pirates, kept pace at his side. *Probably one of the other prisoners.* Then he spied the two pirates from the previous day who had nearly captured him hiding in the bushes—Red and Hands—along with a few other nasty-looking sorts. Sage noted that Red looked a little worse for wear, but after that branch to the head, who could blame him? As for Hands, he seemed intent on watching the prisoners. He had his cutlass in hand, swinging with each step, while his other hand kept fingering something in his shirt.

What's he got there? wondered Sage, as he focused the telescope on Hands's hidden object. Then, as it brushed free of Hands's shirt, a gasp broke from Sage's mouth, and the words, "The amber stone!" hissed out.

CHAPTER 21

DR. LIVESEY AND Jim Hawkins both stopped in their tracks, mouths hanging agape, as their eyes settled on the Supermarine Spitfire. "Why, I'll be..." muttered Dr. Livesey, as Uncle Dunkirk grinned back at him.

Unable to restrain himself any longer, Uncle Dunkirk strode across the clearing, wanting to be the first to arrive, in case Sage had camped anywhere near Willy C. Thankfully, he noted, there was no smoldering fire pit, no bed of palm fronds, nor any sign at all of a makeshift camp. If Sage had spent the night anywhere near the clearing, he had done an excellent job of covering his tracks.

Uncle Dunkirk stepped up to Willy C's impressive four-bladed airscrew. Reaching out, he lovingly ran his hand down the propeller. The metal was warm to the touch from the morning sun, and Uncle Dunkirk's relief at being back at its side easily matched its radiance. He was back with his traveling companion.

After setting down his box of supplies, Uncle Dunkirk carefully followed the contours of Willy

C's body to the wing, searching the ground for the missing amber stone. Other than grass, scrub, and a few fallen coconuts, there was nothing.

Finally, Uncle Dunkirk stopped directly in front of the cannonball hole. He reached into the tattered hole and carefully probed the interior for any sign of serious damage. When he pulled his fingers free, they were clear of any trace of oil or fuel. Miraculously, the cannonball had missed the fuel line. *That's good*, thought Uncle Dunkirk.

"All right!" barked Hands, facing the prisoners. "We've got a job to do, and only a day to do it. If you need anything, you ask. If you need to go into the woods, you ask, and then you take an escort. If you fail to follow any of these rules, you die. It's as simple as that. Understood?"

As one, the prisoners nodded their acceptance. Then, interrupting Hands, Uncle Dunkirk took control and began issuing orders. "Mr. Hands is right. We have a lot to do in order to get this flying machine airborne, and the first thing we need to do is patch this hole. Dr. Livesey, I think you have a square of canvas in that pack of yours. I'll need you to trim a square patch that covers the hole, with an extra half a foot of material on all sides. Nothing shorter than that."

Dr. Livesey nodded, and quickly busied himself with his pack.

Uncle Dunkirk continued, "Jim, you're going

to be in charge of glue. I need you to mix up that glue until it has a smooth consistency about it. I want it to spread onto the wing as smooth as honey, with no chunks or bits in it. Understood?"

"Yes, sir," replied Jim with a grin. He, too, rushed to work, gathering the glue pot and a stick with which to mix it.

"As for you and your men," continued Uncle Dunkirk, addressing Hands, "I need to push the flying machine out from between these trees. Right now, the damaged wing is shaded from the sun, and I need to make the repairs in the light. If you don't mind lending a hand, I'll need some muscle along the wings."

Hands glared at Uncle Dunkirk as the prisoner ordered his men about, but then ceded to his request. "McGregor, keep an eye on the prisoners. The rest of you, lend a hand," he roared.

The remaining pirates followed Uncle Dunkirk around Willy C, and took note of the handholds he pointed out along each wing. Then Uncle Dunkirk climbed up onto the wing, leaned over the cockpit, and called, "Okay, push!"

The pirates dug their boots into the ground and put their backs into the wing. Muscles strained, and labored groans of exertion broke from their parched lips, but Willy C barely rocked forward.

"Hold on one second," ordered Uncle Dunkirk after a long moment, hiding a sly grin from the pirates. He casually leaned into the cockpit and released the safety brake. *I knew I forgot something.*

"All right," called Uncle Dunkirk, rallying the men for another attempt. "Let's put some muscle into it this time...and *push!*"

Once again, the pirates dug in and pushed with all their might. This time, without the safety brake, Willy C responded and rolled forward easily, and the men were able to cover the remaining ten feet in a matter of seconds.

"That's enough," called Uncle Dunkirk, once Willy C basked in the sunlight. "You can all take a break now."

The pirates all stepped away from the wings and relaxed. Uncle Dunkirk, in the meantime, locked the safety brake, and then gingerly stepped across the wing. As he dropped back to the ground, he found himself face-to-face with Red.

"The amber stone?" asked Ben, glancing over from his side of the tree.

"Oh, it's nothing," dismissed Sage, regaining his wits. "Just a possession of my uncle's." Although Sage's words were calm, his mind was reeling. *Hands has Uncle Dunkirk's amber stone!* No wonder Uncle Dunkirk hadn't flashed to safety yet. He was trapped. A prisoner like the others aboard the *Hispaniola*.

Knowing that he now had no option other than to rescue Uncle Dunkirk, Sage turned to Ben and asked, "Do you think we can intercept my uncle on his way back to the beach?"

Ben fingered the long whiskers hanging off his chin. "We could meet them along the trail easily enough," Ben finally replied. "But those pirates are armed, and I don't think we'd have much chance of waylaying them. Two against five ain't the best of odds, especially when the two are a young lad and a half-starved sailor."

Sage chewed over Ben's comments for a moment, but deep down he knew that Ben was right. Changing tactics, Sage pressed on, "Remember how you snuck up on me in the woods, Ben? You were like a ghost. I had no idea you were there. That's what we need to do. Is there any way you could get me close to Uncle Dunkirk without the guards knowing? I need my uncle to know that I'm okay, that I'm not alone, and that we're working on a plan to break them out."

Once again, Ben rubbed his bearded chin with his fingers. "I think I know just the spot. There's a bend in the trail where the bushes run thick alongside it. I can get you there easily enough, but I can't guarantee you success. It will all depend on where the guards position themselves on the trek back. If they walk loose, you'll have a chance. If they're too close, you'll risk being captured."

"I'm willing to take that chance," announced Sage. "I'm a bit of a gopher, Ben. I was always the last kid found in hide-and-seek because I could always squeeze myself into the tightest of spots. You'll have to trust me on this one. If you can get me close enough, I'll get a message to Uncle Dunkirk. If the coast isn't clear, I'll let him walk by, and we'll stick to our original plan."

Puzzled, Ben asked, "Which is?"

"Ah, yes," replied Sage. "The *original* plan." Taking one final glance at Uncle Dunkirk and the others working across the clearing, Sage tuned back to the two overflowing backpacks and began digging inside. "Let me fill you in."

"Oh, hello, Red," greeted Uncle Dunkirk timidly as Red stepped forward, pressing Uncle Dunkirk back against the fuselage. The giant simply glared back at Uncle Dunkirk, his black eyes boring deep into those of the prisoner.

"While we have this moment alone," stated Uncle Dunkirk calmly, "I'd like to offer you my most sincere apology for the club over the head and the foot to the groin. I was simply protecting myself, and would have done the same to anyone on the ship. I do apologize wholeheartedly for my actions, and I hope you realize that it was nothing personal."

Red continued to glare at Uncle Dunkirk, but for a brief second, a look of surprise seemed to cross the giant's face, then quickly disappear.

"I see Red has grown quite fond of you, Mr. Smiley," said Hands sarcastically.

Uncle Dunkirk glanced over to see Hands watching from the opposite side of the wing. "Yes, he seems to have a vested interest in my well-being," replied Uncle Dunkirk, glancing back at the giant.

"Well, don't let him intimidate you too much," offered Hands amiably. "If anyone has a vested interest in your well-being, it's the cap'n."

"*Ha!*" laughed Uncle Dunkirk. "I have no doubt that Captain Silver has my welfare in mind. That is, of course, until the flying machine is fixed."

"You do have a point there," agreed Hands. "The cap'n has been known to change his mind often." Then, glancing around to make sure no one was watching, Hands lowered his voice. "But sometimes one doesn't need to look too far to find an ally."

Uncle Dunkirk perked up, completely caught off guard by Hands's unexpected comment. He slipped away from Red and scampered to the other side of the wing. When he popped back up to face Hands directly, what he saw nearly drained the color from his face. From a leather band around Hands's neck dangled the amber stone.

Uncle Dunkirk hid his shock, and pressed on. "What *exactly* are you saying, Mr. Hands?"

"All I'm saying," replied Hands quietly, "is that there might be a way for you to slip the hangman's noose. Fix the flying machine, and we'll talk some more. But keep this in mind, Mr. Smiley—if one word of our conversation reaches any of the crew, you'll be taking a very short journey off the plank. And if that happens, your only hope of survival will be the speed with which you can swim."

Ben watched curiously as Sage burrowed deeper into one of the backpacks, yanking the occasional obstacle out and setting it aside. Finally, Sage pulled out two small canvas bags, which he held up proudly.

"*Voilà!* Our toiletry bags."

"Toiletry bags?" asked Ben curiously.

"Yes, toiletry bags," replied Sage. "Little bags full of everything you need in the bathroom." He unzipped Uncle Dunkirk's kit, and displayed its contents to Ben. "You see, there's a toothbrush, toothpaste, deodorant, shampoo, scissors, nail clippers, cologne...."

Sage's voice trailed off as a pair of items inside the kit caught his eye. He grinned as he looked up at Ben's curious face. "And another little something for you, Ben. A razor and shaving cream."

At the mention of shaving, a light behind Ben's eyes flicked on. Sage watched as Ben took the metal razor and turned it over in his hands, trying to decide how it worked. Finally, realizing that razors probably didn't look like this in Ben's time, Sage offered, "Just leave it for now. It's a newfangled model from the colonies. I'll help you figure it out in a minute."

Then, grabbing his own toiletry bag, Sage unzipped the top and announced, "More importantly, we have the one item we need to get aboard the *Hispaniola* tonight." He pulled out the small yellow box of *Kids' Cough*.

CHAPTER 22

BACK IN THE clearing, Uncle Dunkirk sifted through the possibilities of Hands's comments. He didn't trust Hands any more than he trusted Silver, and he knew without a doubt that Red would gladly snap his neck. However, Hands had Uncle Dunkirk's amber stone hanging round his neck, and it was imperative that the necklace be retrieved. If not, he and Sage could be stuck on Treasure Island forever.

The repairs to Willy C kept everyone busy throughout the remainder of the morning, and into the afternoon. Dr. Livesey had carefully trimmed a perfect square of canvas, which Uncle Dunkirk had pasted to the wing. Then, while the glue was drying under the hot sun, they frayed a few thick strands of rope so that a few thinner strings of twine could be pulled free. They then lashed the twine around the wing as a precaution, in case the canvas was blown loose mid flight.

The remainder of the afternoon had been spent covering the canvas and parts of the wing in coat after coat of glue, in an attempt to harden the canvas to a consistency solid enough to serve as a patch. As the sun finally fell toward the ocean, Hands rose from his relaxed position sitting against a tree, and wandered over to Uncle Dunkirk. "It's nearly time for us to return to the ship. Have the repairs taken?"

Uncle Dunkirk prodded the canvas with his index finger, and found that the glue had hardened. He tapped it a few more times, testing its strength and the give in the wing. Each time, the canvas held strong.

"It appears fixed," replied Uncle Dunkirk with a sigh. It had been a long day, and the sun had drained much of his strength. "Of course, I won't know for sure until I get up into the air, but the patch seems to have a fair amount of strength."

"Good," said Hands cheerily. "The cap'n will be pleased." Then, under his breath, the coxswain added, "Unfortunately for you, my friend, that means your time aboard the *Hispaniola* is surely nearing an end."

"I wouldn't be so certain of that," replied Uncle Dunkirk. "After all, the wing might be fixed, but the flying machine still needs a pilot, and I'm the only one who knows how to fly it."

"Well, that may be the case," continued Hands. "But the cap'n is a selfish man. Once he learns the magic behind flying, I wouldn't be surprised at all to find you out on the plank."

Hands was pressing for a deal, so Uncle

Dunkirk decided to find out what cards the coxswain held—and what he was willing to ante up in return. Keeping his voice low, Uncle Dunkirk asked, "You said earlier that we'd talk once the flying machine was repaired. What is it, exactly, that you want to talk about?"

Hands peered about cautiously, making sure no one was within earshot. "A partnership, Mr. Smiley, plain and simple. You, me, and Red."

Exasperated, Uncle Dunkirk spat back, "You know as well as I do, Mr. Hands, that Red would break every bone in my body in the blink of an eye. Why should I trust him? And why should I trust you?"

"Because you don't have a choice," replied Hands bluntly. "Face it, Mr. Smiley, your days are numbered with Cap'n Silver. The second he knows how to pilot the flying machine, he'll feed you to the sharks."

"Ah, yes," Uncle Dunkirk groaned sarcastically. "The infamous nick o' time."

Hands's ears perked up at the mention of the sadistic pirate torture. "You've heard of the nick o' time?"

"Oh, yes, Captain Silver introduced me. It sounds quite barbaric."

"Oh, it is," agreed Hands. "It's one of the most disturbing things I've ever seen. And believe me, Mr. Smiley, I've seen some horrors in my lifetime.

The nick o' time ain't for the faint of heart. And in all my years at sea, I've only seen one man survive."

"You mean someone actually lived through it?" asked an incredulous Uncle Dunkirk.

"Yes," replied Hands casually. "And he's standing right over there." Hands motioned toward Red, who was leaning against a tree, keeping a watchful eye on Jim Hawkins and Dr. Livesey.

Then the realization hit Uncle Dunkirk like a lightning bolt from above—*the tribal tattoos.* "Those aren't tattoos on his back?"

"They're nicks," confirmed Hands. "They've just been colored over with black ink. I did it myself the night they pulled Red from the water. I colored every last nick on his back."

"But why?"

"I did it to help Red hide the shame. He's an ox, all right, and a little daft at times, but he survived. He made it out of the water *alive.* And no matter what his crime was, he earned the right to walk like a man, and not be shamed by the marks on his back."

Uncle Dunkirk looked across the clearing at Red and saw him in a new light. There was no doubt in Uncle Dunkirk's mind that the giant was tough—*just look at the size of him*—but surviving the nick o' time? That was unheard of. "Why was he only nicked on the back?" asked Uncle Dunkirk.

"That was a sign of respect from the cap'n.

You see, Red did wrong, there's no doubt about it, and maybe he even deserved to be lashed to the back of the boat. But Red had already proven himself as a fighter aboard the *Hispaniola*, and he'd stood beside the cap'n through thick and thin. Cap'n nicked only his back out of respect for Red's past deeds."

"You'd think he'd be a little nervous having Red on board after condemning him to the nick o' time," mused Uncle Dunkirk.

"Left to his own devices, the cap'n probably would have left Red to drown. But Silver would have lost the respect of his men. You should have seen the men, Mr. Smiley, hooting and hollering at the top of their lungs like kids, while Red grappled with that shark. And when Red went under, the ship went as quiet as a church. Not a peep from anyone. Everyone just stared at the water, waiting for a sign—blood, bubbles, anything. And then Red surfaced, *alive*. He served his penance in the water. All sins have been forgotten."

"But not in Red's mind?" asked Uncle Dunkirk, slowly piecing the puzzle together.

"Would you forget?" asked Hands. "Could you *ever* forget? No, Red has his demons. He might truly dislike you, Mr. Smiley, but if you put it into perspective, a boot to the groin and a knock on the head ain't much when compared to what the cap'n did."

Uncle Dunkirk pondered for a moment or two, and then he cast a line. "So what is this partnership that you mentioned?"

"Why, it's simple," replied Hands. "You teach me the magic to pilot the flying machine, and in return you get your life. A fair bargain, if I ever did hear one."

"Why don't you just take it now?" asked Uncle Dunkirk, thinking out loud. "I'm sure you and Red could easily overpower the other guards. The wing's fixed, and we're a long way from the ship. What's stopping you?"

"Unfortunately, time is stopping me today," replied Mr. Hands matter-of-factly. "The cap'n wants us all back on board by six bells. If we don't return by then, he'll send another landing party ashore, and I'll be the one raked over the coals. No, I think patience is the key. Red and I can wait another day. Tomorrow, you'll teach us the magic, and by tomorrow night you'll be a free man."

Uncle Dunkirk stared at Hands. He knew that Hands's words were nothing more than hot air. However, Uncle Dunkirk still held a few aces, and he felt it was time to give the coxswain a peek at his cards. "I'll go along with you, under one condition. If you want to learn to pilot the flying machine, you'll have to give me a little more than just my life."

Hands squinted suspiciously. "And what

might that be?"

Uncle Dunkirk pointed to Hands's chest. "The stone you wear around your neck. It's mine. I must have dropped it when your men jumped me. It's not worth much, but it has personal value. It was given to me by an old friend, and I want it back. If you give me the stone, I will teach you how to fly. And trust me, Mr. Hands, when I'm done with you, you'll be able to soar through the sky like a bird."

Hands thought about the proposition for a minute. "You have a deal," agreed Hands confidently. "Tomorrow, you teach me the magic, and I give you the stone."

"And my life," added Uncle Dunkirk.

"Agreed," replied Hands, with a smirk. The coxswain spat into his palm and held an open hand to Uncle Dunkirk. Uncle Dunkirk played along, and spat into his own palm before shaking hands with the devil.

CHAPTER 23

LATER THAT AFTERNOON, as Sage and Ben watched from their hiding spot in the woods, Sage noted that the prisoners were preparing to leave the clearing. "Ben, it's time. They're leaving."

Ben looked up in a daze from the ground. His back was against the trunk of the tree, and the small pocket mirror from Uncle Dunkirk's pack was clenched in his hand. At his side, the razor and shaving cream sat discarded, and a pile of white hair lay at his feet.

"Whoa!" Sage exclaimed, at the sight of Ben's clean-shaven face. Under that long mat of white hair, Ben possessed a handsome face. He had a strong chin and a friendly smile to go along with his twinkling blue eyes. His slightly beaked nose twitched and crinkled sporadically, as if searching for the companion that had hung for so many years below it. "You look so young!"

Ben smiled at Sage, and then continued to gaze at himself in the mirror from numerous angles. "You know, in all these years, I'd forgotten what I looked like," he said forlornly. Then, rubbing his hand across his face, he said, "It feels good to lose those long whiskers. Trust me, Sage, never grow a beard. They're nothing but trouble."

Sage grinned at the new Ben Gunn before him. He had seen a big change in the marooned sailor over the past two days. It was amazing what a little companionship, along with a fresh pair of clothes and a razor, could do for one's morale. Sage's final wish for his new friend was to get him off Treasure Island and back to civilization, and he hoped that he could somehow make that wish come true.

"I hate to ruin the moment, Ben, but the caravan's almost ready to move out."

Ben jumped to his feet, placing the mirror carefully into the toiletry bag, and then stuffing the kit into the backpack. "Let's go then. We'll have to move fast, so try to keep up with me."

Ben and Sage sneaked a peek around the tree, and watched as the men slipped into the woods on their way back to the *Hispaniola*. When all seemed clear, Ben led Sage deeper into the trees. The woods quickly closed in around them, blocking out the light and heat from the sun, and reintroducing them to Treasure Island's other world—a shaded kingdom of brilliant flowers, lush trees, and exotic plants.

Sage nipped at Ben's heels as the man raced through the woods, springing over fallen logs and dashing between the towering trunks of trees.

There was an excited twinkle in Ben's eye and a spring in his step as his new hiking boots trod effortlessly over the soft earth.

Finally, Ben slowed to a stop, and motioned for Sage to stay quiet. Holding his head high, Ben began to pivot from side to side as he listened to the otherworldly sounds of the forest. Sage followed suit, lending his ears to the search. Between the playful birdsong and the windblown rustle of leaves, the distinctive sound of boots tromping carelessly through the woods floated on the air.

"They're almost here," whispered Ben. Then, pointing to a large tropical bush directly in front of them, Ben instructed, "They'll pass on the other side of this bush. Get on the ground, and crawl in nice and tight along the base. Then pull a few branches down to conceal yourself. That should put you right next to your Uncle when he walks by." Then, with some feeling, Ben added, "But be careful, Sage. If they hear you ...."

Ben left the thought unsaid as Sage gave the man a reassuring pat on the back. Then, dropping to his chest, Sage crawled forward until he was completely sheltered under the bush's thick canopy of leaves and branches. Then, he gently leaned on a few of the larger fronds, careful not to break them, and bent them downward until he was completely hidden from view.

Once ready, Sage glanced back over his shoulder, but Ben had already vanished. Even wearing Uncle Dunkirk's blinding Hawaiian shirt, Ben was like a chameleon, effortlessly fading into the scenery around him. Sage turned his head back toward the trail, and almost yelped in surprise as a pair of black leather boots stomped into the ground barely inches from his face.

"Move along, now," barked the gravelly voice attached to the boots. "The sun's dropping."

Only after the boots moved on did Sage exhale, as his heart jackhammered against his ribs. He then quietly pressed his cheek against the ground, peering cautiously down the trail.

From this new vantage point, Sage could clearly see legs slogging around a bend in the path. It appeared, from first glance, as if a slight separation had grown between the prisoners and the pirates during the hike—nothing much, just a few additional yards between each person. And other than a few gruff verbal prods to "move along" or "keep going," there was no other conversation.

While he waited, Sage counted the pairs of legs that he saw, trying to keep a running tab of both pirates and prisoners. So far, two pirates had ambled past, and a third was just rounding the corner.

A moment later, Sage perked up as the unmistakable legs of Uncle Dunkirk, clad in khaki pants and wearing sturdy hiking boots, moved into sight. Sage quickly determined that there was a gap of about fifteen feet between Uncle Dunkirk and the next man in line. It was going to be tight, but Sage was determined to make it work.

As Uncle Dunkirk slowly advanced upon Sage's hiding spot, Sage whispered the two words that he knew would instantly catch his relative's ear: *"Uncle Duncle."*

On the trail, there was an immediate reaction. Uncle Dunkirk stopped dead in his tracks. He glanced about, trying to spot Sage. Then Sage tapped the top of his boots twice, and wagged him down with his finger. Uncle Dunkirk bent down on one knee and feigned tying his laces.

By now, the next man in line had sidled up to Uncle Dunkirk. "Everything all right, Dunkirk?" asked a friendly voice, between pants.

"Fine, just fine," replied Uncle Dunkirk offhandedly. "Just need to tie my shoe."

With a friendly clap on Uncle Dunkirk's shoulder, the man passed on the right and continued on down the trail.

While this exchange was taking place, Sage glanced back up the trail, and noted that Jim Hawkins was next in line. Of all the prisoners and pirates, Jim was the easiest to spot, as his legs were much shorter than those of the others.

"Uncle Dunkirk, we're coming to save you

tonight," whispered Sage hastily.

"Are you with Ben Gunn?" asked Uncle Dunkirk softly, tugging on his shoelace.

"Yes," Sage replied. "We're coming aboard tonight. Be ready."

Just then, Jim Hawkins passed by Uncle Dunkirk. "I can slow down if you'd like, Mr. Smiley."

Uncle Dunkirk smiled up at the lad, and replied, "No, that's fine, Jim. Just fixing my shoe. I think Dr. Livesey could use a little company, though."

Once Jim was out of earshot, Uncle Dunkirk quickly picked up the conversation. "Sage, listen. Don't come tonight. I need one more night to work on a few loose ends. Come tomorrow night. Understand?"

Sage was caught by surprise, but knew that Uncle Dunkirk would have his reasons for wanting to delay the rescue attempt. "Okay," replied Sage. "Tomorrow."

"Also, prepare the fort," added Uncle Dunkirk, glancing quickly over his shoulder. Hands had just slipped around the corner, and Red was following close on his heels. "Make sure it's ready for anything. I'll explain everything later. Be careful."

"I will," replied Sage. Then, before it was too late, he added, "Hands has the amber stone."

"I know. I'm working on that." With that, Uncle Dunkirk lifted himself off his knee and continued down the trail. Sage lay perfectly still, until the last two sets of legs continued on past the bush and were soon out of sight.

CHAPTER 24

LATER THAT NIGHT, in the makeshift brig, Uncle Dunkirk and the other prisoners discussed the day's developments— including the discovery of Uncle Dunkirk's "amazing flying machine." While Captain Smollett and Squire Trelawney both seemed momentarily suspicious of this strange twist in Uncle Dunkirk's tale, Dr. Livesey and Jim Hawkins both spoke freely, and stood by Uncle Dunkirk. Finally, when the drama had died down, and everyone reached the same conclusion as before—*we're all prisoners*—Uncle Dunkirk was able to report on the progress of the day. "The flying machine is fixed, or as good as it ever will be on this island. Dr. Livesey and Jim did a great job of helping to repair the wing, but I really won't know how strong the patch is until I'm airborne."

"Now that the flying machine's fixed, what do you think Silver will do?" asked Jim Hawkins, from his perch on the edge of one of the bunks.

"I should think that's a fairly simple answer," replied Captain Smollett. "Silver will use the flying machine for his own wicked purposes. With a machine that can soar hundreds of feet in the air..."

"Actually," interrupted Uncle Dunkirk, "it can fly thousands of feet in the air."

Captain Smollett looked up with shock—this sort of technology was still far in the future—but he quickly regained his formal bearing, and continued, "With a machine that can fly *thousands* of feet in the air, Silver could easily rule the high seas. Instead of sailing the main shipping channels in hopes of crossing paths with a schooner, Silver could actually soar high above the ocean and spot his victims miles away. The oceans we sail will be his private domain."

"Can we stop him?" asked Dr. Livesey.

"Without another flying machine, it will be next to impossible to stop Silver," ventured Uncle Dunkirk. "The shot I took through the wing was pure luck. A thousand-to-one chance. If I'd spotted the *Hispaniola* in the lagoon, I would have had no trouble dodging its guns."

"So we have to stop him," Jim Hawkins stated bravely.

"Precisely, Jim," agreed Uncle Dunkirk. "It's up to us to stop Silver before it's too late."

"And how do you propose we do that?" asked Squire Trelawney. "Now that the flying machine is repaired, we must consider that our time as prisoners is nearly done. How can we stop Silver, when he holds all the cards?"

Uncle Dunkirk looked over his shoulder at the

locked cabin door, and then motioned the men to gather in close. Once they were huddled up, Uncle Dunkirk lowered his voice and explained his plan. "Silver may hold most of the cards, but we still have a few aces up our sleeve. While we were hiking back to the ship, I made contact with my nephew."

There was a murmur of surprise from the group, and Dr. Livesey and Jim both shared an astonished look. "And how did you do that?" asked Dr. Livesey. "There were eyes on us all day."

"It was on the trail, during the hike back to the ship," explained Uncle Dunkirk. "I heard my nephew whisper my name, so I stopped, and acted as if I were tying my shoe. Sage was hiding below the leaves of the bush in front of me."

Dr. Livesey shook his head in amazement. "What a clever young man."

Uncle Dunkirk continued, "Sage is with Ben Gunn, and you'll be glad to know that they're both safe. I've asked them to prepare the fort on the island. They'll make sure that it is secure and well stocked. Then, tomorrow night, they're going to sneak aboard the *Hispaniola* in the dead of night and free us. If all goes well, we'll be off this ship in just over a day's time."

"What makes you think that we still have a day?" whispered Squire Trelawney breathlessly. "With the flying machine repaired, we could all be walking the plank at the crack of dawn."

"An excellent question, with an easy answer," grinned Uncle Dunkirk. "Silver *wants* the flying machine. You can see the hunger in his eyes. He's asked to try out the plane once it is fixed. We're going tomorrow, and I'm going to give him a ride he won't forget. I guarantee you, gentlemen, that when we land, Silver will be convinced that the flying machine is in need of some serious repair. That should buy us a little time. After all, we only need one more day."

"And once we're in the fort, what then?" asked Captain Smollett, his military mind breaking down the plan into its smallest details. "Silver's men have muskets, pistols, and cutlasses. We're all of seven men, and we're severely outmanned. Silver could row a cannon ashore and blow the fort to pieces. What are we supposed to fight back with? Sticks and stones?"

"I don't think you'll have to worry about Silver or his men," replied Uncle Dunkirk. "Once we are free of the *Hispaniola*, you'll all be safe within the fort. At worst, you might have to defend the fort for an hour or two. But that shouldn't prove too difficult a task. Silver won't have enough time to mount a well-planned assault in only a few hours. And even then, I don't think his military skills can match those of your own, Captain Smollett."

Captain Smollett nodded appreciatively at the

compliment. "But you must agree that we can't keep Silver at bay for long?"

"Without proper weapons, I would agree," replied Uncle Dunkirk. "But Silver will have his hands full protecting the *Hispaniola*."

"From what?" asked a puzzled Captain Smollett.

"From me," answered Uncle Dunkirk with determination, "and Willy C."

CHAPTER 25

THE NEXT MORNING, a lengthy caravan of men snaked its way through the woods of Treasure Island, with Long John Silver slithering in the lead. It was a glorious day—the sun was shining brightly, and there was hardly a hint of a breeze. And for the day's special occasion, Silver wore a spectacular long, purple coat, with intricate gold stitching and shiny brass buttons. To further commemorate the day's importance, the pirate had taken a razor to his face, leaving his cheeks glowing fresh and pink, but he hadn't bothered to extend his efforts with the soap, passing completely on a bath.

He looked like a man without a care in the world as he strode forward to meet his destiny. Today, he, John Silver, would take possession of the most unique weapon in the world—a one-of-a-kind flying machine. And tomorrow, he would start his reign as the most-feared man on the high seas. Silver beamed as he imagined his name alongside the legendary pirates Henry Morgan, Edward Teach, Jean Laffite, and William Kidd. Soon enough, people across the modern world would tell the tale of the dreaded buccaneer of the skies, Captain Long John Silver.

As the caravan finally wound its way out of the forest and into the clearing, Silver caught his first glimpse of the flying machine, which Dunkirk had told him was named Willy C, and his rank breath caught in his throat. "Hello, my treasure!" he purred to himself.

Willy C sat ten feet out from the trees, basking like a cat in the morning sun.

Silver stared in awe at this sleek flying machine before him. Its lines were smooth and aerodynamic, almost like a hand-hewn blade. Willy C was a dazzling gem, and Silver was completely enraptured. He saw himself in command, soaring high above the clouds, and lording over his new kingdom as Master of the Skies.

With these visions dancing through his head, Silver hurried across the clearing as fast as his pegged leg would carry him, until he stood directly in front of Willy C. Then, reaching out with reverence, he gently ran his palm along the plane, feeling the warmth of the sun through his fingertips. As Silver basked in the excitement of his new toy, the remainder of the caravan gradually wound its way into the clearing, and formed a half circle, waiting expectantly in front of the plane.

Silver waited patiently for the murmurs of the

astounded sailors, many of whom were also seeing the flying machine up close for the first time, to stop. Then, having carefully practiced some words in his cabin through the wee hours of the morning, Silver spun dramatically on his heel and bellowed his speech. "Today, gentlemen, you will all be witness to history in the making. You should feel privileged to be here, for this is a moment that will be spoken of for ages. Your children's children will talk about the day that the noble field of pirating took a grand step from the ocean into the skies."

Silver used his flare for the dramatic to full effect, raising his hand grandly and pointing to the heavens to punctuate his words. As he paused, however, he was met with only his crew's uncomfortable silence. Although his crooked smile was still plastered to his face, his eyes darted about nervously. Sensing that the Captain was waiting for some sort of recognition, Hands tentatively clapped. When Silver's eyes glinted appreciatively, the rest of the men quickly clued in and followed suit, applauding this historic moment and the Captain's words.

After soaking up the applause for a moment, Silver held his hands up to silence the crew, and then continued. "What I am about to do today is not for the weak of heart. It is a task that requires a true man to take the lead. A man who is not afraid to soar like an eagle, and take possession of the world's next great frontier—the skies above. Today, I, Long John Silver, will lead the charge into the future, and into history!"

Once again, scattered applause echoed throughout the clearing, and Silver was pleased to note that it came without prompting. His twisted smile held perfectly still for a three count, and then he discarded it from his face. He turned on his heel and strode to Willy C's wing, while the men cheered.

But as Silver moved toward the wing, reality seeped into his sun-baked brain, and a hairline crack appeared in his plan. Although he had stayed awake most of the night planning his historic speech, Silver had forgotten one key element: what to do next.

As his crew waited for him to take command of the skies, he realized that he was in a bit of a pickle. He had never been in a flying machine, or even seen one before today. And, of course, the concept of piloting a flying machine was completely lost on him. With a bitter sense of dread seeping into what should have been his finest moment, Silver was desperate to remain calm and in control before his men. As nonchalantly as possible, he turned back to the crowd, and called, "Mr. Smiley!"

In front of the plane, heads turned this way and that as the crew searched for the prisoner.

Moments later, Uncle Dunkirk slipped through the throng, and joined Silver at the wing. "You called, Captain Silver?"

Silver plastered the fake grin to his face for the benefit of his crew, and then he dropped his voice so that only Uncle Dunkirk could hear him. "This is your infernal machine, Smiley," snarled Silver. "How does it work?"

A broad grin threatened to curl across Uncle Dunkirk's lips, but was quickly suppressed. "As I've told you before, Captain Silver, a flying machine is very intricate. It requires months of schooling on land, followed by months of training in the air, for one to become a pilot."

Silver brushed aside Uncle Dunkirk's remarks. "I was never one for schooling or books, Mr. Smiley. But in all my years of plying the seas, I have piloted many a ship through the worst conditions imaginable. I've ridden out the harshest storms and the deadliest typhoons, and I've weaved ships through coral banks so deadly that their teeth could rip a ship's keel to shreds in a matter of seconds." Then, glancing up at the sky above Willy C, he added, "I'm sure I won't have a problem piloting a vehicle through the open skies. After all, what could I possibly hit? A bird?"

"Captain Silver, you are right about the open sky. There's not a lot to hit up there. However, there are two major obstacles to take into account—getting off the ground, and then landing back in this clearing."

"How difficult can it be?" snapped Silver. "Up is up, and down is down."

"Well, let me put it like this," retorted Uncle Dunkirk firmly, "if you try to fly by yourself today, I guarantee you will not be alive tomorrow."

Hearing this, a flash of psychotic anger glimmered behind Silver's black eyes, but Uncle Dunkirk quickly pressed on. "Please, hear me out. I'm not threatening you. I'm just trying to explain it as simply as possible. You see, in order to get off the ground, a flying machine requires massive amounts of fuel. In the colonies, we use something called 'gasoline.' It's very much like the kerosene in your lanterns, and sitting in the flying machine is like sitting on a moving powder keg. So if you were to crash into those trees while landing, the flying machine, and *you*, would explode in a blast one hundred times worse than a direct hit from the *Hispaniola*'s largest cannon."

Silver's anger subsided slightly as Uncle Dunkirk's explanation gradually settled in. Uncle Dunkirk quickly pressed on. "If, by some stroke of luck, you managed to get off the ground, without training you would *never* be able to land in this clearing. If you were to try, you'd either plummet into the ocean or crash on the island. Either way, your historic moment is over. And so is your life."

Silver considered Uncle Dunkirk's words. He had brought his crew to the clearing to witness his historic moment in the limelight, but he hadn't figured that piloting a flying machine would be so difficult. Then, a seed of suspicion sprouted in his mind. *What if Smiley is lying?* It was definitely an option worth considering. After all, any delay in Silver's historic moment meant another reprieve for the prisoners.

"If you are playing me for a fool, Mr. Smiley," snarled Silver, "you are treading water in a whirlpool. Sooner or later, you'll go down."

Uncle Dunkirk held his hands up. "Please, Captain, I'm telling you the truth, and I can prove it. Just take a look inside the cockpit. That's where the pilot sits. One look, and you will see that I am not playing you for a fool."

Silver agreed with a tentative nod of his head. Wasting no time, Uncle Dunkirk led the pirate around the right wing, and instructed him on how to climb up. Once both men were standing on Willy C's wing, Uncle Dunkirk slid open the canopy and stepped aside.

Silver leaned forward warily and peered into the cockpit of the flying machine. Before him, a vast array of dials, meters, buttons, and toggle switches were imbedded in the forward control panel. A stick with a handle stuck up out of the ground, and two shiny pedals also sat on the ground, waiting to be depressed. It was unlike any bridge he'd ever seen before, and Silver realized without a doubt that Smiley was right. Piloting a flying machine was not a simple matter.

However, Silver was determined that his moment in the sun would not be diminished. He had promised his crew a historic occasion, and he would deliver. "I see that there are two seats in this flying machine," remarked Silver casually. "So it is possible for two people to fly."

"Yes, there is a rear seat for a passenger," confirmed Uncle Dunkirk. Then, he added, "It's just an idea, Captain, but if you'd like, I can pilot the flying machine, and give you a demonstration of its abilities in the air."

It was a brilliant suggestion, and the only way for Silver to save face in front of his crew. Hiding his enthusiasm for the idea, Silver mumbled nonchalantly, "I guess that might work." Then, turning back to the crew, he bellowed grandly, "From the ocean to the skies! History in the making, gentlemen!"

Once again, there was a smattering of applause from the men standing around the plane. Uncle Dunkirk clambered over the side of Willy C and into the front cockpit. Then he turned to direct Silver into the rear compartment. Once safely in, the pirate stood proudly on his seat, and pumped his arms into the air, continuing to play the conquering hero.

Bursting his bubble, Uncle Dunkirk said, "You might want to tell them to get out of the way."

"What?" hissed Silver through clenched teeth, his brightest smile still frozen on his face.

"Your men," replied Uncle Dunkirk brusquely. "They're in the way. Tell them to get out of the way or they'll be mowed down."

"Oh," muttered Silver. Then he barked at the crew as if he were manning the *Hispaniola*'s bridge through a tempest. "Get out of our path! History is about to pass by!"

While the crew shuffled out of the way, Uncle Dunkirk ran through a battery of pre-flight checks. Willy C appeared ready to take off, but the damaged wing was still untested. Then, glancing over his shoulder, Uncle Dunkirk called out, "You might want to strap on the seatbelt, Captain Silver. It's that black buckle on both sides of your seat. It works just like a belt. Slip the thin side into the slot of the larger side, and then push the ends together until you hear a click."

Staring at the two buckles of the seatbelt as if they were a pair of magician's rings, Silver banged the ends together noisily, before noticing the slot on one side. Then, following Uncle Dunkirk's instructions, he slid the thin side into the slot and pushed. An audible *click* greeted him.

"Now, don't be surprised by the noise,"

warned Uncle Dunkirk. "A flying machine can get pretty loud." With that, Uncle Dunkirk powered up Willy C and sparked the ignition. The plane instantly belched a cloud of black exhaust, and then sputtered to life.

In the clearing, there was an immediate reaction. With the first loud backfire, crew members from the *Hispaniola* scattered as if war had been declared. They dodged for the safety of the woods, covering their heads and diving for cover. A few of the braver men went so far as to unsheathe their cutlasses and stand their ground, waiting for the mysterious attacker to fire once more.

In the rear cockpit, Silver's fists were clenched nervously, and his palms were greased with perspiration. The plane was vibrating wildly, and the roar of the engines was like nothing he'd heard before. It was the shrill shriek of a banshee, the chilling cry of the devil, and the thrilling rumble of pure power all wrapped into one unmistakable blast, and Silver almost felt at home. With an evil grin now draped across his face, Silver realized how enemies would cower at the sound of the powerful flying machine.

"From the oceans to the skies!" called Uncle Dunkirk as he released the parking brake, and Willy C started to roll across the clearing.

Chapter 26

SAGE NEARLY JUMPED out of his skin as Willy C's engine turned over in the distance, its reverberation shattering the peaceful serenity of Treasure Island. The morning had been long and hard as he and Ben worked furiously to prepare the fort to withstand a siege from Silver's men.

They'd begun the day by gathering as much food and firewood as possible, since they did not know how long they would be cooped up within the walls of the fort. To arm and protect themselves, they had sifted through Flint's treasure and collected three jeweled daggers. Then they scoured the woods and gathered as many long branches as possible. They whittled down the ends of the branches to points, providing themselves with a fair supply of handmade spears. But their chores took a backseat once Willy C's engine interrupted their task, and sent a nervous rush surging through the both of them. Glancing anxiously at Ben, Sage asked, "Do you think Uncle Dunkirk managed to escape?"

Ben searched the sky, trying to locate the source of the foreign noise. "I'm sure he wouldn't leave you on the island," Ben answered reassuringly.

Sage shaded his eyes from the bright sun and peered across the island. He could pinpoint the general direction of the clearing, but a thick wall of trees blocked his view of the inner island. Even so, Sage continued to stare anxiously over the treetops, hoping to catch a brief glimpse of Willy C.

A moment later, the pitch of Willy C's engine rose from a loud, steady purr into the super-charged growl of takeoff. "They're coming," announced Sage. He knew that the sudden change in pitch meant that Uncle Dunkirk was probably accelerating for flight.

Ben quickly sidled up to Sage, and stared after the boy's pointing finger. Suddenly, their patience was rewarded as Willy C blazed over them like a shooting star, sending a loud *whoosh* of air cascading over the fort. Sage and Ben both spun to follow the plane's bullet-like trajectory, and Sage managed to catch a quick glimpse of Uncle Dunkirk sitting in the pilot's seat. Then a feeling of dread crept over him as he noticed that Uncle Dunkirk wasn't alone—someone was sitting in the rear cockpit.

"Did you see them?" blurted Sage. "Uncle Dunkirk was in the front, but I don't know who was in the back."

"I saw them," replied Ben, "And I wouldn't worry about your uncle escaping. That wasn't a prisoner in the back. That was Long John Silver."

Sage stared after Willy C as it rocketed past the island's coral reef and started to climb high over the ocean. The plane was flying on an even keel, the wingtips steady, as it headed farther and farther out to sea. Then, just as Willy C began to fade into a speck on the horizon, the plane began a gentle turn to the right, and it circled back toward Treasure Island.

"Uncle Dunkirk must be giving Silver a demonstration," Sage said. Oddly, Sage felt a little better knowing that Long John Silver, rather than one of the other prisoners, was riding in the backseat of the plane. Although Silver was the enemy, his presence in Willy C was confirmation that Uncle Dunkirk hadn't deserted his nephew on the island. But a worm of anxiety continued to tunnel into Sage's gut. The day was young, and who knew what surprises it still held.

"Come on, Ben," Sage called out, tearing his eyes from the sky. "We have another load to haul down from the cave, and a lot of work to do before night falls. Let's stay in the shadows, though. We don't want to be seen."

CHAPTER 27

LONG JOHN SILVER gawked out the canopy window as Willy C roared across the clearing. The gentle bumping he had felt when the flying machine first started to move forward had been replaced by a teeth-jarring shudder that shook him down to his soul. He clenched his fists uneasily, and watched as the grinning faces of his crew rolled past the window. The trees surrounding the clearing blurred into a solid wall of green. Even under full sail, with a howling wind at his back, Silver had never traveled at this rate of speed, and he hated being at the mercy of another helmsman.

Suddenly, the vibrations that rocked the plane stopped as the flying machine lifted into the air. Excitement tingled throughout his entire body as he watched the ground fall away, and the plane rise higher.

Glancing to the front, Silver's eyes suddenly bugged in horror. The wall of trees that marked the far end of the clearing approached rapidly, and Uncle Dunkirk's chilling words came back to haunt Silver—*it's like sitting on a moving powder keg*. Shielding his face with his arms to screen the rapidly approaching terror, Silver cried out, "Higher, man, higher!"

At the front of the plane, Uncle Dunkirk pulled back lightly on the stick, and rocketed Willy C over the treetops at the clearing's edge, sending a blast of leaves skyward. The plane continued to climb, soaring higher over Treasure Island, and whizzing past Mizzen-mast Hill, Ben Gunn's fort, and finally over the lagoon to the ocean.

As Willy C soared over the choppy waters of the ocean, Silver's fright gradually began to subside. He was still alive. There had been no fiery crash, no explosion—there was only the constant thrum of the flying machine beneath him.

Slowly lowering his arms, Silver peered tentatively out the window. As his eyes took in the scenery below, he was overcome by a feeling of awe. The flying machine was soaring over crystal blue waters, and the vista was breathtaking.

From this altitude, Silver could clearly see Treasure Island's treacherous coral reef, as sharp and deadly as the jaws of a great white shark, running in a jagged line across the coast. Just a little more than a week ago, Silver had personally threaded the reef from the bridge of the *Hispaniola*, and now he could clearly see the route that he had sailed. One false move, and the *Hispaniola* would have been nothing more than shredded tinder on the ocean bottom. Silver puffed out his chest with pride, congratulating himself for his unparalleled skills as a seaman.

As Uncle Dunkirk continued his aerial tour, Silver watched as the turquoise waters surrounding Treasure Island suddenly turned a murkier shade of greenish-blue, and then a darker, more impenetrable blue. Silver knew that as the water darkened, the ocean floor fell. How deep the ocean was below him, he had no clue. But like any man who made his life upon the seas, he had no inclination to ever see its bottom.

Most of all, Silver was astonished by the height at which the flying machine could fly. From their present vantage point, he could easily see from horizon to horizon. The ocean's dark waters bled to the edges of the world, and Silver knew that with the flying machine, everything in between was within his grasp.

"I'm going to turn back toward the island," said Uncle Dunkirk from the front of the plane. While Silver had been gazing hungrily at his new kingdom before him, Uncle Dunkirk had been carefully monitoring the right wing. The canvas patch seemed to be holding strong. The wing had responded well to take off, and it didn't seem to be hampering the flight so far.

Leaning on the stick, Uncle Dunkirk gently banked Willy C to the right, giving Silver a breathtaking view of Treasure Island in the distance. The lush, green island seemed to rise out of the ocean like the shell of a tortoise, completely encircled by water. The island's three large hills, which seemed so large on the ground, now looked miniscule as Willy C completed its turn and raced back toward them.

"How are you enjoying the ride so far?" asked Uncle Dunkirk conversationally.

"It's everything I had hoped for," replied Silver enthusiastically.

"I'm glad to hear that," said Uncle Dunkirk. Then, with a mischievous glimmer in his eye, he added, "I'm going to have to try a few aerial maneuvers to make sure the repairs to the wing hold. You might want to hang on."

Without a second's pause, Uncle Dunkirk yanked the stick hard to the left and put Willy C into a dizzying barrel roll. The plane spun round and round in a blistering 360, and Uncle Dunkirk could hear Silver bouncing heavily off the cockpit walls in the back. After three complete rolls, Uncle Dunkirk eased off the stick and returned Willy C to an upright position. Then he flew on as if nothing had happened.

"Are you mad, man!" cried Silver angrily from the back. "You almost killed us!"

"Relax," soothed Uncle Dunkirk. "That's just an aerial maneuver. It's called a barrel roll. It's very effective in defending yourself from gunfire." Then, with an even larger grin, he added, "And this is a loop-de-loop."

Once again Uncle Dunkirk pulled back on the stick and Willy C rose in a gentle arc up into the sky. As the arc steepened, the plane's debilitating g-force thrust Uncle Dunkirk and Silver like rag dolls back into their seats. The aerial maneuvers of the flying machine proved too much for Silver. A low howl softly filled the cockpit, and then it became louder and longer as the terror of the moment overwhelmed the pirate. "*Ooooooooooooooh!*" cried Silver.

Ignoring Silver, Uncle Dunkirk pulled Willy C tighter and tighter through the loop until the plane was turned completely upside down. An assortment of coins and miscellaneous objects fell free from the pockets of Silver's long coat, and rattled noisily onto the canopy's ceiling. Then, as Willy C began to ease back into a dive, the objects once again took flight, bouncing off the cockpit walls and clattering back to the floor.

Uncle Dunkirk watched calmly as the altimeter spun wildly, and the ocean rose below them. When Willy C began the final curve into the bottom of the loop, Uncle Dunkirk eased up on the stick to bring them upright once again. In a moment, they were back flying on an even keel.

"You're a madman!" cried Silver furiously from the rear cockpit. "You're trying to kill us!"

"Captain, please," pacified Uncle Dunkirk. "I'm just showing you what the flying machine can do. Maneuvers like this are necessary to test the strength of the craft, and right now I have a few lingering doubts about that wing. I don't know if you can feel it back there, but it still seems a little shaky up front."

The flight so far had been an unqualified success. The repairs to the wing were holding strong, and Willy C seemed to show no signs of impairment. "There's just one more maneuver that I need to try," said Uncle Dunkirk. "If the repairs to the wing hold, we should be okay."

Once again, Willy C tilted up, and once again, Silver slammed back into his seat. The plane shot upward, climbing through the sky like an *Apollo* rocket on a trajectory to the moon. Outside the window, the ocean fell away.

Uncle Dunkirk watched the altimeter, and listened carefully to the sound of Willy C's engine. When the whine of the engine began to sound forced, Uncle Dunkirk cut the ignition, and silence enveloped the cockpit.

"Oh-oh," muttered Uncle Dunkirk.

"Oh-oh?" echoed Silver, with a nervous quiver in his voice. "What's *oh-oh?*"

Gravity suddenly took hold of Willy C, and the plane ended its ascent. The front end slowly pitched toward earth, and the wind began to buffet loudly outside the canopy.

"It looks like we've lost our engine," reported Uncle Dunkirk, his voice full of panic. Silver leaned forward and watched as Uncle Dunkirk flicked a number of gauges on the instrument panel, but the engine remained silent.

In the back seat, Silver finally cracked. Although he had held in much of the terror caused by the flight so far, the potential reality of plummeting headlong into the ocean from this altitude proved to be too much for him. A blood-curdling scream escaped from his mouth, and it pierced the cabin with its shrill, high pitch. *"Aaaaaaaaaaaaaaaaaaaaah!"*

Willy C plunged through the sky in a blazing nosedive. The clouds whizzed by in a blur of white, and the dark, threatening ocean rose like an impenetrable wall to greet the plane. The roar of the wind outside nearly muffled Silver's cry, but terror of this magnitude was not easily muted.

Uncle Dunkirk sat in the front of the plane, carefully watching Willy C's instrumentation. Finally, when Willy C had plunged to a thousand feet above sea level, he sparked the ignition once again, and felt the welcome purr of Willy C's engine kick in beneath him.

With a phony cry of joy, Uncle Dunkirk announced, "I fixed it!" before pulling on the stick to decrease their hair-raising plunge. Willy C responded instantly, coasting smoothly out of the dive, and gradually evening out again.

"Are you okay, Captain?" asked Uncle Dunkirk, with mock concern. "That was a close one."

The color from Silver's face had drained, leaving his tanned features pale and drawn. The salt pork and eggs he'd wolfed down for breakfast seeped up his throat like hot lava preparing to erupt, and his stomach flipped wildly. With a visible gulp, he swallowed back his fear, and managed to spit an order past his chattering teeth, "I've seen enough. Put me back on the ground."

Color returned to Silver's cheeks as the embarrassment of his rattled scream came to mind, and for a moment he looked as if he was sporting a thick coating of blush. The pit from which the offensive scream had emanated was now locked tight, and Silver hoped that the key was lost forever. Thankfully, none of his crew had been present to hear his cry, for it wasn't masculine for a man to scream so shrilly, especially when that man was the captain.

"Aye, aye, sir," called out Uncle Dunkirk, and

he aimed Willy C back toward the clearing on Treasure Island. As the Spitfire raced forward, Uncle Dunkirk dropped the airspeed in preparation for landing back in the clearing.

The final few minutes in the air gave Silver the opportunity to regain his composure. He brushed back the long strands of his hair that had been tossed about during the barrel rolls and loop-de-loop, and he managed to swallow back the bile in his throat. Satisfied that he once again had his bearings, Silver glanced out the window just as the plane reached the island.

Down below, Treasure Island's coral reef slowly passed by, followed by the waters of the lagoon. From the air, Silver could see the *Hispaniola* at anchor. A few men who had been left onboard as sentries ran along the deck and waved up at the plane. Silver also noticed the dark outlines of sharks circling the ship, as if waiting for a morning snack.

As the lagoon passed by below, the scenery was replaced by the island's thick, lush foliage, and Silver watched in silence. Mizzen-mast Hill, now level with the plane on his right, stood proud over the island, with Spy-glass Hill and Fore-mast Hill in the distance.

Glancing to the left, Silver spotted the old deserted fort that had been hewn out of the woods. It stood like a lonely sentinel, surrounded by an army of massive trees. Then, just as the plane approached the clearing, something caught Silver's eye.

Peering down, Silver spotted a man walking across the compound of the fort. He had a large pack on his back, and was wearing clothing that easily separated him from one of Silver's crew—a bright, florid shirt. As the man looked up at the passing plane, he seemed startled by its sudden appearance, and ran for cover. Suddenly, a second figure appeared, racing across the compound with a large pack on his back. Noticing the plane, he chased after the first man, and the two of them ducked into the fort's lone shelter. The door to the shelter slammed shut behind them, leaving the compound's grounds deserted once again.

As this puzzling scene played out before Long John Silver, an alarming thought crept to the forefront of the pirate's mind—*After all these years, could Ben Gunn still be alive?* As he pondered the fate of his old friend Ben, the sight of the second man baffled him. *But who's the second man? Another castaway?*

And then, in a moment of chilling clarity, the answer came to Long John Silver. A sly smile stretched over his face, and a wicked twinkle shone through his eyes. All this time, the answer had been right under his nose: the flying machine had two seats.

CHAPTER 28

"GEEZ!" EXCLAIMED SAGE, from the floor of the shelter inside Ben's fort. His blonde hair was pasted damply to his forehead due to the day's exertions, and his heart pounded in his chest. "That was close."

Ben and Sage had been lugging the two backpacks to the fort when Willy C had suddenly passed overhead. It was their third trip up and down the side of Mizzen-mast Hill that day, and their legs felt rubbery and weak. Each weary step had become nothing more than a numbing exercise in foot placement—*one in front of the other, and again, and again.* And it was their state of mental exhaustion that might have been their downfall. They had been concentrating so hard on each torturous step forward that neither Ben nor Sage had heard Willy C coming in for a landing. They'd been caught unaware in the open, and now they were left with the nagging question—*had they been seen?*

As Ben and Sage peered cautiously out the door of the cabin, the sound of Willy C's engine died in the distance. For a long, unnerving moment there seemed to be complete silence in the forest, but then the sounds of nature crept back to the forefront.

"That was a shave too close," muttered Ben.

"So what do you think we should do?" Sage asked. It was already near midday, and Ben and Sage still had a lot of preparations to complete in order to make the fort impenetrable. So far, they had hauled three loads of supplies down Mizzenmast Hill, including a single canvas bag bursting at the seams with gold doubloons. After discussing it with Sage, Ben had decided to lug a single bag of gold to the fort. His reasoning was that in case Silver and his men managed to overpower the prisoners and storm the fort, the bag of gold could be used to negotiate their freedom. After all, just a single glimpse at the glittering pile of gold would send any pirate into a state of treasure fever, and Ben said that he was more than willing to give up every last gold piece for a one-way ticket home.

"I say we make a stand," replied a determined Ben Gunn. "We've come this far, Sage, and I'm not about to keep cowering in a cave. I've been on this island for too long." Ben's exhaustion overcame his fortitude, releasing three years of pent up loneliness and frustration. "I'm tired of hiding, Sage. I want to walk the streets of Cardiff again, and belly up to the bar at the Crown and Anchor."

Ben gazed far into the distance, as if he were already home. "And I want to eat! Oh, do I want to eat! Anything but fish! Maybe a nice shank of beef grilled over an open flame, or a good, thick kidney pie. Or a beef stew with chunks of potato and carrots in a sweet gravy, and a slab of fresh bread to slop it all up."

The marooned sailor grew quiet for a moment, his mind apparently still in Cardiff. Then, with a quavering voice, he continued, "But most of all, I want to see my family again. All these years, my ma and pa have probably thought me dead. That I drowned at sea like many a Cardiff son.

"I want to knock on their door and see the looks on their faces when they see me, standing there, alive." Then, Ben's determined tone returned, and Sage knew by the look in his eye that there was no going back. "No, I say we make a stand, Sage. We carry on with your uncle's plan, and let the chips fall where they may. Because, after three long years, I'm ready to go home."

CHAPTER 29

UNCLE DUNKIRK, LONG John Silver, and Willy C bounced down into the clearing to a triumphant round of applause from the crew. Though Silver's mind was busily analyzing Treasure Island's latest intrigue involving the two mystery men in the deserted fort, he brushed those thoughts aside momentarily to bask in the warm glow of his hero's welcome.

Sliding the cockpit canopy open, Silver stood up grandly, and addressed the crowd, "I have returned! I am invincible!"

Upon seeing their captain alive, especially after that terrifying display in the sky, the crew burst into a spontaneous round of applause. Silver soaked up the adoration, eking out every last clap and cheer, and then he added, "You have just witnessed the future of pirating. Never again will we ply the seas, hoping to cross paths with another schooner. Not only will we *own* the seas, we'll own the *skies*. And mark my words, gentlemen, each and every one of you will be richer than you would have ever thought in your wildest dreams!"

Once again, the crew of the *Hispaniola* broke

into pandemonium, clapping loudly and enthusiastically, and whooping gleefully for their Captain. When the moment passed, Silver climbed out onto the wing and dropped to the ground. Fresh soil had never felt so good beneath his seaman's foot. Uncle Dunkirk then called out, "Captain Silver, a moment, sir."

Silver turned, the ecstatic smile of a conquering hero quickly slipping from his face. He glared up at Uncle Dunkirk on the wing. "Yes, Mr. Smiley, what is it?"

"I need another day or two to work on the flying machine," pressed Uncle Dunkirk. "As you can see, there's something wrong with the engine. It shouldn't seize up in flight like it did. Luckily for you, I was there to fix it, or you could have been killed."

"Yes, I did find that rather curious," remarked Silver, brushing aside the fact that he had never been more terrified in his life—not to mention that he had involuntarily shrieked like a little girl in pigtails. In the back of his mind, Silver wondered if the flaw in the flying machine was just a ploy manufactured by Smiley to buy some time. However, not knowing the workings of a flying machine, Silver had no choice but to allow the extra delay. Although he hated giving in or being played for a fool, he would now have time to weed out the two mystery men in the fort. And if Silver's suspicions were correct about the second man in the fort, Smiley would soon answer for all his lies. "Very well, Mr. Smiley. You have another day. I want this flying machine repaired and ready for flight by tomorrow."

"Thank you, sir," smiled Uncle Dunkirk. "I'll get to work immediately."

As Uncle Dunkirk turned to busy himself with Willy C, Silver spun back to the waiting crew and called, "Mr. Hands!"

The wiry coxswain broke loose from the crowd, and raced to Silver's side. "You called, Cap'n, sir?"

"Mr. Hands, I am leaving Mr. Smiley with the flying machine to make additional repairs," instructed Silver. "Leave a guard of four men here to watch him, and inform them that I want them all back on board by six bells."

"Yes, sir," snapped Hands. "I'll see to it personally, sir."

"No, I'm afraid not, Mr. Hands," replied Silver coolly. "I need to discuss something else with you. Leave Red in charge, under strict orders not to harm the prisoner."

"I'd feel a lot safer watching the prisoner myself, Cap'n," prodded Hands. "You know Red's temper. He's a hothead, and he has it in for Smiley."

Silver had never been one to permit his orders to be questioned—especially not by his coxswain.

His voice was icy as he ordered, "Tell Red that if one hair is missing from the prisoner, I will not show him mercy. He has seen my merciful side once. He will *never* see it again."

"Aye, aye, Cap'n," replied a disappointed Hands. "I'll let him know." With that, the coxswain excused himself, and walked off toward Red.

Captain Silver turned, and bellowed to his crew, "Back to the ship! There is plenty of work to be done!"

The crew groaned audibly. They had enjoyed their leisurely morning watching the magical flying machine soar through the skies.

"Do I hear grumbling?" roared Silver. The crew went mute as all eyes turned to the Captain. Then, to everyone's surprise, Silver's voice softened, and a smile broke across his face. "I said there is plenty of work to be done. For tonight, we celebrate!"

The crew burst into another round of ecstatic applause as Silver carried on, "Tonight we celebrate a new chapter in pirate history! Mr. McGregor, take a few men and hunt us a wild boar! Mr. Hands, unlock the hold and bring up a cask of our best wine! Mr. Toppin, we'll be expecting some music tonight, so gather your instruments!"

The crew cheered madly. With this one small gesture, Silver had solidified his hold on his men. For the time being, the sailors looked as if they had forgotten about the failed search for Flint's treasure.

The promise of the flying machine and the celebration seemed to occupy all thoughts. With a chorus of *hip-hip-hooray*, the men joyously fell into line, and began hiking back to the *Hispaniola*.

Silver watched with a satisfied smirk on his face as his men walked out of the clearing, leaving only Uncle Dunkirk and his guards behind. As the last sailor strode into the forest, Silver called, "Mr. Hands, please join me in the back."

Hearing the order passed along the caravan, a disgruntled Hands slipped out of his place in line and met the Captain.

"What do you know about the old fort near Mizzen-mast Hill?" asked Silver under his breath, once Hands had sidled up beside him.

"Well, there's not much to the place. We've been up there a couple times, and have pretty much picked it apart," reported Hands. "It was the first place we searched after the map came up dry. And McGregor's crew went again just the other day."

"Did they find anything?" asked Silver.

"Absolutely nothing, Cap'n. The fort's in good shape, but there's no sign of habitation—not a speck of food, clothing, or any sign of life."

"That's curious," mocked Silver. "I just saw two men standing inside the fort when I flew over it in the flying machine."

Hands's mouth dropped open. "How could that be, Cap'n? We haven't seen a soul since we landed on Treasure Island. No boats, no campfires at night, nothing."

Silver continued to stroll leisurely down the trail leading back to the *Hispaniola*. He let Hands stew for a moment, and then he asked, "Did I ever tell you how I came to know about Flint's treasure?"

"Begging your pardon, Cap'n, but we all saw your map," replied Hands. Silver had led the first search party, including Hands, to the exact spot on the map where Flint's treasure was supposed to be buried. They had dug for hours and hadn't found a single doubloon.

"Well, there's a little more to the tale than just the map," answered Silver. "You see, three years ago, I was a mate, like yourself, aboard a schooner named the *Tidal Morn*. One day, while we were in port, a sailor named Ben Gunn commissioned the ship. This Ben Gunn claimed that he had sailed alongside Captain Flint, and that he knew where Flint had buried his treasure. The owner of the *Tidal Morn* and Gunn struck up a partnership, and a few days later we set sail for this very island, Treasure Island."

Hands listened intently as Silver continued. "We anchored in the lagoon, and spent the next twelve days combing the island for Flint's gold. In all that time, we didn't see any hint of the treasure. But Ben Gunn insisted that all he needed was a little more time. Since Gunn didn't actually have a map, the owner soon decided that the man was a loon, and that his story was nothing but a seaman's tall tale. So, after promising Gunn that we'd return in a fortnight, while he carried on the search, we hauled anchor and sailed home."

"Leaving Gunn stranded on the island," added Hands, filling in the blank.

"Yes," confirmed Silver unflinchingly. "We left him to rot."

Silver carried on with his tale. "A few months ago, I was in London, when I heard talk of a man who claimed to have a map of Flint's treasure. With a few well-placed coins, I managed to find the man. He was a dreg of a sailor, drunk out of his skull in a shantytown near the wharf. He claimed that he had been aboard Flint's *Walrus* when it was sunk off the coast of Africa, and that he had clung to a barrel for three days before washing up on shore. I befriended the man, and I bought him enough grog to drown a landlubber. When he finally passed out, I found the map hidden in his boot, and took it. The question of whether or not he had actually sailed with Flint didn't make much difference at all once I saw the map. For this map claimed that Flint's treasure was here on Treasure Island. Just as Ben Gunn had."

"So Ben Gunn was right," concluded Hands. "Flint's treasure *was* on Treasure Island." Then, turning to Silver, Hands asked, "And you think this Ben Gunn is still on Treasure Island?"

"Maybe," replied Silver. "Although how he survived on this putrid pile of sand for three long years is anyone's guess. All I know for sure is that I saw two men in the middle of the fort, and judging by their dress, they weren't from the *Hispaniola*."

"But who would the second man be?" asked Hands.

"It's a mystery to me," answered Silver, glancing sideways at his coxswain. For the time being, Silver's theory that the second man came to the island aboard the flying machine would remain the ace up his sleeve. "Maybe he's just another castaway, washed up on shore. Who knows? What we need to do first is confirm if one of those men is Ben Gunn."

"And if he is?" asked Hands curiously.

"Why, it's simple," reasoned Silver. "Find Ben Gunn, and we'll find Flint's treasure. And I know just how we're going to do it."

CHAPTER 30

THAT NIGHT, BEN and Sage worked tirelessly through the dusk, gathering food and water, firewood, and a number of sticks and stones that would have to serve as weapons. The fort was ready, and the two of them were completely spent from the effort—not to mention from the gut-wrenching tension of potentially being spotted. After Willy C's startling flyby, they had quickly closed the gates of the fort, and cautiously peered over the ramparts for any sign of trouble. But other than the odd monkey peering at them curiously from the surrounding forest, they saw nothing to cause concern. Even Ben seemed to calm down after listening to the abundant sounds of nature all around. "If you hear silence in the forest," he instructed, "it usually means trouble's afoot."

As the sun dipped farther into the horizon, deep shadows began to form on the walls of the fort. It was becoming difficult to work in the gloom, so Ben shielded the windows with large palm fronds, and used one of Uncle Dunkirk's waterproof matches to light his homemade coconut husk candle. Soon enough, the room was filled with a warm glow that reminded Sage of summertime campouts in the backyard with his best friends.

Sage dropped to the floor of the shelter and leaned his back against the wall. Ben followed suit. His knees crackled loudly as he bent down, and a ragged groan seeped from his mouth—*"Oooomph."* They were both on the edge of exhaustion, but their night was nowhere near complete. They still had to free Uncle Dunkirk and the other prisoners.

"When do we leave for the *Hispaniola*?" Sage asked, wishing he could just close his eyes for a month or two.

"We can make our way down to the lagoon any time," replied Ben. "We won't paddle out to the ship until the wee hours of morning, though. We want everyone to be fast asleep before we sneak onboard, and that's when the night watch should be less attentive."

"Then I guess I shouldn't get too comfortable," Sage said, rolling over onto his knees, and crawling across the floor to his backpack. "We still have a little work to do."

Digging his hand into his backpack, Sage grabbed hold of his toiletry bag and pulled it out. Then, unzipping the plastic case, Sage removed the small yellow box.

"This is *Kids' Cough*," Sage explained. "It's a natural remedy that you take when you have a head cold. You know, a cough, sniffles, sneezes. But there's also something in there that helps you sleep. An herb or spice, or something."

Ben stared at the box curiously as Sage opened the side flap, pulled a small bottle from inside, and then twirled the dropper out of the top. He passed the dropper to Ben and said, "All you do is squeeze the rubber top. Then drip a few drops into a glass of water, drink it, and *voilà*—it's beddy-bye time."

Ben rolled the dropper in front of his eyes, softly pinching the rubber bulb at the end. As a small stream of *Kids' Cough* spurted out, Ben jumped. Shaking his head in wonder, Ben asked, "And how is this magic remedy of yours supposed to get us on board the *Hispaniola*?"

"Easy," Sage replied. "The one reason Mom gives me *Kids' Cough* is that it helps me sleep when my head feels like it's stuffed with cotton. I say we simply squeeze a few droppers into a container of water. Then we get the guards to drink it. When they do, trust me, they'll be asleep in a matter of minutes, and we can save Uncle Dunkirk and the prisoners."

Ben bit his bottom lip, and seemed to be weighing the logic of the plan. Finally, he asked, "How are you planning on getting the guards to drink the water?"

"I thought we could just sneak a small cask

somewhere on deck where they'd see it," Sage offered. "They have to get thirsty sometime. We just have to wait them out."

"I don't know," replied Ben. "I can see the logic behind your plan, and putting the guards to sleep would do us plenty of good. But I don't know how enthusiastic they'll be to drink the water. That's all they ever drink on a ship. I think we might have to raise the stakes a bit."

With that, Ben rose to his feet, and crossed the room to Uncle Dunkirk's backpack. Opening the top flap, he carefully extracted something wrapped in a rag. As Ben returned to Sage's side, he delicately unwrapped the object, handling it as if it were a fragile piece of art, to reveal a bottle of wine.

"I've been saving this for three years," explained Ben hoarsely. "I had a few of them—a case of twelve—but the others didn't make it past the first couple months. When I got down to the last bottle, I swore to myself that I wouldn't drink it until I was rescued from Treasure Island. But I think we need it more now."

Grabbing hold of the large cork that jutted out of the top of the bottle, Ben began to twist. With an audible *pop*, the cork slipped free. Then, raising the bottle to Sage, Ben asked innocently, "We probably need to empty it a bit, don't we?"

Sage smiled at Ben, and gave him an approving nod. Ben tilted the bottle to his lips and took a small sip—just enough to wet his lips and get a taste of the wine on his tongue. He smacked his lips, and Sage could see the pleasure that the wine gave Ben after three years of drinking nothing more than creek water. The old sailor offered the bottle to Sage, but Sage declined with a shake of his head. "Thanks, anyway Ben. I've got a long way to go until I'm legal." Then, in a determined tone, Sage added, "Now, let's top that bottle off." *Tonight, Uncle Dunkirk's coming home,* he thought.

Ben crossed his legs in front of Sage, and placed the bottle on the floor. Sage inserted the dropper back into the *Kids' Cough*, squeezed the bulb, and then deposited its contents down the neck of the wine bottle. After repeating the process four times, Sage set the *Kids' Cough* down, and passed the wine to Ben.

Once they finished, Ben gripped the throat of the bottle, and roughly twisted the cork back in. He forced it farther down the neck with a few strikes from his clenched fist.

"That should do it," Sage announced, to complete their preparations. Taking the bottle in hand, Sage swirled it around a few times, holding it up to the candlelight to ascertain their success. There wasn't a single trace of tampering in the tempting, fruity vintage. "A few sips of this, and the guards on deck will be in La-La Land," Sage announced happily.

CHAPTER 31

LONG JOHN SILVER strode across the deck, with the festive sounds of a celebration around him. Crew members hoisted pints of grog and merrily toasted the captain as he passed, and Silver amiably accepted their praise.

The ship's cook, Lippert, had grilled the wild boar to perfection, and he stood over the juicy carcass, trimming savory slices with a dagger in hand. A line of men waited for their share of the feast, while others clamored around the tapped cask of wine, recharging their cups to the brim and drinking heartily.

On top of the forecastle, Tom Toppin's small band of musicians had set up a small stage. Toppin, who played a mean squeeze box, was leading two other crewmembers on a flute and mandolin in a spirited jig that had the men shuffling from foot to foot, and swinging each other round by the arm.

It was a grand celebration, and Silver basked in the warm reception he received from the crew. Still, even he was amazed by how a single cask of grog and a hot meal could buy the confidence of men. *Simple fools, one and all.*

Unfortunately for the Captain, business was at hand, and the celebration would have to wait. Silver managed to navigate his way through the men, accepting numerous pats on the back and an endless array of toasts, before he reached the entrance to the forecastle. Looking about, he spotted McGregor a few feet away, shuffling merrily to Tom Toppin's jig, and singing off-key in that grating Cockney accent.

"McGregor," called Silver, "a moment, please."

McGregor quickly drew next to the Captain, and followed Silver into the bowels of the forecastle. Once outside the door to the prisoners' quarters, Silver turned and instructed, "Wait for me here, and enter only if you hear any sign of trouble."

"Aye, aye, Captain," slurred McGregor cheerily. Silver selected one key from a ring of keys at his side and inserted it into the large lock. With a *click*, the lock unclasped, and Silver slipped into the prisoners' room, closing the door firmly behind him.

"Good evening, gentlemen," greeted Silver formally from the doorway. "I hope that your meal tonight meets with your approval."

The startled prisoners looked up from their places around the cabin. Each had a half-eaten plate of grilled boar in front of him, and a glass of wine. Though the prisoners seemed to appreciate the Captain's generosity with the celebratory dinner, they looked as if they questioned the sincerity of it. Squire Trelawney, on the other hand, looked as if he had buried his face in his plate.

"The boar is marvelous!" raved Squire Trelawney, smacking his greasy lips. Through a mouth crammed with freshly chewed pork, he added, "I *must* know what spices your cook uses."

Silver ignored the squire's upper-crust ramblings, and carried on, "I am here to inform you about our future plans on Treasure Island." For the majority of the day, Silver had measured his numerous options in his cabin, while the crew prepared for the celebration. With the flying machine, Silver stood to gain great wealth and unlimited fame. However, a spark of blistering anger had burrowed deep within his gut, and Silver was having difficulty ignoring it. They had been on Treasure Island for more than a week now, searching in vain for Flint's treasure. And all that time, Ben Gunn had been watching from the shadows, and laughing as Silver's men bumbled about from spot to spot. There was no doubt in Silver's mind that Ben Gunn was in possession of Flint's treasure, and as he brooded over the issue, a plan came to mind. A plan that would net him both the flying machine *and* Flint's treasure.

"It has come to my attention that there is a

man on the island named Ben Gunn," Silver announced suddenly. Although his black eyes quickly searched each of the prisoners, watching for any sign of recognition, no one seemed to take the bait. Undaunted, Silver carried on, "He is hiding somewhere on the island, but he has been sighted by the old fort." Then, after a slight pause, Silver dropped a bombshell. "And he isn't alone."

Uncle Dunkirk had been holding his breath nervously since Silver mentioned Ben Gunn. He had prayed silently to himself, hoping that Sage had not also been spotted, but now the pirate's words pierced Uncle Dunkirk's heart like the icy shaft of an arrow. Silver knew that Sage was on the island. Now it was just a matter of time before the boy would be caught.

"I have my suspicions as to who the second man is," continued Silver mockingly, toward Uncle Dunkirk. "And by tomorrow, those suspicions will be confirmed."

"Why? What's going to happen tomorrow?" asked Jim Hawkins nervously.

"Tomorrow, young Master Hawkins," replied Silver, "one of you will be sent to the fort, along with Mr. Hands and a few of my men. Your task will be simple——negotiating with Ben Gunn for every last doubloon of Captain Flint's treasure."

"And what are we negotiating with?" asked Dr. Livesey.

"Your lives," replied Silver coldly.

Uncle Dunkirk rose to his feet instantly. "I'll go." He knew that Silver would probably turn him down, as the pirate most likely suspected that the second man had come from the flying machine, but Uncle Dunkirk had to take the chance. After all, this could be his last chance to see Sage, and formulate a plan to fall back on before it was too late.

"No, I don't think so," said Silver. "I think it would be best to keep you safe on board. After all, you are the only one who can pilot the flying machine, and I wouldn't want to put you at any risk."

"Then you must send me," announced Captain Smollett, stepping forward. "It's the only fair thing to do. After all, I am a captain of the sea, and have personally overseen many delicate negotiations. Plus, I need not reassure you, Captain Silver, that I am a man of my word. If you send me, you will have my word of honor that I will return."

"While I have no doubt about the value of your word, Captain Smollett, unfortunately, I must once again refuse," opposed Silver calmly. "Might I remind you that a number of the crew served directly under you? I wouldn't want you poisoning their minds again, now would I?"

With his pronounced *knock*, step, *knock*, step, Captain Silver strode across the room to stand directly in front of Jim Hawkins. The young lad looked up nervously, but then he slipped on his most defiant face, as if daring Silver to underestimate him. "Jim Hawkins," ordered Silver, "tomorrow, you will join my men on Treasure Island. It will be up to you, and you alone, to negotiate for the lives of every prisoner. It is a daunting task, but one that I know you are up to."

"But Jim's just a boy!" called Dr. Livesey. Shoving his chair back, Dr. Livesey jumped to his feet, and stood his ground before Silver. "Quit picking on the lad! Send *me*. Send a man, and leave Jim out of this madness."

Silver turned and faced Dr. Livesey like a bloodthirsty panther. His hands, which had been tucked behind his back, now slipped into his long coat, only to reappear with two loaded pistols. Leveling them directly at Dr. Livesey, Silver warned, "You had best keep your opinions to yourself, Dr. Livesey. *I* am Captain of the *Hispaniola*, and *I* will decide who stays and who goes. Tomorrow, Jim Hawkins goes to Treasure Island."

Dr. Livesey glared at Silver with a look normally reserved for rotting sewage. With his temper bubbling over, the doctor finally broke and lashed out, "You are as much a captain of this ship, as I am Jean Lafitte. You're nothing more than a lying scoundrel who holds the leash to a few dozen dogs that do your bidding. You're a sorry excuse for a human being."

Then, turning to face Captain Smollett, Dr. Livesey issued a defiant salute at the fallen captain. Surprised, Smollett rose quickly to his feet, snapped to attention, and returned the crisp salute.

"This is *Captain Smollett's* ship," pronounced Dr. Livesey. "And he alone is the captain of the *Hispaniola*."

Silver glared angrily from behind the barrels of his pistols. "If that is your opinion," growled Silver, "then I will have to do something about it."

Turning to the door, Silver barked, "McGregor!" With a loud *bang*, the door crashed in on its hinges, and the drunken sailor stumbled in, loosely clasping his cutlass. He spun around, searching for trouble. "Take Captain Smollett and lock him in the brig!" ordered Silver. Then, turning back to face Jim Hawkins, Silver decreed, "I will give you until six bells tomorrow to negotiate with Ben Gunn for your lives. If you don't return to the *Hispaniola* with every last doubloon of Flint's treasure, Captain Smollett will walk the plank."

A startled gasp escaped from Dr. Livesey's mouth. This hadn't been part of their plan. Now Captain Smollett would be as good as dead if their rescue plan failed.

"Wait, Captain!" sputtered Dr. Livesey apologetically. "I'm sorry. I spoke out of anger. I allowed my frustration to overcome my good sense. I was clearly out of line, and I apologize sincerely. *Please*, Captain Silver, don't take my insolence out on Captain Smollett. It was my impertinence that brought this about, not his."

With a fiendish grin, Silver replied, "Please, Dr. Livesey, there's no need to apologize. You simply stated the truth. Captain Smollett *is* the true Captain of the *Hispaniola*. You know it, I know it, and the crew knows it." An icy chill descended upon the cabin, as if a ghostly Siberian wind had swept across the ship as Silver continued. "I think it's high time that we remedy that misconception for good."

CHAPTER 32

IN THE DARK of night, Ben and Sage made their way through the forest. The tropical splendor of Treasure Island had disappeared with the sun, leaving a more sinister terrain. Slivers of moonlight peeked through the twisted canopy of branches high above, and every time Sage dared to glance up, he felt as if giant, gnarled claws were hovering over him, ready to snatch him from the ground the second he turned his back.

Ben, on the other hand, strode on calmly. Half his time on Treasure Island had been spent in the dark of night, and Ben seemed to have left his fear behind him long ago. As well, living in a gloomy cave looked as if it had done wonders for Ben's night vision. With eyes as keen as an owl's, Ben picked his way effortlessly through the forest and led them safely to the edge of the lagoon.

As Sage waded through the final few feet of brush and onto the fine sand of the lagoon's beach, his eyes were drawn instantly to the *Hispaniola* across the water. From various points on the ship's deck and rigging, lanterns hung and sparkled in the night, like glittering diamonds laid against a background of black velvet. The cheerful sound of music wafted over the water, and they could see dark outlines of the crew dancing and cavorting on deck. Obviously, a riotous celebration was in full swing on the *Hispaniola* tonight.

"This could take some time," Sage moaned, dropping to the sand and pulling his knees in tight against his chest. To Sage, it looked as if this party showed no signs of slowing.

"Actually, this might work in our favor," suggested Ben. Sitting next to Sage, Ben reasoned, "The men will feast until their stomachs bulge, drink till they drown, and dance until their legs give out. Then they'll sleep like the dead all night. By the time we slip aboard, a blast from a cannon wouldn't wake them."

Sage heard the wisdom in Ben's words, and his mood visibly brightened. As fatigued as he was, he really didn't mind losing a little more sleep in order to improve their odds of success. Through the long hours of the night, Ben and Sage watched the celebration slowly quiet down. Once or twice, Sage dozed lightly, jerking awake every few minutes to find Ben staring straight ahead, his eyes never wavering from the *Hispaniola*. Finally, as the night deepened, the lanterns on the ship were gradually snuffed out until only a single one remained, burning like a lone beacon near the forecastle.

Sage woke with a start as Ben gripped his elbow and whispered, "It's time." He rubbed his eyes with the back of his fingers, yawning widely, and then he rose to follow Ben back into the wall of foliage. Like phantoms, they crept along the outskirts of the lagoon, circling round until the *Hispaniola* was anchored directly to their left. Then, next to a large banyan tree, Ben revealed a small skiff that he had handcrafted from a fallen tree years ago to fish in the lagoon.

As Ben dug his feet in, he took hold of the front of the skiff and yanked it loose. The skiff slid forward a few feet along the sand. Sage braced his hands against the back of the skiff and helped Ben push it down to the edge of the water. Once there, they waded up to their knees, and then carefully slipped aboard.

Ben took hold of the single oar that he had fashioned from a branch and quietly dipped it into the lagoon, paddling away from shore. As they glided across the water, Sage gazed down into the normally translucent waters, now nothing more than murky blackness, and wondered what creatures were ominously circling below. With a shudder, he pushed all thoughts of sharks from his head, and concentrated on their mission—rescuing Uncle Dunkirk and the prisoners.

As they neared the *Hispaniola*, the sound of conversation gradually grew in volume. The dark outlines of two guards could be seen near the forecastle, and they were obviously engaged in an animated conversation about the Captain's "magical flying machine." Words like "soaring" and "bird" drifted out over the water as Ben slipped the skiff snugly against the longboat, which was tethered to the side of the *Hispaniola*'s hull.

Ben gestured for Sage to be quiet. Then, grasping the bottle of wine in one hand, he climbed the rope netting that hung along the side of the *Hispaniola*. The creaks and groans of the rope ladder were veiled by similar sounds emanating from the ship.

"I'm telling you, Bloom," bragged one of the guards to the other, "it was like watching a hawk at play. It soared high above amongst the clouds, spun like a top, and dived like a gull. I never saw nothing like it before."

Ben stole a cautious peek over the side of the rail, and spotted the two guards near the forecastle. Their attention was focused on their conversation, and not on the task of guarding the ship. After all, the *Hispaniola* had been anchored in the lagoon for more than a week now, and Treasure Island wasn't exactly a hotbed of activity.

Ben slid his hand through the rail and carefully laid the bottle of wine on its side. Then, ducking his head down below the deck, he held his breath, muttered a silent prayer, and released the bottle. A moment later, the *Hispaniola* rocked gently on the lagoon's current, and the bottle rolled noisily across the deck.

The two guards jumped at the sound, and quickly advanced with their swords drawn. They cautiously raked the deck, peering into shadows and nooks, before one noticed the capsized wine bottle. He stooped to pick it up.

"It looks like the celebration ain't exactly over, O'Malley, me mate," he said through a mouth of toothless gaps. "Hands must have forgot to stow one of the Captain's bottles. And it's full!"

The second guard quickly snatched the bottle from the other's hand, and raised it to his left eye—a black patch covered the other. He saw that the bottle *was* full. He clenched the cork between his back teeth, bit down hard, and twisted the cork free. Then, turning aside, he spit the cork over the deck rail.

Down below, in the skiff, Sage waited quietly for the guards to take the bait. He had heard the bottle roll across the deck, and the excited words of the guards. And now, as Sage looked up, he saw a small object soar over the deck rail in the moonlight, arc through the air, and begin to drop. He watched as it fell like a stone, plummeting until it landed with a wooden *plonk* in the middle of the skiff. Looking desperately over his shoulder, Sage saw that it was a cork, and he realized immediately that it should have made a *splash* as it fell into the water.

Sage glanced up at Ben, who was still hanging from the netting, pressed as tightly against the ship as possible. The resigned look on his friend's face said it all. They had come so far, risking life and limb, only to be discovered because of a cork spit carelessly over the side. There was nothing for them to do, and nowhere to go. They were trapped—sitting ducks.

On deck, O'Malley lowered the bottle suspiciously, and muttered, "Didn't hear no splash." He crossed to the deck rail, his cutlass still dangling from his free hand.

Just as he leaned to glance over the side, his companion, Bloom, exclaimed, "Gimme that!"

"Hey! Save some for me!" bawled O'Malley, his suspicions instantly forgotten. Pushing off the deck rail, he chased Bloom across the width of the ship, as they jostled for possession of the bottle.

Glancing up at Ben, Sage let out a relieved sigh. He reached back, took the cork in hand, and held it up for Ben to see. Ben nodded. Then, hanging his hand over the side of the skiff, Sage quietly released the unlucky cork into the lagoon, and watched it bob away.

Within minutes, the thirsty guards had consumed the entire bottle of wine. Ben and Sage knew this as fact, because both had heard a *kerplunk* as the discarded bottle was dropped into the lagoon. Luckily, the two guards had opted this time to discard the empty bottle on the other side of the *Hispaniola*, nowhere near Ben's skiff.

Ten minutes later, as silence descended on the *Hispaniola*, Ben risked another glance over the deck rail, and then waved Sage up. Sage quietly clambered up the netting to meet Ben. The two guards had settled down comfortably, and were sitting with their backs propped up against the mainmast. Both stuck their legs straight out, and their mouths hung groggily open. Their eyes were closed, and their chests heaved smoothly, the gentle rise and fall of the ship lulling them deeper and deeper into sleep. Sage's sleeping potion had worked.

Ben slipped cautiously over the rail, and found a club that he could use to stifle the guards if they so much as stirred. However, the gruff sound of their drunken snores quickly pushed any doubt aside—the guards were not only sleeping, they were on a two-week vacation to La-La Land. Just as Sage had predicted.

Sage grasped Ben's hand as he scampered

over the deck rail. From the embankment on Mizzen-mast Hill, they had spied the prisoners being herded into the forecastle, and now Ben and Sage headed in the direction of its door.

As the forecastle had only a single entrance, they had to creep directly past the sleeping guards. Unfortunately, in order to clear room for a small dance floor for that evening's celebration, a number of crates and wooden kegs had been stacked alongside the rail. The sleeping guards, who were now snoring at full bore, had their legs extended straight out—effectively blocking Ben and Sage's path.

Ben went first, stepping gingerly between one of the guard's legs. The crusty old sailor was deep in sleep. His chest rose and fell like the tide, and a long, ragged snore sputtered from between his rubbery lips. Occasionally, he would issue a small, nostalgic whine, almost as if he were visiting a favorite haunt in his dreams, but then he would simply smack his lips loudly and nod off again. Wasting no time, Ben took another step, and crossed to the opposite side.

Next up, Sage followed Ben's cautious path, and placed a foot between the other guard's open legs. Sage had just planted his right foot on deck, when the toothless guard suddenly stirred. Sage froze, balancing on one foot as the pirate's head lolled back and forth, his lips smacking wetly.

Suddenly, the guard's cheeks puffed out like a jazz trombonist's, and he expelled a noxious *burp* of sour wine fumes directly into Sage's face. Sage bit back the urge to cough, and restrained himself from brushing aside the foul cloud. Stepping quickly, he crossed over the guard's other leg, and sidled up to Ben, who watched nervously.

As they continued across the deck to the forecastle, Ben put his lips to Sage's ear, and whispered, "They should be down in the forecastle somewhere. But be quiet, there are crew quarters below, too."

Ben took the door handle, slowly twisted it, and cautiously swung the door open. A slight *squeak* emanated from the rusty hinges; however, to Ben and Sage, it sounded as loud as the peal of a church bell. Noting that the guards were still fast asleep, Ben and Sage closed the door behind them, and then stole down the stairs into the main corridor.

Once inside, closed doors greeted Ben and Sage on either side of the corridor, and the sounds of drunken snoring came from all sides. The loud gruff snores seemed to shake the walls, but they were the perfect distraction for masking Ben and Sage's intrusion.

Ben crept quietly from door to door, twisting doorknobs, but not opening doors. His reasoning was simple. The prisoners would be stowed in a locked cabin, and if a door wasn't locked, chances were it housed the crew. As Ben and Sage made their way down the dark hall, they soon enough found what they were looking for—a door with a large padlock.

"How do we get in?" whispered Ben.

Sage looked at the lock, and realized that it shouldn't prove too much of a challenge. The mechanism looked ancient and had a keyhole the size of his index finger. It wasn't anything like the complicated dial locks they used in school.

"Step aside," Sage whispered. He dug his hand into his pocket and pulled out a handful of miscellaneous knickknacks—a few loose coins, his lucky Jim Hawkins compass, some multi-colored pocket lint, and his house key.

Sage turned the house key over in his hands, looking at the various edges, and then shrugged his shoulders—*it's worth a try*. He stuck the key into the lock's hole and began to wiggle it around. The size of the ancient keyhole gave him plenty of room to maneuver, and Sage knew exactly what he was looking for. Back in Spruce Ridge, he had learned the complicated art of picking the lock on the bathroom door with a toothpick, a feat that came in handy whenever he had the playful urge to douse his father with a bucket of ice water when his father was in the shower. It was a skill that Sage never thought he'd ever have to apply outside of his own home.

Seconds later, as Sage tinkered away, something gave on the opposite end of the key. Carefully, he pushed the key back, depressing the spring, and with a *click*, the locking mechanism released.

Ben and Sage exchanged a surprised look. Sage slipped the lock off its hinge, and then, as quiet as could be, Ben twisted the doorknob and slowly opened the door.

CHAPTER 33

LONG JOHN SILVER woke to incessant knocking on his door the morning after the celebration. The captain's head was clouded by wine from the night before, and he had a headache that seemed to split his skull right down the middle.

Lifting his head groggily from the pillow, Silver bellowed, *"What?"* The knocking stopped, and the door creaked open a crack.

The shaggy-haired head of a crewman peeked apprehensively around the door. "Begging your pardon, Captain, but there's a problem, sir."

Silver bristled. *Why can't I get one good night of sleep without being interrupted by my idiot crew?* Firing a look of complete disgust at the crewmember, Silver sneered, "And what is it now? No fresh water for breakfast? No one on deck to order you about? Or does someone have an upset tummy?"

"Actually, I'm feeling quite chipper," replied the crewman stupidly. "Mr. Hands just asked me to inform you that the prisoners are gone."

In a whirlwind of silk and cotton, Silver threw his sheets aside and jumped out of bed. He was dressed in a three-quarter length nightshirt, and he crossed the cabin like a cobra rushing in for the kill. Sensing his imminent demise, the crewman at the door bolted, and raced back on deck with Silver fast on his heels.

Storming out on deck, Silver stumbled as the morning sun blinded him momentarily. He picked himself off the ground, brushed off his nightshirt, and stood tall. His sleep-mangled hair poked out every which way, giving him a fleeting resemblance to Medusa. Shielding his eyes with his hand, Silver drew in a deep breath, and then roared like a lion, *"Haaaaaannnnnnds!"*

As if a starter's pistol had just gone off, the men on deck scattered, making themselves as scarce as possible. Some scurried up the riggings, while others dodged behind casks. When Captain Silver was in one of his moods, it was best to simply vanish from sight.

"Haaaaaannnnnds!" screamed Silver again, dropping his hand from his eyes and storming across the deck.

The forecastle door burst open, and Hands raced out. He clutched a cutlass, and the menacing bulk of Red towered behind him, holding a lantern.

"Hands! Where are my prisoners?" demanded Silver.

"Cap'n, we've searched everywhere on board,"

reported Hands. "And they're not here. They must have slipped off sometime in the night."

Fury coursed through Silver's veins like molten lava, bubbling and burning deep inside him. His nostrils flared, and his eyes bulged. A wiry blue vein appeared instantly next to his right eye, and as it throbbed, it was matched in time by a nervous twitch beside the same eye. "What about Smollett?"

"Smollett is still locked in the brig," replied Hands, with relief. At least he had one good piece of news for the Captain.

"And what about our guards? What became of them last night?"

"They claim they were drugged, sir," replied Hands. "They say that they found a bottle of wine on deck, and that after they drank it, it knocked them clean out."

"And where is this mysterious bottle of wine?" growled Silver.

"Well," Hands offered, shuffling his feet from side to side, "the men say they tossed it overboard."

"How *convenient*," snapped Silver. "Have both the guards locked in the brig along with Smollett. They will pay dearly for their blunder."

"And the prisoners? Shall I prepare a search party, Captain?" asked Hands.

"Arm a dozen men, Mr. Hands," replied Silver calculatingly. "However, there's no need to launch a search. I know exactly where they'll be. Send a man down to the brig and have him guard Smollett. And when I say guard, I mean *guard*. No one sleeps on duty!"

"Yes, sir!" snapped Hands in reply.

"Most importantly, I want you to protect that flying machine. Put a half dozen guards on it at all hours, around the clock. I don't want Smiley or the prisoners going anywhere near my prize."

"Yes, sir," replied Hands.

"Finally, I want you to take a crew of men to the old fort. You'll find the prisoners locked up inside, along with Flint's treasure and Ben Gunn. Tell them that I am still willing to barter for their lives. We will give them their freedom in exchange for Flint's treasure."

"What if they won't give it up, Captain?" asked Hands.

"Oh, they will," replied Silver smugly. "They already know what the consequences will be. If every ounce of Flint's treasure is not on board the *Hispaniola* by six bells tonight, Smollett walks the plank. Then we'll blast that fort to bits with our cannon."

CHAPTER 34

UNCLE DUNKIRK PEERED over the battlement from inside the old fort and looked at the wall of trees encircling them. The sun had risen two hours ago, and it warmed his weary back as the temperature gradually rose. *It won't be long now before they come knocking.*

The prisoners had said that they spent the majority of the night wide awake, listening to the raucous carousing on deck, and hoping that the celebration wouldn't interfere with their rescue. As the hours passed and the party died, the prisoners had told Sage and Ben that they turned their attention to the sounds of the ship—the endless creaks and moans of shifting lumber, the irritating *squeak-squeak* of a lantern swinging on its hinge, the soothing sound of water lapping against the hull. However, just as their resolve to stay awake had begun to falter, they heard a sound that instantly roused their lagging spirits—two magical words whispered from the darkness: *"Uncle Duncle."*

The remainder of the rescue had been a blur of adrenalin and anticipation. After exchanging a few silent smiles, the prisoners had all crept onto the deck, tip-toed over the legs of the two sleeping guards, and clambered down the rope ladder to the skiff. With the small vessel piled high, the group pushed off, dipping their oars into the lagoon and paddling for shore.

Once on the beach, the prisoners finally felt secure enough to take a moment to thank their saviors with a hearty round of handshakes, backslaps, and even a hug or two. Uncle Dunkirk swept Sage up in his arms and squeezed mightily. "I knew you could do it, Sage," he said with a twinkle in his eye. "You're a Smiley after all."

After proper introductions had been made, they had set off through the forest to the old fort, where they would barricade themselves from Long John Silver and his pirate horde.

"Do you see anything?" Sage asked, as he quietly slid next to Uncle Dunkirk on the battlement.

"Nothing yet, but they'll be coming soon," replied Uncle Dunkirk with a smile. As he looked at Sage, a feeling of great affection swept over Uncle Dunkirk. Finally, he said, "You know, Sage, I'm proud of you. This hasn't exactly been the vacation I was hoping to take you on, but you've been a real trooper. You've managed to survive on a deserted island, elude pirates, and even stage a daring rescue on an enemy ship. You're a hero, Sage. And I have to say, I'm proud to have you as a nephew."

"Thanks, Uncle Dunkirk," Sage replied, with cheeks flushed red. "But in all honesty, it's been a pretty cool summer vacation."

Uncle Dunkirk tilted his head back and laughed. He tousled Sage's hair, and said, "Now that's the spirit! You're going to have lots of stories to tell as you grow up. You really are."

"That is, *if* you grow up," called out a strange voice, rudely interrupting their conversation. Uncle Dunkirk quickly tucked Sage behind him for protection, as, twenty yards in front of them, Hands stepped out of the forest and into the clearing.

"Ah, Mr. Hands," greeted Uncle Dunkirk. "We've been expecting you."

As the wiry coxswain stepped a few more paces into the clearing, Uncle Dunkirk whispered to Sage from the corner of his mouth, "Warn the others."

Ducking down below the battlement, Sage slipped off the ledge to the compound floor and dashed to the shelter to sound the alarm.

"That was a very impressive ploy last night," congratulated Hands. "You should have seen Cap'n Silver. He was furious! Madder than a bee chasing a pot of stolen honey."

"Well, I'd apologize for our sudden departure," retorted Uncle Dunkirk, "but it is a prisoner's duty to escape."

By now, Hands had completely crossed the clearing and stood just feet below Uncle Dunkirk, staring up at him in the battlement. "However, I'm not here to trade stories. The cap'n has sent me to barter for your lives. I thought we might discuss the terms face-to-face, like gentlemen."

"Why should we negotiate with Silver?" asked Uncle Dunkirk. "After all, we already have our freedom."

"Yes, but one of you is still in captivity," answered Hands. "Cap'n Smollett is still locked tight in the brig." Then, he added, "That is, until six bells tonight."

Out of the corner of his eye, Uncle Dunkirk spied movement as the rest of the prisoners took their positions around the fort.

"Why? What happens at six bells?" asked Uncle Dunkirk.

"At six bells, Cap'n Smollett walks the plank," replied Hands indifferently. "That is, unless we can come to an agreement."

"And what might that be?"

Hands glanced over his shoulder, and Uncle Dunkirk followed his gaze. Inside the forest, a half dozen men waited patiently for Hands's signal to attack. Each man wore a menacing look and clutched a cutlass. However, one man stood head and shoulders above the others—Red. The giant clutched a thick wooden club, which he lobbed back and forth between his hands threateningly.

Lowering his voice so that only Uncle Dunkirk might hear, Hands carried on, "I thought now would be a good time to discuss our partnership, Mr. Smiley. There might be something in it for the both of us."

Uncle Dunkirk smiled to himself. He had read Hands perfectly. The coxswain was nothing more than a sea urchin who was desperate to make a buck for himself. However, Hands still had the amber stone in his possession, and Uncle Dunkirk needed it to leave Treasure Island far behind.

"Leave your cutlass and knife where you stand," ordered Uncle Dunkirk. "Then come to the main gate. You'll be let in. But let me warn you, Mr. Hands, if there's any funny business while you're inside the fort, *you*, not my nephew, will be the one who won't live to see another day."

Hands unsheathed his cutlass and dropped it to the ground. Then he reached into the sash tied round his waist and, from it, drew a long, sinister looking dagger, and placed it on the ground next to the cutlass. Then Hands strolled up to the main gate and waited.

Taking a last glance at the woods surrounding them, Uncle Dunkirk called down to Dr. Livesey, "Open the gate quickly, and let Mr. Hands in. However, if you hear me call, close the gate as fast as you can."

Jumping into action, Dr. Livesey lifted the wooden brace that secured the gate and quickly pulled it open. As the door swung inward, Hands casually strolled into the compound and stopped to wait. Once Dr. Livesey secured the gate, he turned and aimed the point of his wooden spear at Hands's chest.

"There's no need to worry about him, Dr. Livesey," called Uncle Dunkirk. "He is unarmed, and we have his word that he will act like a gentleman. Now, if you don't mind, please take my place on the battlement while I have a few words with Mr. Hands. But be careful, Hands is hiding a few friends in the woods."

Uncle Dunkirk jumped down into the compound, and led Hands into the shelter. Once inside, they took their seats on two wooden benches and continued negotiating, out of earshot of the others.

"Well, here we are, Mr. Hands, just the two of us," stated Uncle Dunkirk. "What do you want?"

"Why, Flint's treasure, of course," replied Hands, equally bluntly.

"Why do you think we have Flint's treasure?" asked Uncle Dunkirk innocently.

"Because Ben Gunn was one of the men that saved your skins," retorted Hands. "He's been hiding all this time on the island, watching from the woods. I know it, and so does Cap'n Silver. And he hasn't been alone, has he? He's been with that little nephew of yours. What did you call him? *Sage?*"

Uncle Dunkirk bristled at the mention of Sage's name, but he had to stay calm. "Never mind my nephew, Mr. Hands. He is of no concern to you, and he's not part of these negotiations. This negotiation is about Flint's treasure, and who gets it—you or Long John Silver."

"Well, being that Cap'n Silver isn't exactly present, why don't we keep this negotiation between ourselves," volleyed Hands. With that, he dug his hand into his shirt and yanked the amber stone free. "Your necklace *and* your freedom, for the treasure."

"And what of Captain Smollett?" asked Uncle Dunkirk.

"Forget Smollett," suggested Hands callously. "You barely know the man, and he's as good as dead anyway. The cap'n doesn't like to be bested, and you've gone and humiliated him in front of the entire crew. Knowing the cap'n, Smollett will walk the plank whether I show up with Flint's treasure or not."

Uncle Dunkirk weighed his options for a moment. The amber stone was much more valuable to him than a trunk full of treasure and gold baubles. However, Sage had told him that the treasure was still hidden in a cave on the side of Mizzen-mast Hill. Even with a few of the prisoners lending a hand, it would be next to impossible to transport it all to the ship before six bells.

Then, of course, there was the possibility that Hands's negotiations were nothing more than a ploy to trick the prisoners into leaving the safety of the fort. Silver's men could easily be waiting in the forest, ready to pounce upon the first prisoner that crossed their path.

Either way, there were too many variables to be measured, too many options to weigh. Silver's word was worth nothing to the prisoners, so Flint's treasure would remain where it was, safe inside Ben's cave. There was no other reasonable option.

That left Captain Smollett at the mercy of Long John Silver. And Uncle Dunkirk was certain that, on this occasion, Silver's word would ring true. At six bells, Captain Smollett *would* walk the plank and plunge into the shark-infested lagoon. And there was nothing they could do about it. *Or was there?*

Finally, Uncle Dunkirk spoke: "I have an offer for you, Mr. Hands, that will not only solidify our partnership, it will also make you a very rich man. Look around you. Flint's treasure is not in the fort. However, I can have every last chest stowed into the flying machine by midnight tonight. You take your men and return to the ship, and we'll gather the treasure. Then, in the dark of night, you sneak off the ship to the flying machine, and I'll fly you and the gold anywhere you want to go."

"How do I know you're not fibbing?" asked Hands suspiciously.

"Because I am your partner, and not Long John Silver's," assured Uncle Dunkirk. "And because I am willing to make you a down payment right now. Even if I were fibbing, which I assure you I'm not, the down payment would be enough to keep you in riches for quite some time."

With that, Uncle Dunkirk rose and crossed the room to his backpack. Sage had already told him about the canvas bag of gold doubloons that Ben had brought to the fort. Ben's quick thinking was about to buy them their freedom.

Digging his hand into the backpack, Uncle Dunkirk pulled the canvas sack free, and dropped it on the floor at Hands's feet. At the unmistakable sound of gold doubloons jingling within, Hands instantly perked up.

"This is a bag of gold doubloons from Flint's treasure. It's one of many, and more than you would ever earn in a lifetime at sea. To show you I am a man of my word, I will give it to you now. What you do with it is your concern. You can bury it in the sand for all I care and not share a cent with anyone. This transaction will be our little secret."

Uncle Dunkirk could see greed descend over Hands's eyes like a green window shade as the coxswain calculated the thickness of the canvas sack, and the amount of booty inside. A pencil-thin mustache of perspiration had formed on Hands's upper lip, and his beady eyes bulged covetously. The man barely seemed able to restrain the primal urge to rip open the canvas bag at his feet.

"As a sign of *your* good faith, I will require the necklace," continued Uncle Dunkirk. "Not a bad deal, if you ask me—a worthless piece of jewelry for a bag of Flint's treasure."

After a moment's hesitation, Hands smirked, and then scooped up the amber stone and tossed it over. Uncle Dunkirk pulled the necklace from the air and felt the warmth of the amber stone in his palm. He held it to a shaft of light that streamed through the shelter's window, and caught a quick glimpse of the magical starburst encased within. With a relieved smile, Uncle Dunkirk tied the amber stone securely to his neck, and tucked it safely against his chest.

"Partners," offered Hands, extending his hand.

With the amber stone now back in his possession, Uncle Dunkirk had no qualms about taking the offered hand and shaking it warmly. "Partners."

CHAPTER 35

AS THE *HISPANIOLA'S* bell pealed six times, Long John Silver stood at the deck rail, alongside Hands, staring intently at the far shore of the lagoon.

"It appears as if our generous offer has fallen on deaf ears," announced Silver. "Mr. Smiley has failed to meet our demands."

"I'm surprised," added Hands, lying through his teeth. Hands knew that the prisoners wouldn't come anywhere near the *Hispaniola*, and he consoled himself for lying to the Captain by picturing the bag of gold doubloons he had hidden in the rotting carcass of a fallen tree. In fact, Hands had been rather enjoying himself all afternoon. He'd been fibbing to the Captain since his return to the ship by stating that the prisoners would deliver Flint's treasure to the lagoon's shore by six bells, in exchange for their freedom and the life of Captain Smollett.

"Smiley assured me that Flint's treasure would be on the beach by six bells," fibbed Hands. "'*Every last doubloon,*' he'd said."

"Well, he can sleep fitfully, knowing that Smollett's death was on his cowardly hands," spit Silver without remorse. "Tomorrow, we'll load a cannon into the longboat and row it to shore. Then each and every one of those prisoners will perish under my blade when we blast the fort's walls to tinder."

With his course of action decided, Silver turned his back on the far shore and ordered, "Have the prisoners brought up from the brig, and gather the men. At least we'll have a little entertainment for the crew tonight."

A few minutes later, Captain Smollett and the two other prisoners, the sleeping guards O'Malley and Bloom, were led from the brig at sword point. They climbed the stairs of the forecastle and stepped out onto the deck, where a murmuring crew stood gathered.

A table had been placed near the deck rail, and at it sat Silver, Hands and Mr. McGregor—the *Hispaniola's* kangaroo court. The three prisoners were prodded to stand directly in front of the table.

Silence descended over the deck as Silver looked over each of the prisoners. Although the pirate's face was sober, his eyes glittered with enjoyment as he saw the fear in each man's face.

Finally, Hands stood, cleared his voice, and announced, "Gentlemen, you have each been charged with a crime against this ship, the *Hispaniola* and it's cap'n, John Silver."

Captain Smollett stood as the image of a professional soldier. His back was ramrod straight, and his eyes stared forward, unblinking, while O'Malley and Bloom cowered like blubbering children beside him.

"Billy O'Malley and Richard Bloom," declared Hands, glancing briefly at his two shipmates, "you have been charged with neglecting your shipboard duties. Your disregard for your duties as night watch allowed four prisoners to escape. Do you have anything to say on your behalf?"

Billy O'Malley stumbled toward Silver and managed to blubber a plea. "But, Captain, sir, we was drugged! We was knocked clean out!"

Bloom joined the plea. "Have mercy, Captain! Have mercy!"

"Quiet!" barked Silver, slamming his fist to the tabletop, and silencing the two guards. "Your disgraceful conduct has allowed four prisoners to escape. For that, you will pay the price with *twenty* blows to the back!"

O'Malley and Bloom recoiled in terror as Silver passed his harsh judgment. *Twenty blows!* Several hands seized them from behind and dragged them across deck to the mainmast, where they were lashed by their arms. The two prisoners cried out in terror, pleading for mercy, but their calls fell on deaf ears. Silver had pronounced the sentence, and there was nothing anyone could say that would change his mind.

"Leave them be for a moment," instructed

Silver, over the crew's excited chattering, "while we deal with our next prisoner." Then, turning to Smollett, Silver announced, "Mr. Smollett, you have been charged with high treason."

Captain Smollett's military bearing finally crumbled upon hearing Silver's wildly fabricated charge, "*Treason*? *I* am the captain of the *Hispaniola*! *I* have served my country well, and *I* have done nothing to merit these false claims! *You*, on the other hand, Silver, are the mutinous scum that should be hanging from the yardarm!"

"You see!" cried Silver to his crew, pointing at Captain Smollett. "He says *he* is the captain of the *Hispaniola*. That is high treason!"

Pure hatred seemed to burn behind Captain Smollett's eyes as he glared at Silver. "Mark my words, Long John Silver, you will pay for *your* treasonous ways." Then, addressing the crew, he added, "And so will each and every one of you, for joining forces with this ruffian! What has it gotten you? Where is the treasure Silver promised?"

Smollett's words seemed to touch a chord with the crew, for they sparked another round of murmurs.

"I think you've had your say," growled Silver. "Unfortunately, it is your word against mine, *Mister* Smollett, and yours is about to be silenced." Then Silver smirked, before barking out an order. "Break out the plank! Mr. Smollett is going for a little walk!"

CHAPTER 36

"IT'S ALMOST TIME," announced Uncle Dunkirk, as he peered through Sage's telescope from the embankment outside Ben Gunn's cave.

Once Hands had departed from the fort, and returned with his men to the *Hispaniola*, Ben, Sage, and Uncle Dunkirk had made the trek back up the side of Mizzen-mast Hill to Ben's hidden cave. Dr. Livesey, Squire Trelawney, and Jim Hawkins had all stayed behind at the fort to guard it against any surprise attacks.

Upon first entering the cave, Uncle Dunkirk had been awed by the glittering chests of gold, diamonds, and other precious stones. However, unlike most men, he didn't give much thought to the wealth and privilege that the treasure would allow him. Instead, Uncle Dunkirk was first and foremost a historian, and he was fascinated by thinking of where these glittering prizes had come from, and what each jeweled piece signified.

Once the treasure had been prepared and stowed for the next phase of Uncle Dunkirk's plan, the three men set a rotating watch on the *Hispaniola*. Taking turns peering through the telescope, they watched intently as the drama unfolded on deck, once the three prisoners were placed in front of Silver.

Raising the telescope to his eye, Uncle Dunkirk watched as Captain Smollett was paraded in front of Silver's court. He felt great admiration for Smollett as the captain stood at attention throughout the ordeal. But the gravity of the situation settled in when a crewman swung open a small gate on the left deck rail, and two other sailors slid a wooden plank to hang over the water. Hands had not been lying when he said that Captain Smollett would walk the plank at six bells.

"Sage," called Uncle Dunkirk, lowering the telescope, "I want you and Ben to hurry back to the fort. Make sure everything is packed up and ready to go. But keep an eye peeled for Silver's men. You never know what that madman might do."

Sage nodded. "But where will you be, Uncle Dunkirk?"

"I have a few things to take care of," replied Uncle Dunkirk. "But I'll see you back at the fort. Just promise me you'll be careful."

Sage crossed the embankment and embraced his uncle tightly. "I promise. You be careful too."

Uncle Dunkirk released his nephew and ruffled his hair. "Don't worry, Sage. I'll be fine. I have our little friend back." With that, Uncle Dunkirk pulled the amber stone from beneath his shirt.

"The amber stone!" exclaimed Sage excitedly. "How did you get it back from Hands?"

"I swapped him for a bag of Flint's gold," grinned Uncle Dunkirk.

"Good deal."

"A *bargain*! Everything is working out just as I planned. Now, you'd better get a move on."

Uncle Dunkirk watched Ben and Sage descend Mizzen-mast Hill. He was proud of his nephew, and the way that he had handled himself throughout everything. When he looked at Sage, he saw glimpses of himself—a *younger* self, to be sure, and with a grin Uncle Dunkirk recognized that Sage was definitely a *true* Smiley.

Then, turning his mind back to the present situation, Uncle Dunkirk prepared for the next stage of his plan. Raising the telescope to his eye, he watched as Captain Smollett was prodded onto the plank. *It's time*, Uncle Dunkirk thought, compressing the telescope and slipping it into his pocket. Then he crept to the edge of the embankment and peered cautiously over the precipice.

The face of Mizzen-mast Hill was a dizzying five hundred foot drop that hung off the side of the rise at an intimidating sixty-five degree angle. Though it was nowhere near unconquerable to a trained mountaineer, the slope was a daunting sight to Uncle Dunkirk, who needed to build up a rapid amount of speed in a short amount of time.

He just hoped that he'd be able to move quickly enough to transport himself from Mizzen-mast Hill to the *Hispaniola*, and not somewhere in between, for the foul beasts in the lagoon weren't too fond of visitors.

The sun dropped rapidly as Uncle Dunkirk prepared himself. Its bottom edge already touched the horizon, and the sky above Treasure Island had an ominous appearance to it, as blood-red fingers of dusky light seemed to reach out of the ocean. Uncle Dunkirk shivered, praying that it wasn't a sign of things to come. Then, taking a deep breath, he stepped out over the abyss.

Uncle Dunkirk plunged down the side of Mizzen-mast Hill for a good fifteen feet, waving his arms frantically to stay upright, before his feet struck the ground once more. Struggling to keep his balance, Uncle Dunkirk pushed off with his right leg, and bounded down the side of the hill, his feet covering three times the distance of a normal step, due to the precipitous angle of the hill. But Uncle Dunkirk pressed on, ignoring the nagging feeling that he was about to lose his balance. With the wind whipping through his hair and whistling noisily in his ears, Uncle Dunkirk cleared his mind, concentrated on a location, and called out, "With wings of wind, I fly!"

He felt a familiar flash of pure energy and was momentarily blinded by the brilliance of the light. His mind reeled, and he felt as if he were floating through time, traveling at a remarkable rate of speed.

Then, in the blink of an eye, he crashed back to reality. He sensed the dizzying surge of energy slip away, and the dazzling burst of light that glowed red through his eyelids faded away to nothing. Best of all, Uncle Dunkirk felt solid ground beneath his feet, and not the water of a premature landing in the lagoon. Opening his eyes, Uncle Dunkirk found that his calculations had been right. He had successfully flashed to the bridge of the *Hispaniola,* and was hidden from view behind a large water cask that he had spotted through the telescope from Mizzen-mast Hill.

His arrival on board the *Hispaniola* was greeted without any fanfare. At this precise moment, every eye on ship was firmly locked on Smollett, as he shuffled to the edge of the plank. Without a second to spare, Uncle Dunkirk raced out from behind the water cask and dashed across the deck. He dodged a triangular stack of cannonballs, and then jumped over a pile of netting, landing in full stride, like an Olympic hurdler. Other than these few objects, the deck was mostly clear. The crew was pressed against the rails, hanging from the rigging, and leaning over the forecastle and the quarterdeck. The only major obstacle between Uncle Dunkirk and the plank was the broad back of Long John

Silver, who stood watching Smollett's sentence from the head of the plank.

Lowering his shoulder, Uncle Dunkirk slammed into the back of the pirate captain, delivering a body check that would have rattled the teeth of any professional hockey player. A gusty *whoosh* of air exploded out of Silver's mouth as he slammed, belly first, into the deck rail. Then, bouncing off the railing, the pirate toppled backward to the deck, where he lay writhing in pain, and gasping frantically for air.

The crew finally turned its attention to the deck, but it was too late. Uncle Dunkirk had already recovered and was racing down the plank's short surface, chasing after Captain Smollett.

At this point, Captain Smollett had already edged his toes over the shark-infested waters. With a bravery bred into men of true character, he'd shuffled his final step forward.

As Uncle Dunkirk watched, Captain Smollett buckled forward, giving in to his fate. Uncle Dunkirk frantically reached out, hoping to catch a fragment of clothing, or anything that would stop the captain's headlong plunge, but he was a fraction too late.

Without a second thought, Uncle Dunkirk sprinted off the edge of the plank and dove forward. As he fell, his arms encircled Captain Smollett's waist, and his hands clasped tightly, holding strong.

As the pair tumbled headfirst through the air, dropping into the lagoon, and the razor-sharp teeth of the sharks waiting below, Uncle Dunkirk cried, "With wings of wind, I fly!" Then the water closed in over their heads.

CHAPTER 37

LONG JOHN SILVER lay in a crumpled heap on the deck of the *Hispaniola*, shaken and confused. His chest heaved, desperate for air, but with each labored inhalation, an intense jolt of pain rocketed through his back and ribs, as if another log had been tossed on the blazing bonfire in his chest.

Silver managed to shake free of the cobwebs in his head as the blurry visions that danced before his eyes slipped back into focus. His eyes traced the crew-laden mainmast up into the clear sky. *Interesting view*, thought Silver, still in a bit of a daze. Then a number of oddly familiar faces crowded over him, reining him in somewhere closer to reality.

"Captain, are you all right?" asked McGregor, one of the many men leaning over the fallen captain.

Silver blinked a few times, still struggling to understand what had brought him to this odd position. He slowly sat up and winced in anguish as a jolt of pain surged through his body. A sturdy pair of hands slipped under his arms, and Silver felt himself being hoisted up to his feet. Someone else quickly produced a wooden chair, and Silver dropped weakly onto its welcomed surface.

As the seconds passed, Silver was finally able to inhale a good, deep lungful of air. The fresh oxygen did wonders for his mind, dusting the debris away, and calming his frazzled nerves.

"What happened?" Silver murmured, his voice hoarse and weak.

"It was that Smiley fellow," answered McGregor smartly. "I don't know where he came from, but he hit you from behind, and followed Smollett into the lagoon."

Followed Smollett into the lagoon? The words jumbled together as nonsense, but something about them sparked Silver's consciousness, and his mind began to clear.

He was Captain Long John Silver, aboard the English schooner, *Hispaniola*, which was anchored in the lagoon of Treasure Island. He had just sentenced Captain Smollett to the plank, and he'd been watching Smollett shuffle the length of the timber when all had gone black. *Had Smiley really snuck on board to rescue Captain Smollett, only to be dragged into the lagoon with him?*

Disregarding his pain, Silver jumped from his seat, and sent his chair crashing onto the deck. He raced to the deck rail and, leaning over, peered down into the clear blue waters of the lagoon. Directly below the plank, a spherical ripple of water extended out a few yards, as a pack of sharks circled lazily below.

However, something wasn't right about this picture. Something was amiss. If Smollett and Smiley *had* gone into the water, where was the blood? Or the feeding frenzy that would have surely ensued? *Was I knocked out so long that I missed all the action?*

"Where are they?" demanded Silver.

As one, the men turned their heads back to the lagoon. The water was remarkably translucent, and one could easily pick out the rocks and sea plants below. Even scattered remnants of litter tossed off the *Hispaniola* lay discarded on the ocean floor. However, there was no sign of Captain Smollett or Uncle Dunkirk. Incredibly, the men had completely vanished.

"I saw 'em hit the water," offered one of the crew, perched over the lagoon on the main boom. "I *know* I did."

"I did, too," called another crewman from the deck rail. "I saw them go in."

The crew of the *Hispaniola* were scratching their heads in bewilderment, when a voice called out from high above the deck, on the main topmast. "Captain! Captain! On the shore! On the shore!"

As one, the crew of the *Hispaniola* and Long John Silver raised their eyes to the far shore of Treasure Island. There, on the beach, were the two missing prisoners, Uncle Dunkirk and Captain Smollett, jogging across the sand toward the shelter of the trees.

"Load the cannons!" bellowed Silver, and the crew instantly burst into action. Men scampered like agile monkeys down the masts and scurried like mice across the deck, rushing to take up their battle positions.

Neatly-stacked cannonballs were hoisted and slipped into the gaping barrels at the front of the black metal cannons, then pushed securely into place with long plungers. The sound of matches scratching against wood carried over the deck, soon followed by the unmistakable sizzle and spit of fuses lit like sparklers on a birthday cake. Ribbons of pungent smoke wafted through the air, curling up into the sky, before the first cannon exploded.

Ka-Boom!

The first cannonball soared over the lagoon. It seemed to hang in midair for a moment before slamming into the forest on the far side of the beach, with the sickening *crack* and *crunch* of shattered wood. It was quickly followed by a second, a third, and soon a whole volley of cannonballs, arcing high, and wreaking havoc on the far shore.

Ka-Boom! Ka-Boom! Ka-Boom!

As the barrage continued, Silver stalked the deck furiously, watching his crew load charge after charge into the blazing cannons. He barked frantic orders at the men, urging them to "Hurry up!" and "Fire that gun!", but a knot in his stomach told him that they were already too late. Captain Smollett and Uncle Dunkirk had slipped out of sight moments ago, and they were now sheltered from the *Hispaniola's* brutal onslaught by Treasure Island's thick, lush forests.

"Mr. Hands!" cried Silver suddenly, changing tack. Silver's men passed his call along the length of the ship, from blazing cannon to cannon. But as word reached the far side of the ship, it was met with blank stares from the crew members. Hands was nowhere to be found.

Finally, one of the gunners, pointing with a powder-blackened finger, yelled, "Captain, in the lagoon!"

Silver charged to the rail and glanced over the side. He was joined a fraction of a second later by Red. With looks of complete astonishment, both men saw that Hands was rowing steadily toward shore, already halfway across the lagoon. The coxswain had left his post, not to mention the ship, during a siege.

"*Hands!*" screamed Silver furiously between cannon blasts.

Across the water, Hands stopped rowing for a moment, and looked back at the *Hispaniola*.

"Hold fire!" barked Silver, and once again the

crew passed the order down the length of the ship. Once the guns had gone silent, Silver turned back to the lagoon and called again, "Hands! What in *blazes* are you doing?"

Cupping his hands around his mouth, Hands called back, "Don't worry, Cap'n! I'll get them!"

Silver seethed. *He* was the captain, and *he* gave the orders. Why would his coxswain set out by himself in the middle of a battle?

To boot, with Hands alone in the longboat, there was no way that Silver could launch a landing party to hunt down the escaped prisoners. His coxswain had the only longboat, and with ferocious sharks still massing in the lagoon, no sane man would dare swim its length to fetch the vessel from shore. "Return to the ship *immediately!*" Silver screamed. "That's *an order!*"

Hearing the rage in Silver's voice, Hands began rowing once again. "Sorry, Cap'n. No time to waste!" replied Hands. "I'll capture the prisoners and bring them back!"

With one last backward glance, Hands looked at Red. The giant wore a pained look on his face. Seeing the expression on Red's face, Hands simply smirked and shrugged his shoulders. He had betrayed Red, there was no doubt about it, and somewhere in his wicked heart he felt a slight twinge of regret for betraying the stupid ox. But any remorseful thoughts were quickly gold-plated as Hands realized that without the giant there was twice as much treasure for himself. Not giving Red a second thought, Hands continued to row to shore.

"Hands!" bellowed Silver, his voice cracking in fury. "Get back here! *Now!*"

As Silver continued to yell at the fast-departing longboat, no one noticed Red slip stealthily over the opposite rail and climb down the netting to the lagoon. Hanging from the bottom rung of the net, Red glanced over his shoulder into the water. Although a few of the sharks had departed for richer hunting grounds when their feast didn't arrive, a number still roamed the waters of the lagoon, gliding smoothly beneath the waves.

With a final glance up at the *Hispaniola*, Red slipped a dagger between his teeth and clamped down tightly. Then, fearlessly, he silently slid into the lagoon to join the sharks.

CHAPTER 38

BEN AND SAGE made quick time back to the fort, and were thankful to find the surrounding area clear of Silver's men. Seeing them slip out of the foliage, Dr. Livesey quickly climbed down from the north battlement and lifted the wooden brace, allowing them to enter the compound. Then, Dr. Livesey greeted Ben and Sage with a nervous inquiry: "How did it go?"

"We're not sure," Sage replied honestly. "Uncle Dunkirk said he had some loose ends to tie up and that he'd meet us here. He said to keep an eye out for Silver's men though, and that he wanted us to pack up and prepare to go."

"That sounds good to me," said Dr. Livesey. "Why don't the two of you begin packing up? Jim can lend a hand. I'll keep watch outside with Squire Trelawney." With that, the doctor turned to inform the squire, who was hungrily perusing one of the jewel-encrusted daggers that Ben had acquired from Flint's treasure chest.

Ben and Sage crossed the remainder of the compound to the shelter, where they found Jim Hawkins. The three of them began to pack up the supplies. Anything that could be found elsewhere on the island, such as coconuts for food and rocks for hurling, were discarded. They crammed the remaining supplies into the two backpacks and gathered the pile of remaining spears and set them aside.

They had been working hurriedly for about twenty minutes when they heard an ecstatic cry from the battlement. Racing back out into the compound, they saw Dr. Livesey hurrying to the gate. Once again, he hoisted the brace and swung the gate open, and moments later, Uncle Dunkirk slipped in. To everyone's surprise and enormous relief, he was followed by Captain Smollett.

"Captain Smollett! Dunkirk!" exclaimed Dr. Livesey. "I'm so glad to see you!" There was a flurry of clasped hands and clapped backs as the two men stepped into the safety of the compound.

Sage raced up to Uncle Dunkirk and gave him a relieved hug, elated that he had returned safely and with Captain Smollett in tow.

"How did you do it?" the doctor asked Captain Smollett. "How did you escape?"

"Well, this reunion wouldn't have been possible had it not been for Mr. Smiley's heroics," replied Captain Smollett, running a hand through his hair. Strangely, the top of the captain's head was sopping wet, while the rest of his body was bone dry. "But I'm not really clear on what happened. I was already on the plank, ready to plunge, when I felt someone grab me around the waist. And as I hit the lagoon, I heard a voice—"

"I hate to put a damper on this warm welcome," interrupted Uncle Dunkirk, who also sported the same curious look—a wet head and dry body—"but we don't have much time. Silver's men are probably rowing to shore as we speak." Uncle Dunkirk smiled at the captain. "Let's just say that I used a little magic to save you. There will be time to catch up, but for now, we should keep moving."

"I don't know how you did it," replied Captain Smollett, "but I am indebted to you, Mr. Smiley. You are a true gentleman, and you may count on me whenever you need me. On that, you have my word." Captain Smollett gripped Uncle Dunkirk's hand and shook it firmly.

Uncle Dunkirk nodded to the captain and then turned to Sage. "Have all the preparations been made?"

"The bags are packed and ready to go," Sage reported.

"Good," said Uncle Dunkirk. "Then let's saddle up and hit the trail."

Ben, Jim, and Sage raced back to the shelter. Ben slipped one of the heavy bags over his shoulders, while Jim and Sage each grabbed a shoulder strap of the second pack and hefted it into the compound. Once there, Sage dashed back to the shelter and returned with the small pile of spears. Uncle Dunkirk was issuing instructions: "Dr. Livesey, I'm going to need you to carry one of these backpacks. Ben, I need you to lead everyone back to your cave. Once there, lash the treasure chests closed—"

"Treasure chests?" sputtered Squire Trelawney, who had been hovering over Uncle Dunkirk's shoulder.

"Yes, treasure chests," repeated Uncle Dunkirk.

"And this would be Flint's treasure, correct?" asked Squire Trelawney.

"As a matter of fact, *no*," replied Uncle Dunkirk firmly. "It belongs to Ben. Now, if you don't mind, squire, time's wasting, and we do have work to do."

"Oh, a million apologies," sputtered Squire Trelawney. "I've been on watch all day, and I must be a little uninformed about our plan."

"Just follow the caravan, squire," said Uncle Dunkirk. "I'll fill you in when time permits." Then, turning back to Ben, Uncle Dunkirk continued, "Once in the cave, lash the treasure chests closed. You'll find a length of strong cord in my backpack. Make sure they are lashed tight. Then wait for me to return."

"You're not coming with us?" asked Captain Smollett.

"I'm afraid not," replied Uncle Dunkirk. Then, with a firm set of his jaw, he added, "It's time for me to take this fight to the sky."

CHAPTER 39

UNCLE DUNKIRK WATCHED as the caravan disappeared into the forest. Then he jumped off the battlement and into the compound. Glancing at the sun, he guessed that he had now been off the *Hispaniola* for approximately thirty minutes, and he hoped that his timing wasn't too far off.

Pressing his back flat against one wall of the fort, Uncle Dunkirk took a deep breath and then charged forward, sprinting at full speed toward the far wall. As the small compound passed quickly below his feet, he freed his mind, concentrated on a location, and shouted, "With wings of wind, I fly!"

Moments before Uncle Dunkirk would have crashed headfirst into the opposite wall, there was a brilliant flash of light, and he disappeared from sight. Ben Gunn's fort was deserted once again.

Seconds later, Uncle Dunkirk felt the searing flash dissipate, and he cautiously opened his eyes. He was standing at the edge of the clearing near the bottom of Mizzen-mast Hill, two hundred yards from Willy C. The plane was parked exactly where he had left it after his hair-raising flight with Long John Silver, and the clearing was empty.

With a grin, Uncle Dunkirk jogged across the clearing and up to Willy C's gleaming black propeller. Giving one of the blades a loving stroke for luck, Uncle Dunkirk slipped around the side, ducked under the wing, and then clambered onto the plane. He slid the canopy back and then hastily climbed into the cockpit.

Uncle Dunkirk prepared Willy C for flight, frantically running through a pre-flight check. He tapped the fuel gauge and was a little startled to see that the tanks were only half full. He and Sage had used a quarter tank getting to Treasure Island, and the flight with Silver had burned another quarter tank. Uncle Dunkirk realized that he'd have to watch his fuel consumption carefully if he and Sage expected to return to Spruce Ridge in one piece. Anything less than a quarter tank would leave them flying on fumes, unable to reach the necessary altitude and speed.

Then Uncle Dunkirk flicked the ignition switch, and Willy C's powerful motor roared to life. With the sudden, thunderous explosion of sound, a hundred birds tore from the trees surrounding the clearing and scattered through the skies, away from the deafening noise. Uncle Dunkirk watched as the four-bladed propeller disappeared into a blur before his eyes.

"Off we go into the wild blue yonder," he muttered, as he reached for the hand brake.

Suddenly, there was an audible *click* behind his head, and a familiar voice cooed in his right ear, "Good evening, Mr. Smiley."

Uncle Dunkirk slowly turned his head, and was met with the sight of a black gun barrel pointed directly at him. Following the line of the barrel, he saw Hands grinning behind the cocked pistol.

"I had a feeling you'd be heading this way," said Hands. "I have to say, though, that I'm a little disappointed in you. You're not exactly a man of your word, Mr. Smiley." Then, with a lifeless cackle, he added, "But then, neither am I."

"If you're looking for Flint's treasure," said Uncle Dunkirk, "it's not here."

"Oh, that's all right," replied Hands. "I already have a sack of gold, and something worth a whole lot more—your flying machine. I think I'll just bid adieu to Long John Silver and his band of men right now and leave Treasure Island a rich man. With this gold and your flying machine, I should be rich in wine, women, and song for quite some time."

"So, what do you want from me?" asked Uncle Dunkirk, playing along.

"Why, a ride, of course. I want you to get me off this cursed island and take me back to London.

I've had more than enough of Silver and his search for Flint's treasure. I'm ready for high society to come calling."

"I'll take you to London," offered Uncle Dunkirk. "But you're going to have to lower that pistol. If it were to go off in flight, we'd both be dead."

Hands hesitated. Then he slowly lowered the gun, taking the pressure off the hammer with his thumb. "Just remember," warned Hands. "I'm right behind you, and I can easily put a plug in you."

"Oh, I have no doubt that you would," said Uncle Dunkirk. "I just want us both to get through this alive. Now, I suggest you sit back and relax. It's a long ride back to London."

With that, Uncle Dunkirk reached down and tightened his seatbelt. Then he released the hand brake and gently accelerated the engine, allowing Willy C to roll forward. Once underway, Willy C gradually increased speed, bouncing roughly over every bump and rut in the clearing, before gracefully lifting into the sky.

Hands stared wide-eyed over the side of the plane, watching as it brushed over the tops of the trees, and then left the clearing far behind, climbing higher and higher over Treasure Island.

As Willy C accelerated, the wind gusted against Hands's face with a fury mightier than the angriest storm, tossing his greasy hair to and fro.

"Shouldn't we close the top?" screamed Hands over the din of the wind.

"What?" called Uncle Dunkirk over his shoulder. Although he had heard Hands clearly, he chose to ignore him.

"I *said*, shouldn't we close the top?" bellowed Hands. This time, Hands raised the pistol and rapped the barrel against Uncle Dunkirk's shoulder.

Suddenly, Willy C cleared the trees and soared high above the lagoon. Off to one side, the *Hispaniola* seemed alive with men, dashing here and there, pointing at the flying machine in the sky. Uncle Dunkirk could see the men running for their cannons, and knew that his timing couldn't have been better.

"Look to your left," called Uncle Dunkirk over his shoulder. "It's the *Hispaniola*."

Hands stole a glance over the side of the plane and down at the ship at anchor below. Cupping his hands around his mouth, Hands called out, "Ahoy, mateys! Look at me! I'm a bird!"

Hearing Hands's cry, Uncle Dunkirk grinned and called behind him, "Well, then, how about showing them your wings?" With that, he slammed the control stick to the left and threw Willy C into a barrel spin.

In the rear cockpit, the smile on Hands's face evaporated faster than an ice cube at the equator as he felt the plane start to spin and his body lift out of his seat. He had the oddest sensation in the pit of his stomach—almost as if he were floating. Then, as the plane continued through its roll, gravity took hold, and Hands slipped from the safety of the cockpit and into the sky.

Hands glanced to the left and watched curiously as the tail of the flying machine shot past him, before he realized that he truly *was* floating. He was out of the flying machine and floating in midair.

Then, as the wind began to buffet him harder and harder, Hands dared to look down. With a scream that pierced the silence of the skies, Hands realized that he wasn't *floating*. He was *falling*. And, even more horrifying, he was falling from a great height.

Like a rag doll, Hands tumbled head over heels, plummeting through the sky toward the crystal blue waters of the lagoon. Hands realized with satisfaction that he still clutched the bag of Flint's gold in his left hand. Then, looking at his right hand, he noticed that he still held the pistol.

Finally, glancing down, Hands spied the slinky outlines that crisscrossed beneath the surface of the lagoon. The sharks were patrolling their territory, waiting patiently for a trespasser to cross their threshold. Pointing the pistol down, Hands cried, "Here I come, you foul beasts!" and fired his only lead pellet into the water below.

Seconds later, he crashed into the waters of the lagoon.

CHAPTER 40

IN STUNNED SILENCE, Sage and the others watched the rippling waves of the lagoon. Endless rings pushed farther and farther out from the point of impact. Long seconds stretched into a minute, but Hands did not surface. After a moment's silence, Dr. Livesey commented bluntly, "I guess that we won't be seeing Mr. Hands again."

As the caravan had trekked through Treasure Island, they'd heard the unmistakable roar of Willy C taking flight. It had been Captain Smollett who had first spied Hands sitting in the passenger seat, and together they had watched the pirate plunge through the sky.

"Well then, what are we waiting for?" Sage asked, knowing that they still needed to get to safety. "Let's get moving!"

Moving with an extra surge of adrenaline, the caravan tackled the final stretch of Mizzen-mast Hill. Soon enough, the final embankment neared, and Ben lent a hand to help the others clear the final hurdle.

"This is it?" spit Squire Trelawney, brushing flecks of dirt and dust from his finery. He took a long look at the vines that hung over the entrance to Ben's cave. "You expect *me* to go in *there?*"

Captain Smollett stepped forward and moved the vines aside. Then, stepping through, he replied over his shoulder, "Squire, you are welcome to stay outside to greet Long John Silver."

With Captain Smollett's suggestion hanging in the air, the squire quickly dashed through the mouth of the cave before the vines swung back into place. He shuddered upon entering the cave, and his eyes darted nervously from top to bottom, side to side.

Once Ben crossed the cave and lit a candle, however, the squire's demeanor changed completely. Any outward sign of fear disappeared as Ben's candle illuminated the four chests of gold.

"Is that Flint's treasure?" asked Squire Trelawney, his voice hushed in awe.

"That it is," replied Ben nonchalantly. "Every last doubloon."

Without a second thought, Squire Trelawney raced across the cave and, like a child in a candy store, dug his hands into the chests. Gold doubloons rained through his fingers, and a greedy laugh bubbled out of his mouth. "Why, this is more gold than the king has!" giggled Trelawney.

The other members of the party watched the squire's display with shock. He was acting childish and giddy. If there was, in fact, an ailment known as gold fever, the squire was not only stricken, he was possessed.

Finally noticing the odd looks of the others, Squire Trelawney managed to abruptly contain his laughter. He dropped his handful of gold coins unceremoniously into the chest, took hold of a jeweled dagger, and strolled casually across the floor. Then suddenly, he spun clumsily, seized Jim Hawkins around the chest, and backed toward the cave entrance. "I'm sorry, gentlemen," he announced, brandishing the dagger against Jim's throat, "but I'm afraid I'm going to have to confiscate this treasure."

A look of sheer surprise painted everyone's face. Although the dagger looked purely ceremonial, there was no doubting the sharpness of its blade, nor the fear in Jim's eyes.

"You must be daft!" sputtered Dr. Livesey. "Let go of Jim immediately! The treasure belongs to Ben."

"Yes, well, I seem to be the only one armed at the present moment, and I say that the treasure belongs to *me*," replied Squire Trelawney ruthlessly. "Now, drop those twigs that you call spears and kick them over to me."

Around the cave, everyone dropped his hand-hewn spear and kicked it toward the squire. Captain Smollett, one of the men closest to the mad squire, followed his kick with a carefully orchestrated stumble, which brought him a few feet closer to Jim. However, the squire seemed to notice the ruse, and warned, "That's close enough, Smollett. You can be sure that I do know how to use a blade. Although I may not look it, I've been tutored by the best."

"As have I," growled Captain Smollett. "I demand that you drop that dagger now, Squire."

"Why?" taunted Squire Trelawney. "What will you do, Smollett? You with your expert training. You couldn't even stop a maniac like Long John Silver from stealing your *entire* ship! And you call yourself a *captain* for His Majesty!"

Fire burned behind Smollett's eyes, but without a weapon, there wasn't much that he could do. In fact, there wasn't much that anyone could do. If they all rushed the squire, Jim could be killed. The squire had the upper hand.

"How do you expect to guard us all?" asked Dr. Livesey. "After all, you're only one, and there are four of us."

While the men argued, Sage thought he spied a shadow cross the entrance to the cave. He thought to cry out a warning, but then realized that it could be Uncle Dunkirk, flashing back to the cave. Sage held his tongue and watched, fascinated, as a massive arm, thick with muscle, slid through the vines.

"Why, it's simple," replied Squire Trelawney. "You will tie up the others, and then Jim Hawkins will tie you. Once that is done, I'll—"

Suddenly, the smug look on Squire Trelawney's face vanished, replaced by an expression of shock. The hand that had slipped through the vines had clutched a fistful of the squire's shirt, and yanked the squire back through the vines and out of the cave. Luckily, in that brief moment of surprise, the squire had loosened his hold on Jim, and the boy had been able to twist free.

Captain Smollett and Dr. Livesey rushed after the squire, pausing only to snatch two spears off the ground. They advanced through the vines, and to their surprise, they found Squire Trelawney locked in a powerful bear hug as Red's massive arms squeezed the air out of him. The squire's face had turned a bright shade of red, and dollops of sweat peppered his face. His feet kicked wildly, raining blow after blow against Red's tree-trunk thighs, but the giant barely winced. Instead, he clutched tighter in retaliation.

"Let go," Trelawney wheezed. "Please, let go!"

Cautiously advancing toward the squire, Captain Smollett and Dr. Livesey raised their spears and pointed them at the pirate. "Let him go, Red. Now!" Captain Smollett ordered.

Instantly, Red unclasped his hands and let the nearly unconscious squire drop to the ground. The squire crumpled to the ledge and curled up into the fetal position, coughing uncontrollably. His chest heaved, searching vainly for air, and a ribbon of saliva dangled loosely from his bottom lip.

"Where's the rest of them?" barked Captain Smollett, the business end of the spear still pointed at Red's chest.

"There are no others," replied Red calmly. "Just me."

With a nod from Captain Smollett, Dr. Livesey circled carefully around Red and peered over the side of the ledge. He expected to see a war party of pirates scaling the side of Mizzen-mast Hill, but there was no one.

"He's telling the truth!" Dr. Livesey exclaimed, both surprised and confused.

"I didn't come to capture you," continued Red.

"Then why did you come?" asked Captain Smollett.

Shuffling his feet nervously, Red hung his bulbous head and stared at the ground. The giant mumbled quietly, "I wanted to go with you."

"What?" sputtered Dr. Livesey. "You want to *go with us?*"

"Yes," answered Red. He glanced up from the ground to meet Dr. Livesey's eyes. "I don't want to be a pirate no more. I just want to go home."

"And why should we trust you?" pressed Captain Smollett.

"I just saved the boy, didn't I?" offered Red. "I could have let the squire carve him from ear to ear, but I didn't. The boy's hurt no one, and he didn't deserve to be harmed."

"Yes, but that could have been a trick," countered Dr. Livesey. "How do we know that Silver isn't surrounding the hill as we speak?"

Sighing, Red slid off his vest to expose his muscular body. Turning slowly in front of Dr. Livesey and Captain Smollett, Red exposed his broad back, which was covered completely in small ornamental tattoos. "Do you see these marks?" Red asked, over his shoulder. "These aren't the marks of battle or bravery. They are the sign of a coward's torture. Silver gave them to me. He did this. And do you know *why?*"

Captain Smollett and Dr. Livesey stared back at Red blankly, shocked by the brutality of the scars on the giant's back.

"When Silver took command of the ship, I had to go along with the mutiny. I apologize to you, Captain Smollett, for not standing my ground, but I didn't have a lot of mates on board who would have stood alongside me. And I thought Silver's crew might take me in as one of their own.

"But Silver had other ideas. He thought that he could make an example out of me. After all, if he could topple the biggest man, no one would dare stand up to him." Red's voice cracked with emotion, but he carried on. "He called me to his cabin late one night after dinner and charged me with a false deed. Silver claimed that I'd been overheard threatening to turn the crew in to the authorities once we reached port. It was an outright lie, but it was his word against mine.

"I was sentenced, seized by the men, and lashed to the mast. And then Silver personally delivered the punishment. Brandishing a dagger, he cut dozens of tiny nicks on my back—one after another, until my back came to look like this. Once done, I was lashed to the back of the longboat, and then dragged through the water."

"My God, man," sputtered Dr. Livesey. "How did you survive?"

"I managed to free my hands underwater," answered Red. "And I released myself from the longboat's wake. The water was so clear that I could see hundreds of feet around me. I spun round, searching for sight of a shark, knowing that now I'd at least see it coming."

"And did you?" asked Dr. Livesey, engrossed. "See a shark, I mean?"

"Oh, I did," replied Red. The giant's eyes looked into the distance. "I saw one. It must have been fifteen feet long, with a jaw big enough to swallow me whole. And it was smiling something fierce. He was on my trail, and I knew that my time was drawing to a close, so I turned to face my fate."

"And then?" pushed Captain Smollett.

"And then," shrugged Red nonchalantly, "I slugged him."

"You *what?*" sputtered Dr. Livesey in disbelief.

"I slugged him," repeated Red. "I pulled my arm back and belted him on the nose."

"What did the shark do?" asked Captain Smollett in amazement.

"Well, surprisingly enough, he scampered off. Stayed well away, too. I managed to swim all the way back to the longboat, and I was pulled over the side without a single scratch. Since then, I haven't had much fear of the beasts."

Captain Smollett and Dr. Livesey shared a quick glance. The abused giant had been as much a prisoner as any of them, and now he simply wanted to be free.

"Please," begged Red. "You can bind my hands if you want, or keep me lashed to a tree, for all I care. But I just want to go home. The men aboard the *Hispaniola*, they were never my friends. They're nothing to me. Please, have mercy. Take me with you."

As Captain Smollett listened to the giant's

plea, he slowly dropped the tip of his spear. Seeing this, Dr. Livesey followed suit. With his hand extended in friendship, the captain stepped forward. "Welcome aboard, Red."

CHAPTER 41

"MR. MCGREGOR!" bellowed Silver from the deck of the *Hispaniola*. All around him, the havoc of battle ensued. The crew scampered about, loading the cannons to blast at the flying machine soaring high above, and the pungent smell of gunpowder permeated the air.

From out of the hectic action, the Cockney sailor dashed up and issued a haggard salute. "Captain, you called!"

"Congratulations, McGregor," announced Silver. "You're now coxswain." Moments before, Silver and the crew of the *Hispaniola* had watched in surprise as the wayward Mr. Hands had tumbled from the sky and splashed down into the lagoon. They'd also noticed, to the morbid delight of the Captain, that Hands hadn't bobbed back up to the surface.

A look of disbelief washed over McGregor's face, and he stammered, "Why...why, thank you, Captain."

"Now hoist anchor and get us out of this blasted lagoon!" ordered Silver, wasting no time on ceremony. "I want the wind at my back when I blow that flying machine from the sky."

McGregor peered across the deck to the horizon and noted that the sun had nearly set. "But, Captain, the sun's almost down, and these waters are treacherous as it is."

Silver glared at McGregor and muttered between clenched teeth, "Rule number one, Mr. McGregor—what I say *goes*. Is that understood?"

"Yes, Captain, sir. Understood," bumbled McGregor. Then, turning on his heels, he bellowed over the din of the deck, "Prepare to hoist anchor! We're setting sail, boys!"

As one, the men of the *Hispaniola* glanced at McGregor uncertainly. They looked to their captain for confirmation, but there was no mistaking the look on Silver's face. The men abandoned their positions at the cannons and raced to their sailing stations.

Within minutes, the crew of the *Hispaniola* had hoisted the anchor off the floor of the lagoon and raised the small foresail. The remaining sails were being unfurled by the crew, ready to be hoisted on a moment's notice once the *Hispaniola* reached open water.

Soaring high above Treasure Island, Uncle Dunkirk watched the frenzied action aboard the

Hispaniola, and grinned. Everything was going according to plan. Silver had hoisted anchor, and was sailing out to sea. That meant that Sage and the others would be safe on the shore. Now, it was just Silver's deadly schooner, the *Hispaniola,* against Uncle Dunkirk's trusty Spitfire, Willy C. *It's time to settle this score once and for all.*

Leaning on the stick, Uncle Dunkirk dropped Willy C into a blistering dive. The plane shot through the sky, blazing down toward the darkening waves of the ocean. At one hundred feet, Uncle Dunkirk leveled the Spitfire off, tilting the wings slightly to bring its course directly in line with the *Hispaniola.* Then, seconds after Willy C slipped over the boundaries of the lagoon, it rocketed over the tops of the *Hispaniola's* sails like a blazing comet.

All along the ship, terrified crewmen dove to the deck, covering their heads with their arms and cowering from the angry roar of the demon flying machine. Only Silver remained standing. He waved furiously after the flying machine.

"Come on, McGregor!" roared Silver, with a taste of battle in his mouth. "Put us out to sea!"

Like a locomotive slowly gaining steam, the *Hispaniola's* foresail snapped and fluttered under the light evening breeze, and the ship began gliding across the lagoon. Silver raced up the stairs to the quarterdeck and seized control of the rudder. The coral reef surrounding Treasure Island was razor sharp, and Silver trusted no one other than himself to navigate these waters.

As the *Hispaniola* slipped out of the lagoon, Uncle Dunkirk circled lazily above, taunting Silver and his crew. Willy C was safely out of cannon range, but Uncle Dunkirk made sure that he was close enough for Silver to hear the Spitfire's powerful engine. Like a cavalry trumpet calling troops to combat, the thrum of Willy C's motor was leading the *Hispaniola* out to battle.

The *Hispaniola* broke free of the lagoon and slipped past the final treed cove into deeper waters. McGregor peered over the side of the rail, and saw that the normally translucent waters had darkened in the dusk, making navigation through the coral bank all that much harder. He also noticed, to his surprise, that the lagoon's chief inhabitants, the sharks, seemed to be following the ship as if it were the Pied Piper. After days of feasting on scraps thrown from the ship, the creatures weren't about to let their main food source sail away.

"Captain, it's getting quite dark," McGregor noted, hoping that Silver might exert a little more caution.

"Then we'd best hoist another sail and get out to sea all the much quicker, Mr. McGregor," spat Silver. "Hoist the fore topsail and main topsail!"

Two more sails blossomed high above the *Hispaniola*, and the billowing wind quickly filled their seams. The ship surged forward, adding a few more knots to her speed, and steaming closer to the hazardous coral reef that ringed the island.

With McGregor standing ready at his side, Silver watched as the flying machine circled a few hundred feet over the ship. "Like a hawk waiting for its prey. That's how we'll deal with that infernal flying machine, Mr. McGregor," explained Silver. "It's all about timing—when the bird swoops, we'll blast it from the sky."

Then, brusquely, Silver ordered, "Mr. McGregor, have four cannons loaded, two per side, and have them aim high, toward the flying machine."

"But, Captain," sputtered McGregor, glancing warily at the angry waves crashing over the reef. Free of the lagoon's natural shelter, the ocean winds gusted steadily from the east and thrashed the waves about. "The reef is—"

"Rule number *one*, Mr. McGregor," reminded Silver coldly. "What I say..."

"Goes," mumbled McGregor in reply. McGregor took another nervous glance at the reef and then relayed Silver's order: "Man guns two, four, eight, and nine. Load charges and await my order."

The cannon teams raced to their positions and quickly loaded their guns. Once the balls and gunpowder had been properly tamped into the barrels, the men stood by, awaiting further orders.

From the cockpit of Willy C, Uncle Dunkirk watched as the *Hispaniola* cruised into deeper waters and neared the edge of the coral reef. *It's now or never*, thought Uncle Dunkirk, and with a final glance at his target, he took action.

Pushing the stick forward, Uncle Dunkirk once again dropped Willy C into a furious dive. As the ocean's churning waves raced up to greet him, Uncle Dunkirk leveled the plane off at ten feet. He blazed over the waves, kicking up a wall of salty spray that seemed to chase the Spitfire. The *Hispaniola*'s port side loomed in the distance, and Uncle Dunkirk could see Long John Silver standing on the quarterdeck, bellowing orders to combat the impending attack. Focusing on his target, Uncle Dunkirk continued to push Willy C forward at top speed.

"Here it comes, Captain!" called a lookout from the mainsail. Silver watched hungrily as the flying machine raced across the water toward him. Smiley was flying on a collision course with the ship and, Silver noted with a satisfied smirk, was in direct line with his cannons.

"Captain, should we fire?" asked one of the gunners, hovering a match over his cannon's short wick.

"Just wait," stalled Silver, holding his hand up like a starting flag. He glared across the water, almost daring Uncle Dunkirk to blink, as the flying machine blazed closer and closer. He knew that the contraption would have to pull up eventually, and when it did, it would be exposing its broad underside. That was when he'd give the order to fire. Smiley wouldn't have anywhere to go, and one of the *Hispaniola*'s cannons would tear the flying machine to shreds. *Just a few seconds longer.*

Uncle Dunkirk stared out his cockpit window at the *Hispaniola*, which was beginning to loom large. The waves surrounding the boat got fatter and rougher, crashing against the side of the ship, and throwing sheets of spray in every direction. On the quarterdeck, the unmistakable form of Long John Silver stood, glaring angrily at Uncle Dunkirk, with an arm held upright in the air. As Willy C rapidly closed the distance to the ship, Uncle Dunkirk finally blinked and pulled back on the stick.

"Now!" yelled Silver. He threw his arm down and watched as the gunner's flame touched down, sending sparks off the cannon's wick. Time seemed to stand still aboard the *Hispaniola* as the wick slowly vanished.

Willy C responded instantly to Uncle Dunkirk's touch and arced upward, its bottom completely open to a volley from the cannons. Pulling the stick to the right, Uncle Dunkirk tilted the wings across the *Hispaniola*'s port side, coming close to Silver's guns.

Just then, as the port's cannons roared, sending their deadly contents racing skyward, Silver heard a *crunch*, and the ground beneath his feet shook violently.

"We're on the reef!" cried the lookout in terror, from high above the mainmast.

With Treasure Island's stormy current forcing the *Hispaniola* forward, the schooner's port side was dragged violently along the reef. Timber snapped like kindling as the serrated corral thrashed the ship's underside into shreds. Water surged over the deck, throwing men, casks, and crates about as if they had been tossed into a typhoon.

Through this all, Silver stood alone on the quarterdeck, shaking his head in bewilderment. The *Hispaniola* was sinking. His proud ship was going to the bottom of the ocean.

In stunned silence, Silver watched as his men dashed frantically about the deck, desperately searching for something, anything, to keep them afloat. The longboat, which might have saved a few men, sat abandoned by Hands on the shore of the lagoon. And other than a few small bobbing casks, there was nothing resembling a floatation device anywhere.

As each successive wave grated the *Hispaniola* like cheese against the coral reef, the crew gave in to the inevitable and finally began to jump ship. In ways of options, there weren't many. One could either swim for it—and hope to elude both the razor sharp coral and the man-eating sharks long enough to reach shore—or one could be sucked down into Davy Jones's locker with the ship.

Suddenly the door to the forecastle sprung open and McGregor stumbled out with a large cask of wine in his arms.

"What do you think you're doing, Mr. McGregor?" asked Silver incredulously. "The ship's going down, and all you can think about is *wine*?"

"I'm not much of a swimmer," answered McGregor timidly. "I thought I might be able to float to shore."

By now, the last of the crew had dropped into the churning water alongside the *Hispaniola*. Silver watched them splashing about, as they attempted to stay above the choppy waves and fight off the hungry predators below.

"Let me help you," offered Silver, crossing the deck to the port rail. "I'll toss you the cask once you jump in."

Nervously, McGregor handed the cask to Silver. "You promise?" he asked, as he hoisted his right leg over the rail.

"Of course I promise!" spat Silver angrily. "Now get off my ship!"

McGregor launched himself off the rail, trying to put as much distance between himself and the crumbling carcass of the *Hispaniola* as possible. As he surfaced, sputtering water from his lips and splashing about madly, he called, "The cask, Captain. The cask!"

Silver just grinned back slyly before replying, "Thanks for thinking of your captain, Mr. McGregor. You made a fine coxswain."

Over the din of the collapsing ship, an incessant buzzing filled the air, and Silver glanced up to see the flying machine soar over the *Hispaniola*. The cannon balls had missed their target, and as Silver turned to follow the plane's path as it soared over the lagoon toward the mainland, he saw the machine's wings waggle from side to side, as if saying a final good-bye.

With a final shudder, the ribs of the *Hispaniola* collapsed under the weight of the waves, and the ship began to slide beneath the water. Long John Silver took one final glance toward Treasure Island, gripped the cask of wine firmly, and then felt the cold waves of the ocean rise around him.

Silver floated amongst the wreckage, listening to the cries of suffering seamen all around. Pieces of wood and tinder floated everywhere, and a few men hung tight, kicking savagely at the sharks that swarmed below them. In the distance, Silver spied McGregor struggling to stay afloat as he was pulled out to sea by the tide, but the sailor's flailing arms soon disappeared beneath the waves, not to reappear.

A wave lifted Silver and the cask, and carried them toward the coral reef. Looking into the translucent waters, Silver watched as the brightly colored reef passed below him, and then, as the wave passed, felt its razor sharp barbs tear at his shirt. A raw scrape scoured his waist, clouding the water around his body with a trickle of blood. Another wave lifted him up and carried him over the reef and back into the lagoon, bobbing freely.

Silver glanced over his shoulder and watched as the last of his men slipped beneath the waves. All that remained of the *Hispaniola* were the two tall masts that still stood proud, rising out of the ocean, but they too were slowly sinking beneath the waves.

As Silver watched the masts slip beneath the surface, a massive grey fin cut through the waves before him, patrolling the edge of the reef. It swam alongside the jagged coral wall, slinking farther to the left, before turning back to shore, in direct line with Silver and his floating cask.

Silver kicked frantically, aiming for the closest shoreline two hundred feet away, but the cask simply turned a lazy circle in the water. Glancing back, Silver noted why. *My peg! A lot of good it does me for swimming.*

The cask slowly spun back toward the coral reef, and Silver looked up, facing his foe. The shark's snout broke the surface and its massive mouth yawned open, rows of serrated teeth glittering wetly inside.

Silver screamed the same high-pitched, girlish shriek that he'd first let loose in the back of the flying machine, before the shark's mouth swallowed him from head to chest, and slammed down with a sickening *crunch*.

CHAPTER 42

THE FOLLOWING DAY, Sage woke with a wonderful sense of excitement and anticipation. After the joyous victory celebration of last night, he and Uncle Dunkirk had been up until the early hours of the morning, trying to work out a dilemma—how to get their friends back to London *and* get themselves back to Spruce Ridge with barely any gas left in Willy C's tank, and, of course, only two seats.

Sage knew that they had come too far, defeating Long John Silver and his pirate horde, to fail now. He'd thought of his friend Ben, and how the marooned sailor longed to return to Cardiff. He'd thought of the other people he'd met—Dr. Livesey, Captain Smollett, Jim Hawkins, and Red—and realized how much each of them had come to mean to him in such a short time.

And just as he'd glanced over the now-familiar island, taking in the many landmarks of his summer vacation—the lagoon, the fort, the thick forests below Mizzen-mast Hill, the clearing—and thinking that this final obstacle was insurmountable, inspiration had struck. Today,

Sage's plan would be put to the test.

"All right, everyone, rise and shine," called Uncle Dunkirk cheerily, as he strolled back into the cave. "We've got a few things to take care of before we bid Treasure Island adieu."

Soon after everyone had risen, Uncle Dunkirk put them all to work. The remaining supplies and necessities were crammed into the two backpacks, while items that seemed useless or too cumbersome were discarded into the back of the cave.

Ben was assigned the duty of packing the treasure, as it rightfully belonged to him. For the sake of convenience, Uncle Dunkirk suggested that Ben divide the treasure into manageable loads for all to carry. However, even when the backpacks were laden with gold doubloons and dazzling gems, there were still two full chests of gold remaining against the cave wall.

"Leave it be," Ben decided abruptly. "We already have more riches than we'll ever need."

"What do you mean by *we?*" asked Jim Hawkins innocently as he rolled the sleeping bags into tight bundles.

"You keep what you carry," offered Ben. "I'd have it no other way."

"Excuse me, Ben," interrupted Dr. Livesey with a startled tone, "but did I hear you correctly? We *keep* what we *carry?*"

"Aye, Doc," grinned Ben. "Whatever you can

lug, you can keep. Why just one sack of Flint's treasure will keep you in the high life for years."

Ben's announcement caught everyone off guard. With a single charitable gesture, he had effectively made wealthy men out of them all. They happily gathered their allotted sacks of treasure—now more than willing to carry the extra weight—and hoisted their sacks, shaking them merrily so that the valuables inside rattled and jingled like the sweetest- sounding noisemakers, and then slung them over their shoulders, testing the weight.

Squire Trelawney sat with his back against the wall, sobbing loudly. "You *keep* what you *carry*! You *keep* what you *carry*! What a load of bollocks!" Finally, after everyone had had their fill of the squire's endless rambling, a gag was fashioned out of one of Uncle Dunkirk's shirts, and the squire was silenced.

Once everyone was packed, the caravan stepped out onto the ledge, ready for its final trek across the island. Ben stood inside the entrance, holding the vines back with his arm, and looking over the cave that had been his home for the past few years. His handmade table and chairs sat in the back corner like a lonely reminder of a previous existence.

"Kind of sad to leave?" asked Sage, sliding up beside his friend.

"No, not really," replied Ben evenly. "I'm just glad that this day's finally arrived." Then, with a smile, Ben added, "I'm going home. I'm finally going home."

Leaving the cave behind, the group crept over the ledge and began the slow process of trudging down the side of Mizzen-mast Hill. Although the descent was difficult under normal circumstances, it was doubly so with each of them lugging as much of Flint's treasure as humanly possible. The going was even harder for Red, who also pulled Squire Trelawney along on a tight leash. However, the grueling work was far overshadowed by the grand atmosphere of the day. Everyone was ecstatic to finally be underway, and conversation was light and playful all morning.

At the bottom of Mizzen-mast Hill, the caravan entered the forest once more, and Sage took the lead on the trail to the clearing. As they slipped into the clearing, the welcome sight of Willy C greeted them, but to the surprise and dismay of everyone, Sage trudged on by. He led them back into the forest behind Willy C and continued trekking through the woods.

After only a few more minutes of hiking, Sage saw the sun streaming through the canopy, and knew that they had arrived. Spying the gnarled branches of a familiar life-saving tree, he dropped his two packs of gems and jewels, and said to Uncle

Dunkirk, "This is it. The spot I told you about."

Uncle Dunkirk added his pack to the pile, and then crept carefully forward. Firmly grabbing one of the tree's branches, he leaned out as far as possible, and glanced over the edge of the abyss that Sage had nearly plummeted down the day they arrived on Treasure Island.

Uncle Dunkirk turned to the gathered men. "Sage and I have a little dilemma that we've purposely kept from you. You see, we weren't sure how to get everyone home, as the flying machine is nearly out of fuel. While I was trying to come up with a plan last night, Sage reminded me of an adventure I took a number of years ago. And in that adventure, we found our answer. Have any of you heard of a leap of faith?"

"A leap of faith?" asked Dr. Livesey.

"Yes, it's quite simple, really," replied Uncle Dunkirk. "There's a remote island in the Pacific Ocean called Pentecost Island. On that island every year, a tribe celebrates its yam harvest with a ritual called the *Nagol*, which they've been performing for over one thousand years. The elders of the tribe select a number of vines from the forest. Once they climb a seventy-five foot tower, they tie these vines to their ankles. Then, they take a leap of faith and jump off the tower. If their measurements are correct, the vines take up the slack just before their heads brush the ground."

Sage watched as confusion seemed to cloak the eyes of the others. After all, from their perspective, what did a ritual performed at a yam harvest have to do with escaping Treasure Island?

To clarify things, Uncle Dunkirk added, "What I am asking each of you to do is to put your trust in me and take a leap of faith off this cliff. I guarantee you that when you open your eyes, you will be back home."

Dr. Livesey chuckled nervously. "You have to be kidding, Dunkirk."

"I've never been more serious in my life," replied Uncle Dunkirk. Then, turning to Captain Smollett, he asked, "Captain, remember the magic that saved you from the sharks in the lagoon? It's the same magic. It worked once, and I guarantee you it will work again. All you have to do is take my hand and walk off the cliff. The magic will keep you safe. Do you trust me?"

Sage watched as Captain Smollett struggled with the request. After all, who wouldn't be nervous, given the task of walking off a cliff? Yet if it hadn't been for Uncle Dunkirk, Captain Smollett's life would have ended in the lagoon of Treasure Island as chum for the sharks. Squaring his shoulders, Captain Smollett marched forward to stand before Uncle Dunkirk. "I promised that you could count on me, Dunkirk, and I am a man of my word. I'm with you. I'll take the leap of faith."

Now there were three standing bravely before the others. Sage looked at Ben, and he could see the worry lining his friend's face. Catching Sage's eye, Ben winked and then groaned, "Ah, why not. It's still better than spending another year on this island." With that, Ben stepped forward.

Sage grinned as he turned to Dr. Livesey and Jim Hawkins. Both stood quietly, seemingly pondering the stretch of imagination that was required for Uncle Dunkirk's leap of faith. Then, just as the tribesmen on Pentecost Island placed their faith in a length of vine, the two decided to continue betting on Uncle Dunkirk. Sharing a quick glance between them, they stepped forward together.

And finally, with a shrug of his thick shoulders, Red stepped up, tugging Squire Trelawney behind him. Although no one bothered to lift the gag from Squire Trelawney's mouth, they all agreed that his garbled cries from behind the cloth were words of submission, although his terror-stricken eyes told a different tale.

Then, with Flint's treasure secured firmly to their backs once again, Uncle Dunkirk asked them all to form a line along the edge of the embankment. Uncle Dunkirk instructed everyone to clasp hands tightly. He explained that under *no circumstances* should they let go. There was magic in their embrace, he explained, and the magic would quickly disappear if the bond was broken.

Once they were all in position, Sage glanced down the line and spotted each man sharing a look of apprehension with his neighbor. They had come so far, and only had a short distance to travel now. A single leap of faith would lead to a world of luxury and comfort back home.

"Gentlemen, this has been a grand adventure," announced Uncle Dunkirk, as he dug a hand into his shirt and grasped the amber stone. "But I'm afraid it's time to say farewell to Treasure Island."

Then, as one, they strode forward, sliding down the embankment and over the cliff.

CHAPTER 43

MOMENTS LATER, THEY suddenly appeared on the streets of London, in front of London Bridge. A number of shocked looks from passing bystanders greeted them, but they simply ignored the gawkers, as they were too overwhelmed by the sights and sounds that surrounded them. As if announcing their presence, Big Ben tolled six times loudly, its resounding peal echoing over the city.

"Well, gentlemen, here you are, back in London," stated Uncle Dunkirk officially. Then, grabbing the arm of a young boy who was racing past, Uncle Dunkirk asked, "Young man, what is today's date?"

"Why, August the seventh," he replied helpfully.

"And the year?"

"It's 1789," he added, with a curious smirk. "Same as yesterday."

Uncle Dunkirk dug into his pocket and placed a gold doubloon into the boy's hand before releasing him. The boy blinked twice at the coin, then glanced at Uncle Dunkirk, before bolting away on a cloud of joy.

Meanwhile, the men all glanced about in awe,

taking in the familiar sights of their hometown, and laughing out loud at the strange and curious magic that had brought them there.

Finally, Captain Smollett strode up to Uncle Dunkirk and Sage. "Dunkirk, I don't know how you did it, but you got us home. You are a man of your word, and I would gladly take another leap of faith at your side."

"Thank you, Captain. I appreciate your words," replied Uncle Dunkirk.

"As for you, young man," continued Captain Smollett, turning to Sage, "I expect great things from you. Make us proud."

Sage grinned and replied, "Thanks, Captain. I'll try." Then, noticing the strange look on Ben's face, Sage asked, "Are you all right, Ben?"

Since miraculously appearing back in London, Ben had stood in awe, spinning round and taking in sights he had long thought lost. Turning to Sage, he smiled and said, "You know, I was right about you. You really are a sorcerer."

Suddenly, the marooned sailor stepped forward and wrapped Sage in a tight embrace. His voice was hoarse as he spoke. "I can't believe I'm almost home. And I owe it all to you, Sage. Thank you for getting me off that godforsaken island."

"I couldn't have done it without you, Ben," replied Sage, hugging him back.

As Uncle Dunkirk watched their exchange, a

thought suddenly occurred to him. Excusing himself, he dashed into a small shop across the way. A minute later, he returned, grinning broadly. After a last round of good-byes, he and Sage were ready to flash back to Treasure Island.

Waving to their fellow travelers, Uncle Dunkirk and Sage climbed up onto the mortar-block railing of London Bridge. They stared down at the brown water of the Thames rushing beneath them, and then stepped out into thin air.

CHAPTER 44

ONCE BACK ON Treasure Island, Uncle Dunkirk and Sage quickly ran Willy C through a pre-flight check. The patch on the wing still seemed to hold strong, and Uncle Dunkirk was anxious to get airborne, and off the desolate isle.

Before they climbed into the cockpit, Uncle Dunkirk turned to Sage and said, "I almost forgot something." Then, reaching into his shirt pocket, he pulled out a small square of paper with an artist's sketch of London Bridge on it. "I grabbed you a souvenir of London. It's about as close as I could come to a postcard this time around, since they haven't invented them yet. I picked it up in that little store next to London Bridge. I think the poor chap nearly had a heart attack when I told him to keep the change from my gold doubloon. But it never hurts to do your part to support the arts, Sage."

Sage took the fragile-looking card in hand and beamed at the image of London Bridge. The meticulously sketched illustration had obviously taken some time, and it had been rendered by an artist with a talented hand. "Thanks, Uncle Dunkirk.

This one means more than all the others combined. I'll add it to my collection, and keep it safe."

Then, with one eye on the gas gauge and the other on the altimeter, Uncle Dunkirk piloted Willy C up through the Caribbean sky. As the gas gauge needle dipped severely, the ever-faithful Willy C soared to the proper altitude, carrying Sage and Uncle Dunkirk high above the ocean.

With one final look at Treasure Island far below, Uncle Dunkirk dropped the plane into a dive, and bulleted toward the earth. This time, rather than squirming with terror anticipating their impending crash, Sage sat back and enjoyed the thrilling ride. Sage grinned as the clouds flitted by his cockpit window and the ocean rose rapidly to his right.

Treasure Island had, surprisingly, been an exhilarating summer vacation for Sage. He had personally joined Uncle Dunkirk on an amazing adventure, rather than having to read about it on the back of a postcard, and he couldn't wait to share every thrilling detail with his friends. But, as they plummeted faster and faster toward the sea, Sage suddenly felt uncertain. He knew his friends would love to hear about his adventures, flashing to Treasure Island with Uncle Dunkirk's magical amber stone, and matching wits with Long John Silver, but would they believe him? Maybe it would be best to start seventh grade as a normal kid, and not the kook with the overblown imagination. But, then again, maybe there was another option.

"You know, Uncle Dunkirk, I'm thinking of starting a journal."

"What kind of journal?" asked Uncle Dunkirk, over the blasting din of the wind outside the cockpit.

"Kind of like your postcards," explained Sage. "Maybe I'll write about my summer vacation on Treasure Island."

"That's a great idea, Sage. All the great explorers keep journals. It can be your own personal recollection of our adventure together."

"And I think I've got the perfect name for it," offered Sage, with a twinkle in his eye. "'The Uncle Duncle Chronicles.'"

"I love it!" grinned Uncle Dunkirk. "With a name like that, how can it fail? Now, why don't you bookmark that thought for a second, and help your Uncle Duncle flash us back home."

As Willy C blazed like a lightening bolt toward the ocean, Uncle Dunkirk and Sage joined voices and called, *"With wings of wind, I fly!"*